"Stories such as *The Orb and Casanova* flaunt Pack's literary brilliance and her ability to grow the world and characters episodically ... Come for the literary sights and sounds, stay for Pack's miraculously fine-tuned imagination."
—*Kirkus Reviews* (starred review)

"Imaginative and filled with insightful dialogue, this story rivets the reader to the page."
—*Janet Carpenter, fantasy author*

"Pack's LIBRARY OF ILLUMINATION series is creative and compelling story telling at its finest."
—*Chris Collora, author*

"... well written, imaginative, fast moving, and leaves you wanting to read more."
—*Reviewer*

Books in the LOI series

The Library of Illumination
FIRST BOOK IN THE SERIES
The Curator*

The Library of Illumination:
BOOK TWO
Doubloons*

The Library of Illumination:
BOOK THREE
The Orb*

The Library of illumination:
BOOK FOUR
Casanova*

The Library of Illumination:
BOOK FIVE
Portals*

Chronicles: The Library of Illumination
Books One through Five*

The Library of Illumination:
BOOK SIX
The Overseer (2014)

CHRONICLES: THE LIBRARY OF ILLUMINATION

C. A. PACK

Artiqua Press

WWW.ARTIQUAPRESS.COM

Artiqua Press

www.artiquapress.com

This is a work of fiction. The characters, incidents, and dialogue are products of the author's imagination and are not to be construed as real. Any resemblance to actual events or persons, living or dead, is entirely coincidental.

Artiqua Press
New York
info@ArtiquaPress.com

CHRONICLES: THE LIBRARY OF ILLUMINATION

ISBN-13: 978-0-9835723-9-8
ISBN-10: 0983572399

ACKNOWLEDGEMENTS

Deepest thanks to my husband, Andrew, and to the rest of my family and friends for their undying support. A special shout out to my brother, Carl Mealie, who corrected my Italian, to his wife Maureen, and to my nephews David, Ian, and Danny who are a never ending source of inspiration. I want to extend my gratitude to author Karen Dionne for her invaluable feedback on my writing, and my friends Carol Scibelli and Barbara Paskoff for allowing me to bounce ideas off them. Special thanks to Dr. Claus Maywald of the Gutenberg-Museum in Mainz, Germany, for explaining the steps that would have gone into producing the Gutenberg Bible in the fifteenth century; and to Susan Murphy for putting me in touch with Joan Kahnhauser of the Emma S. Clark Memorial Library, who helped me learn about some of the technology librarians would love to have in their libraries. Plus, a big thank-you to editor Neal Hock, who cleaned up my punctuation and pointed out the problems caused by my inability to remember what I've already written; and to Jeanine Henning for her cover design. Finally, a big hug to my cousin Joann Colucci, who inspired the original *Library of Illumination*.

In memory of Mal

C:L ◎ I

PROLOGUE

The Curator

A GUST OF cold air coming in the window made Mal shiver, but not as much as the keening that followed it. He turned in time to see the enormous beak of a flying lizard just two feet away. And then, darkness.

And so it began ...

THE TEXTURE OF the paper, the scent of the ink, the vivid contrast of dark print in relief against a creamy page— Johanna loved everything about books, reading them, touching them, owning them. She found illuminated manuscripts and finely bound texts intoxicating, and she appreciated the beauty of richly colored plates illustrating the books she read. Just like someone with drug or alcohol dependence, she always looked for her next fix.

She often dreamed of having her own library, a

large wood-paneled room with floor-to-ceiling shelves filled with ancient dictionaries and atlases and centuries-old fiction. She envisioned the books that would populate the space: *The Iliad*, *The Odyssey*, a Gutenberg Bible, a first edition of *Through the Looking Glass*. Between the banks of shelves, natural light would stream in through tall windows. She could almost hear the crackle of flames as they devoured logs in a fireplace, adding atmosphere and warmth to the library of her dreams. She sighed when she thought about the gentle stretch she would feel in her thighs every time she climbed the circular stairs to a narrow balcony that circled the perimeter of the library's second story. That's where she would keep her old favorites by Poe, Shakespeare, and Brontë. Of course, her muscles would thank her as soon as she settled into the down-filled cushions of a leather sofa and propped her book on top of the soft cashmere pillow on her lap. It would be the perfect setting for reading one of her beloved tomes.

B-B-B-R-R-R-I-I-I-N-N-N-G-G-G!

Johanna hated the telephone and everything it represented. It rudely rang with no regard for what she was doing at that moment. The ring tone sounded brassy and irritating, and the people on the other end of the line were, for the most part, annoying and picayune. However, speaking to those callers happened to be an integral part of her job. "I'm a people person," she had blathered to the man who was about to become her employer. He hired her specifically to deal with clients, and all day long an unending stream of customers called, each one demanding her time and attention, with no thought that perhaps Johanna deserved the same courtesy from them.

When she first took the job at Book Services, she had high hopes about working with precious manuscripts all day, researching ancient texts, or perhaps learning bookbinding and repair. But she quickly found out the only book involved in her job contained the work orders she filled out as the calls came in. She was just another worker bee in a hive filled with countless drones.

"Where's my delivery?" "You sent the wrong books." "I don't want this anymore. Come back and get it." Demanding. Obnoxious. Exhausting. At the end of each day, she dragged herself home, bone tired and too weary to do anything except eat dinner and fall into bed with a book. Always with a book. That's when her life began, for only when she immersed herself in the pages of a well-written story did Johanna feel like life was worth living. No wonder. She'd had a tough childhood—orphaned when she could barely walk and brought up in an institution best described as utilitarian, which brooked no signs of independent thinking. Books were her only means of escape.

Johanna had grown into a curious and imaginative child, forced to bury all indications of innate intelligence if she wanted to avoid punishment and humiliation. And being preternaturally intuitive, she quickly learned to conform.

ONE FRIDAY EVENING, at the end of a particularly trying day, her boss waited until after she punched out on the time clock to tell her to pick up a package and deliver it to Mr. Henry Morton at Bay House in Exeter. "It's an emergency."

She had never heard of Mr. Morton, nor did she feel inclined to go out of her way on her own time on a rainy Friday evening to deliver a package to him. But jobs were scarce, and she needed to keep hers if she wanted to keep a roof over her head, even if the roof leaked and urgently needed to be repaired. She silently cursed but audibly agreed, and trudged out to her car.

She had trouble finding the address where Mr. Morton's package awaited her. That part of town had an abundance of winding lanes and gloomy buildings that were not clearly marked. When she finally pulled up to the structure that she *believed* matched the address her boss had given her—for the building had no number— she was surprised to find an old library she never knew existed. The name carved in the limestone lintel had nearly worn away:

The Library of Illumination

Johanna remained in her car for several minutes, listening to raindrops drum against the roof. The Library of Illumination looked closed, but she was already there, so she might as well see if anyone was inside. She ran to the building and pushed against the narrow double doors. They opened into a drab vestibule with a scarred wooden floor and dark patterned wallpaper. A small overhead fixture emitted just enough light to enable Johanna to see a worn brass plaque with narrow gills fastened to the far wall. A button that looked like a doorbell had the words *What do you seek?* engraved beneath it.

She pushed the button, but didn't hear it ring. *Just my luck,* she thought. She waited a minute and then pressed it a second time. She was again greeted by silence.

She thought about leaving and telling her boss no one had been there. She looked out the door. The rain had turned to hail, and she could hear it pitting the outside of the glass.

Annoyed, she pushed the button again, and when nothing happened, she started poking it over and over again, tears of frustration stinging her eyes. She was supposed to be home, not here wasting her time in a strange place in this dark, depressing warren of a neighborhood, just so her boss could curry favor with a client.

"YOU—CALL—THIS—ILLUMINATION?" she shouted, violently stabbing the button to emphasize each word.

Suddenly, the wall sprang open, and she stared into the room of her dreams. Books lined polished wooden shelves that soared overhead for several stories—so high, in fact, that the shelves actually looked like they got lost in the clouds. But of course that was impossible. She chalked it up to her need for food.

Johanna leaned her umbrella against the wall. Rivulets of water streamed down the nylon fabric and across the floor. Like a caravan of parched men lost in the desert, the old, dry floorboards welcomed the moisture, absorbing it immediately. She brushed droplets of rain from her sleeves before entering the library.

Inside, what she saw mesmerized her. The aged glass in the windows looked wavy and translucent, and although she knew a storm raged outside, these windows admitted a warm glow. Flames danced among the logs inside a two-story fireplace, and as the heat embraced her, she could smell the aroma of pine and cedar.

"Hello?" she called out.

When nobody answered, she wandered over to a large refectory table that stood off to one side. It was covered with some of the most beautiful books Johanna had ever seen. Forgetting why she was there, she inspected a thick volume on astronomy. The leather cover had a fine patina, and she carefully turned the delicate parchment pages, until the beauty of a richly colored plate illustrating the solar system arrested her attention. It was so finely detailed, she felt like she could hop right into it and glide through space. She stroked the picture with her fingers, feeling the silky smoothness of the page, but froze when a three-dimensional image appeared in midair, right in front of her. Each brightly colored planet rotated on its axis as it circled around the sun. She studied Earth and swore she could see the storm clouds now pelting Exeter with hail.

Johanna closed the book, and the solar system disappeared. Intrigued, she gingerly walked around the room until she spotted a faded, green linen book with the words *Noah's Ark* embossed in gold on the cover. She opened it to the page recounting the animals that had boarded the ark. Her head snapped up when the roar of an elephant assailed her. There it stood—one of a pair— with its trunk held high, right in the middle of the library. She watched as a goat meandered out from behind the pachyderm, picked up a first edition of *Moby-Dick*, and started devouring it.

"Oh no!" she screamed, as she slammed the book shut. The animals disappeared, and the half-eaten Herman Melville novel dropped to the floor.

Johanna felt beads of sweat forming on her upper lip. She always perspired when scared or nervous. If she had learned anything from her childhood experiences, it was that the damaged book could mean big trouble. For her. She picked up the book and looked for an inconspicuous place to put it. Stashing it behind the leather sofa seemed like a good idea; however, she wasn't expecting what she found there. In a heap on the floor lay a scrawny little man, whose nearly bald head was punctuated by only three tufts of fluffy, white hair. He sported a pair of broken wire-rimmed spectacles that had been taped back together, and wore baggy corduroy pants and a threadbare cardigan sweater that had a tiny pin attached to it, identifying him as *Malcolm Trees, Curator.* She put her face close to the man's nose and mouth to check if he was still breathing.

"You're stealing my air."

Her heart nearly stopped. "You're alive, then?"

"Just barely. I really don't have a choice. I must remain here to watch over these books."

Johanna got down to business. "I'm here to pick up a package for Mr. Morton."

"Yes, of course," the old man replied. "If you'll do me the favor of helping me off the floor."

"What happened to you? Did you fall?"

"No. I was cranking the window shut when a wind gust lifted the cover of a book on paleontology. A pterosaur flew out and knocked me over."

He ignored her shocked expression as he continued. "Thank goodness I held on to the window crank. As I went down, I pulled the window closed. The book cover dropped back into place and that stopped the pterosaur in its tracks, or there would have been a mess in here. We're lucky it was an Istiodactylus and not one of its larger brethren, or I dare say, things might have ended differently, and you may have been attacked as soon as you entered the door."

"I wouldn't have liked that," she responded. "May I have Mr. Morton's book now?"

"Yes, yes, of course, just be careful with it. It would never do to have gangs of Bengal tribesmen running all around Exeter, looking for witches to kill."

Johanna must have gaped at the man, because he quickly added, "Don't worry. The book is securely wrapped in brown paper and all tied up with twine in a nice, neat package. You should be perfectly safe."

She reluctantly took the package, and found her way back to the vestibule. The door slammed shut behind her, and once again, the world grew dreary. She looked around for her umbrella, but it was gone. *Great.*

She made a mad dash for her car, and carefully navigated the roads of Exeter, looking for Bay House. When she finally found it, she realized she would have to run for the door with the book stashed under her coat to protect it.

Johanna hurried, even though the walkway was slick. She hoped she wouldn't slip and fall and somehow give free rein to the fury of the men in the book she carried.

She banged the door knocker several times. *Manners be damned.* She just wanted to deliver the book and go home.

A large, muscular man pulled the door open.

"Mr. Morton?"

"You have the book?"

"Yes, I do. And it put me through quite a bit of trouble." She pulled the book from under her coat and fussed with the string that bound it.

The man pulled the book from her hands and slammed the door in her face.

"Hey," she screamed, banging the knocker. "I want a receipt for that, and I'm not leaving until I get one." But she waited in vain. In the rain. And when a bolt of lightning cracked overhead, she retreated to her car and slowly made her way home.

Johanna arrived at Book Services the following morning to find the pile of work on her desk had more than doubled in size. She glared at her colleague Lucinda. She felt sure the older girl worked late for the sole purpose of dumping unwanted work on Johanna's desk. Lucinda appeared to be as busy as ever and didn't looked up.

B-B-B-R-R-R-I-I-I-N-N-N-G-G-G!

Johanna closed her eyes, just for a moment, and wished she were somewhere else. The phone continued to ring until she reluctantly picked it up.

"I want to see you in my office."

Disgusted, Johanna threw her purse under her desk. *I'm only two minutes late,* she thought, and she'd spent more than an hour of her own time the previous evening making a delivery for her boss. *What does he want from me, blood?*

When she got to his cramped cubicle, he motioned for her to sit down. "How did everything go last night?"

"Fine. I got the package and delivered it to Mr. Morton, who, I might add, refused to give me a receipt for it. He just slammed the door in my face and left me standing there in the rain."

Her boss reached behind him and pulled out her umbrella. "Here. I believe you left this behind."

"I didn't leave it behind. I leaned it against the wall so it wouldn't drip water everywhere, and when I left, it wasn't there. Were you following me?"

"No. And I'm not interested in the history of your umbrella. I just want to know what you saw when you went to the ... uh ... library."

"What do you mean, what I saw?" Visions of a half-eaten *Moby-Dick* flashed before her. Had the little old man complained about her?

"Well, leaving your umbrella behind would imply that you were either there for some length of time or left in a hurry because of some atrocity."

She wouldn't really call the goat an atrocity, and she hadn't actually seen the pterosaur. However, she had been there more than a few minutes, soaking in the wonders of her dream library and the enchanted books it held.

"It took me a while to get in, you know. I think the bell is broken."

"I've never gotten in," he replied offhandedly. "Every time I turn to leave, I hear a rush of air behind me. By the time I turn back, the parcel is sitting on the floor, waiting for me. It's the oddest library I've ever been to. How can anyone look for a book there?"

Johanna broke out in goose bumps; not just a minor plumping of her hair follicles, but major zit-sized goose mountains. *He's never been inside.*

Her boss warily eyed the tiny elevations on her skin. "Are you all right?"

She rubbed her arms with an exaggerated motion. "It's all this rain we've been having. It chills me to the core. And standing outside Mr. Morton's house waiting for a receipt didn't help. I may be coming down with something."

"I'm sure if you work your way through it, you'll be just fine. Pros play hurt, Johanna. Don't you forget that." He shooed her out of his office.

She knew he would react that way. God forbid anyone might need to take off a day from work; that simply was not allowed. They were given one week of vacation a year, and employees who took sick days received no pay. They were each forced to sign an agreement accepting those conditions before they were hired.

A WEEK LATER, her boss again waited until the last minute to ask Johanna to pick up a book and deliver it to the priory in Exeter.

Why does it have to be Exeter again? Why can't it

be a little closer? At least it wasn't raining. She left work and steered her way to the library. She thought she'd find it more easily, considering she'd been there before, but if she didn't know better, she would think it had changed locations. She drove up and down the winding streets for several minutes before she finally found it.

Inside, the vestibule remained unchanged. She pressed the button, straining to listen for a ringing sound. Again, nothing happened. She thought back to her previous visit and what she had said and done. She remembered punching the bell, but couldn't remember what she said. She focused on the small brass plaque. *What are you seeking?*

She pressed the button a second time and said, "I'm here to pick up a book for the priory." Nothing happened. She pressed it again. "I'm seeking entrance." Still nothing.

"Open sesame." "Let me in." "Why are you doing this to me?" "Is this thing broken?" With each request, her voice grew louder and her actions more animated. Disillusioned, she leaned her forehead against the button. "How can you call this a Library of Illumination when no one will illuminate me on how to get in?"

The wall slid open, revealing the splendor she remembered from the previous week.

She stepped inside. The little old man was nowhere to be found. She peeked behind the couch. He wasn't there. Neither was the book the goat had snacked on during her previous visit.

She perused the titles of books scattered about the area until her eyes came to rest on *Little Women*. She had first read it at the age of thirteen, and loved the Louisa May Alcott book so much, she often daydreamed about being Jo. She opened it to a random page and read to herself.

Suddenly, Jo sat before her in a barber chair, arguing with a man over how much he should pay her for her hair. "Twenty-five dollars and not a penny less," she demanded.

Johanna watched in amazement as the barber picked up a strand of Jo's long, luxurious hair and fingered it. "All right. But don't let this get around, or you'll send me to the poorhouse." He combed her hair back from her face and tied it with a string. Picking up a pair of shears, he cut off her ponytail and gently placed the locks on a counter. He then snipped Jo's hair shorter and shorter, until he'd littered the floor with her severed tresses.

"Oh, dear."

Johanna slammed the book shut and whirled around to find the little old man staring at the floor. "I ... I ... I came to pick up a book for the priory," she stammered.

"I have it right here. But I must ask you to linger a moment and help me out. My lumbago is acting up." He shuffled across the room and opened a narrow closet hidden in the wall paneling. "In here. There's a shovel and a broom. Would you please sweep up those hair clippings? I wouldn't want to slip and fall."

Johanna took the broom and shovel and returned to where she had seen Jo getting a haircut. Jo may have vanished, but bits of her hair lay all over the floor.

A foul odor emanated from the broom as Johanna swept. She wrinkled her nose.

The little old man apparently noticed. "That broom still stinks, does it? I tried cleaning it, but I guess I didn't do a good job. I must need new spectacles. But it's your own fault, you know. Those animals from *Noah's Ark* left quite a mess last week, and I believe that was all your doing."

Noah's Ark? Johanna thought about the elephants and other animals. She had been so busy trying to get the book away from the goat that she hadn't given much thought to what the other animals may have left behind.

"What should I do with this?" She jiggled the shovel containing the pile of loose hair.

The little old man pulled on a handle near the closet door. It opened up into a chute. "In here," he answered.

Johanna dumped the snippets, and Malcolm Trees nodded toward the closet. She put the tools away without saying another word.

He picked up a parcel and handed it to her. "Be careful. Templars can be ruthless."

She nodded, and delivered the package as instructed.

THE FOLLOWING MORNING, Johanna found a huge pile of work on her desk, no doubt due to another nocturnal visit from lazy Lucinda. She busied herself with getting it done, so she wouldn't have to stay late.

Johanna's boss startled her. "How did it go last night?" He had actually come out to her desk to ask about the book delivery, rather than call her into his office. Even Lucinda stopped typing and gawked at him.

"Fine," Johanna answered, not offering him any additional information.

He stared at her in silence for a minute or so, then walked away without saying another word.

"What's that all about?" Lucinda asked casually.

"I have no idea," Johanna answered. "Why don't you ask him?"

Lucinda returned to her typing, with a scowl on her face. About the only things she and Johanna had in common were that they worked for the same company and neither of them liked their boss. He reminded Johanna of the cold and calculating headmaster who had used an iron fist to rule the orphanage in which she grew up. She didn't know why Lucinda hated their boss, but she knew Lucinda would never ask him *anything*.

A FEW DAYS LATER, Johanna's boss told her she would have to pick up two parcels and deliver them to two different destinations.

She didn't mind visiting the library, but she hated her boss for intruding on her personal time. She thought he waited until the last minute to ask her to make deliveries as a demonstration of *his* power over *her* job. She wondered if he told her to make two deliveries because he had tried to make one himself and had failed.

"Where are they going?"

"They'll give you the addresses at the library."

"I hope they're local," she said, walking toward the door. "I don't have a lot of gasoline to devote to running all over creation. And my fuel costs are getting out of hand. I asked the garage to send you the bill."

She watched his face turn white, then red, just before the door closed behind her. She hadn't really asked anyone to send him the bill, but saying so made her feel like she was taking back control of her life. She smiled. She didn't do it often, but when she did her face instantly changed, and her beauty emerged.

IN EXETER, SHE again felt like someone had switched the streets around. It took her an extra half-hour to find the library, and it seemed like she stumbled upon it by accident.

She entered the vestibule and walked over to

the button on the brass plaque. She pressed it and said, "Illumination." The doors opened, and she walked inside, smiling at having figured out the key to gaining entrance.

The little old man stood waiting for her. "Feeling pretty proud of yourself, are you?"

"What do you mean?"

"Very few people come to our door, and rarely does anyone gain admittance. It would seem that hardly anyone ever seeks illumination. They punch the button, pound on the door, and rant and rave in general, but no one is going to get in unless they say the right thing.

"You managed to gain entrance the first couple of times through sheer, dumb luck."

He said it matter-of-factly and without malice, but Johanna's smile vanished. Her mind immediately transported back in time to the orphanage in which each child had been treated with such contempt, they couldn't help but feel worthless.

The headmaster of the orphanage had been invited to sit in on the youngsters' weekly spelling lesson. Their teacher made a big fuss over him, and he began drilling the students.

Johanna waited her turn with both enthusiasm and trepidation. She wanted to excel, but she feared humiliation.

"Johanna, spell judgment."

Johanna stood ramrod straight, her excitement building. Her teacher had just gone over the spelling the previous day, and Johanna had memorized it. She really wanted to impress the headmaster, and she now had a chance to shine.

"Judgment, j-u-d-g-m-e-n-t, judgment."

Her teacher nodded his head in approval until

the headmaster shouted out, "Wrong!"

Her teacher just stared, his mouth hanging open.

"There is an E *in* judgment. *J-u-d-g-e-m-e-n-t."*

Johanna knew she was right. She spelled it just the way she had been taught, and she stood her ground. "I spelled it correctly," she stated, with a slight quiver.

"You dare to challenge me?" the headmaster bellowed. "Prepare to be punished severely."

Johanna looked to her teacher for support, but found none.

The headmaster left the room momentarily, and returned carrying a massive Oxford English Dictionary *and a cat-o'-nine-tails. He scanned the well-worn dictionary to letters beginning with* J, *and there it was: j-u-d-g-e-m-e-n-t. It didn't matter that the OED also included the other spelling; only that Johanna be punished for defying him.*

He whipped Johanna five times in front of her classmates. Her teacher had betrayed her by not defending her. Her so-called friends made fun of her afterwards. As a result, Johanna learned to embrace isolation and numb her feelings against pain.

"What impressed me," Malcolm Trees continued, "is how you learned from it."

But Johanna didn't hear his last sentence. She had already switched to self-preservation mode. She masked her feelings of inadequacy with a harsh retort. "Why don't you just give me the parcels then, and we'll be done with it."

"Wait here," he answered, surprised at her sudden

change of mood. Her curt manner made him involuntarily retaliate. "And for heaven's sake, don't open any books."

"Be quick about it, then. I haven't got all night." Her own rudeness shocked her, but she would rather die than let this little old man know he had the power to hurt her.

The first parcel was very large. "You'd better hold this with both hands. It's an encyclopedia, and lord knows what page it might open up to if you should drop it. You could unleash the tidal waves caused by the sinking of Atlantis, the hideous and painful boils from the bubonic plague, or perhaps the bombing of Hiroshima. It could be catastrophic."

"Where's it going?"

"Look here," he said, thumping the top of the package. "It's practically around the corner."

"Is there a second package?"

"Oh. Yes. I have it right here." He walked over to the desk and took a miniature parcel out of the drawer. "I'll slip this into your pocket," he said, matching word to deed. "You had best deliver the larger one first."

The encyclopedia weighed a ton, and Johanna rested it on the refectory table to get a better grip. In doing so, she knocked Charles Dickens' *A Christmas Carol* on the floor, and the Ghost of Christmas Past sprang into action, conjuring up a festive ball. In an instant, Mr. and Mrs. Fezziwig danced around the library, swirling to and fro, knocking more books onto the floor. Suddenly, a young boy in a wheelchair began asking where he could find *The Secret Garden*. Trying to avoid him, the Fezziwigs danced right into a British soldier, who held the body of *Gunga Din*. They all went down hard, causing mass confusion.

"Go," the little old man said, pushing Johanna toward the door. "I'll deal with this."

Johanna suddenly found herself alone in the dim vestibule, clutching the encyclopedia for dear life. She didn't remember actually walking out the door. She felt almost as if the old man had transported her there by magic.

She carefully placed the large parcel on the seat of her car, and drove to the address written on it. The old man had been right about the location. She probably could have walked there if she weren't afraid of dropping the encyclopedia and unleashing who knows what.

After the first delivery, she took out the smaller package and looked at the address. Her stomach lurched when she saw *her* name and address on it. She slipped it back into her pocket and drove home. She wanted to make sure she was someplace safe and familiar before opening it.

Johanna's attached cottage could almost be called ramshackle, even though she worked hard every weekend to keep it from deteriorating. She had a small living room, a smaller bedroom, a tiny kitchen, and a minuscule bathroom—pleasant but humble. It wasn't her dream home, but it was all she could afford. She was only seventeen years old, and she liked being able to say she lived in a one-bedroom flat, even though she had friends with studio apartments larger than all her rooms added together. Now it looked like she would lose her home to a developer who wanted to build condominiums. Her landlord had informed her she would have to move out by the end of the year. *Perhaps my next flat will let me have a cat,* she mused. At least one positive thing might result from her dilemma.

She locked the door and pulled down the shades

before taking out the tiny parcel. It would never do to have a neighbor witness something that might be difficult to explain.

She sat on the diminutive sofa in her living room and gingerly opened the package. Inside, she found a small journal. It had the initials *J.C.* stamped on the front cover. *My initials.* How did the man at the library know her name?

She began to lift the cover but stopped suddenly, breaking into a cold sweat. *What if J.C. stands for Jesus Christ and they start crucifying him here in my living room?* She imagined the crowd roaring for blood. She could practically see the dust rising as Christ dragged the cross to the field of execution. She smelled the sweat of the Roman soldiers leading the way. *Or is that me?*

She didn't know what to do. She thought back to her early years in school, when her teachers forced her to sit through Bible instruction. She had daydreamed through a lot of it, but was pretty sure no one had ever mentioned Jesus Christ keeping a diary. She had to chance it; after all, her address must have been written on the package for a reason.

She opened the cover. The fly page had been dedicated to her:

> *To Johanna Charette,*
> *You seek Illumination.*
> *May these pages embrace your imagi-*
> *nation and feed your soul.*
> *Regards,*
> *Malcolm Trees, Curator*
> *The Library of Illumination*

Malcolm Trees? The little old man in the library had given her a gift. She felt awful about having been rude to him. Maybe she should bake him some brownies to smooth things over. *Does he even have any teeth?* She made up her mind. She would bake light, fluffy muffins. She wouldn't add nuts.

Carefully, she turned to the first diary page. It had that day's date on it. She removed a tiny pen from a loop attached to the book. Then carefully, very carefully, she wrote about the day's events.

As she wrote, she nervously looked up from time to time, expecting to see her words come alive. But every word she wrote stayed firmly on the page.

When she finished, she locked the diary with a tiny key that had been tied to its blue ribbon bookmark and slipped the key into her purse. She hid the diary in the back of a cupboard, behind her supply of bathroom tissue. *It should be safe here.*

JOHANNA BAKED MUFFINS every night and carefully wrapped them in a red-and-white-checked napkin for Mr. Trees, but she received no last-minute requests from her boss to make a delivery. So each night she went home and ate the muffins for dinner, then immediately baked a fresh batch for the next day. She gave up baking after ten days. Her clothing had started to feel snug, and she couldn't afford to keep paying for the ingredients.

The first day she arrived at work without muffins, her boss asked her to make a delivery. That evening, she thanked Malcolm Trees for the diary. He waved his hand in the air as if it were nothing, but she thought she saw a hint of a smile before he turned away.

She was careful not to open any books while there, and watched as he wrapped up a book on the history of tobacco plantations. She accepted it with a nod and a smile and went on her way. Aside from the occasional odor of burning tobacco whenever she hit a bump, there were no mishaps.

As THE WEEKS passed, her boss called on Johanna to make deliveries with increasing frequency. Each time he told her to pick up a book at the library, her joy exceeded the time before. Not that she let it show. It was her secret. She spoke to her boss as little as possible about her visits. Whenever he told her to make a delivery, he stared at her as if he expected her to spill her guts about everything she had seen inside the library, but he'd stopped asking her about it, because when he tried questioning her, Johanna always requested time off as compensation for her trouble.

Every time she picked up a parcel, she diligently wrote about the experience in the tiny diary. It had become second nature. As the year progressed, Johanna had many opportunities to explore the books she saw. In doing so, she met the Headless Horseman from *The Legend of Sleepy Hollow*; nearly fell down the rabbit hole with Alice during her *Adventures in Wonderland*; and listened to Sancho complain about *Don Quixote*.

One day, while she waited for the *Atlas of the Ancient World*, Mr. Trees accidentally dropped the oversize book. She heard him groan as latitude and longitude lines floated over Mesopotamia. The book had split in two. Rather than asking her to wait by herself while he made the necessary repairs, he invited her into the library antechamber. There, he taught her how to repair broken bindings and re-sew loose signatures, the folded pages that make up sections of a book. She paid attention to every detail, and from that day on, he guided her as she helped him fix old tomes in need of restoration.

Everything Johanna had learned in the library was called to task the day she found Mr. Trees pinned down by a lion. He had apparently ducked behind a wingchair, and the lion had jumped up on the piece of furniture, knocking it on top of the old man. Now the beast glared at the curator, and growled menacingly. Johanna scarcely moved as she looked around for the book the lion had escaped from, but didn't see it. She had to divert the animal's attention if she wanted to save Mr. Trees. Her eyes searched the shelves for books written by Edgar Rice Burroughs. If anyone would know how to handle this, Tarzan would.

A copy of *Tarzan at the Earth's Core* lay just a few steps away. She quietly inched her way over to it and opened it, but instead of Tarzan, she encountered Germans operating an airship. The lion roared at the unexpected intrusion. She gently closed the cover, replaced the book, and pulled an earlier Tarzan novel off the shelf.

In the blink of an eye, the King of the Jungle stood before her in all his glory. ALL HIS GLORY. *Not even a loincloth.* She averted her eyes and pointed toward the lion. Tarzan's wild call of the jungle got the animal's attention, and the two faced each other, ready for battle. As man and beast circled each other, Johanna slipped behind the armchair and lifted it off Mr. Trees. He quickly closed the *National Geographic* magazine he held in his hands, leaving a stunned Tarzan looking for the now-missing cat. Johanna backtracked to *Tarzan of the Apes* and closed the cover on that book as well.

Aside from a large puddle of lion drool on the floor and the manly scent of a savage who had never heard of deodorant—much less used it—the library was none the worse for wear. Johanna, already well versed in the location of the cleaning supplies, went about tidying up that afternoon's encounter, while Mr. Trees carefully wrapped a selection of *National Geographic* magazines that Johanna had been called on to deliver.

AND SO IT went. *Every* time Johanna visited the Library of Illumination, she found herself more immersed in the fabric of its existence, and hid her disappointment on days when she wasn't asked to make a delivery.

She thought about the library so often, the rigors of daily life barely penetrated her consciousness. Invitations from friends went unnoticed, as Johanna ignored everything but the library.

One sultry summer morning, she felt restless and decided to visit the library on her own, but even though she had been there dozens of times before, she couldn't find the building. After two hours of searching, she finally gave up and drove home, perplexed and depressed. A second attempt a few days later was equally unsuccessful.

Yet the next time her boss told her to make a delivery, she located the library without difficulty. Try as she might, she couldn't solve that enigma.

THE SEASONS CHANGED, and before Johanna knew it, the trees had lost their leaves and the cold bite of winter made its approach. Soon afterward, an eviction notice arrived. Johanna had forty-eight hours to vacate her home. *How can they do this?* she wondered. *This isn't enough notice.* But as she scanned the sizable pile of unopened mail on her kitchen counter, she found the still-sealed letters announcing her impending eviction.

She called in sick the next morning, needing the day to dump her meager belongings into boxes and find a place to stay. She called a couple of friends, seeking their help, but instead of sympathy, she found bitterness, because she had ignored their invitations for too long and hadn't returned their calls.

That afternoon, she looked at a few apartments and boarding houses, but they were either unfit for human habitation or well beyond her budget. She would be forced to lose another day's pay looking for a place to live.

Relentless rain pounded her windows the following morning. She dragged herself out of bed and dressed in a hurry. No time for breakfast; besides, she had already packed her teakettle and mug for the move to her next flat.

She walked down to the corner for a paper, and struggled to study the real-estate section while attempting to keep her umbrella from turning inside out in the wind. *An extra set of hands would be nice.*

The first place she viewed was a basement flat that had flooded in the torrential rain. "Don't mind that," the landlady told her. "Just place a few towels on the floor by the wall to sop it all up.

The next apartment came with an inebriated live-in roommate. *No thank you.*

Two more dreary prospects dampened her spirits even more. She made up her mind. She just wouldn't leave her old apartment. What would they do? Physically pick her up and throw her on the sidewalk?

Her stomach growled. It was well past noon, and she hadn't eaten all day. She stopped to buy a sandwich and had the bad luck of running into her boss.

"I thought you were sick?" he chided her. "You know, if you don't like your job, there are plenty of people who are more than willing to fill your shoes. Maybe you should come in and clean out your desk."

He was baiting her and she knew it, but she hated giving him the satisfaction of knowing that he got under her skin. "If that's what you want, fine."

As soon as the words came out of her mouth, she knew she had made a mistake. Not because her boss's face turned bright red, but because she realized she would no longer have any connection to the Library of Illumination.

"Don't expect any severance pay," he said brusquely.

She opened her mouth to apologize, but he turned his back on her and disappeared into the rain. She had no recourse but to return to Book Services to clean out her desk. *Great, another box of belongings, with nowhere to put them.*

She didn't have much to pack at work. Just a small potted plant, the cardigan on the back of her chair, and a book. Always a book. Other than that, she kept few possessions at the office, because they had a tendency to disappear.

As Lucinda watched, Johanna went through her desk to make sure she didn't leave anything personal behind. She could actually feel Lucinda's smug smile behind her back. As her final act, Johanna picked up a huge pile of outstanding work orders and plopped them in Lucinda's "In" basket. "These are yours now," she said, with only a hint of satisfaction.

Lucinda's jaw dropped, but before she could utter a word, the sound of an overturned chair crashing to the floor made them both jump. They watched as their boss stormed out of his cubicle and made a beeline for the company president's office. Moments later, he emerged quaking with anger and stomped over to them.

He stuffed a thick envelope in Johanna's hand.

"Severance pay," he mumbled. She wouldn't have been surprised to see steam rising from his collar. He hemmed and hawed for a moment before thrusting another envelope at her. "I've been authorized to give you an additional week's pay if you'll make one more delivery for the library."

Her heart raced. She would get to visit her beloved library one last time and say goodbye to Mr. Trees.

THE WEATHER WAS similar to the first time she had visited the Library of Illumination, and Johanna once again found the little old man lying on the floor, this time in the Magazines and Periodicals section. She leaned over him, careful not to steal his air.

When he didn't immediately open his eyes, she shook him gently by the shoulder. She had never touched him before, and could feel the frail bones of his arm encased in the sleeve of his sweater. She wondered when he had last eaten a meal.

"Please wake up, Mr. Trees. It's me, Johanna."

She picked up an old newspaper and began fanning him, but tiny Lakota Indians started flying off the page and made a racket as they did a war dance right next to him. It reminded her of the Lilliputians in a passage from *Gulliver's Travels*.

Johanna scanned the paper and saw it was dated 1876. The headline story recounted the Battle of Little Bighorn and General Custer's defeat in eastern Montana. She quickly placed the newspaper down, covering the Indians. Their war cries stopped. She prayed they had returned to the printed page and that she hadn't smothered them to death

She looked around, desperately seeking a text that might help her. Her eyes settled on an 1887 copy of Beeton's Christmas Annual. It contained the Arthur Conan Doyle story *A Study in Scarlet*. She grabbed the magazine and opened it up. Sherlock Holmes appeared, but she ignored him, turning the pages until Dr. John Watson showed up.

"Doctor, you've got to help me. That is, you've got to help Mr. Trees."

"What seems to be the problem?" he asked, not at all surprised by his surroundings.

"I don't know. That's why I sought you out." Her voice had a tinge of hysteria.

Watson picked up the old man's wrist and felt for a pulse. He put his ear to the man's chest. "Well, he's still alive, that's for sure. Fetch a glass of water, please."

He sprinkled some of the water onto Mr. Tree's face and lifted the man's eyelids to see if his pupils were dilated.

"Dr. Watson, how wonderful to see you again."

"There you go," Watson answered, as he slipped his hand under the old man's back and helped him into a sitting position. "Catnapping again, Malcolm?"

"Just for a moment, my good man, but I'm awake now, so I'll let you get back to it." Mr. Trees turned to Johanna. "Hello, Johanna. Please close the magazine." Dr. Watson winked at Malcolm just before disappearing back onto the pages of Beeton's.

"My God, Mr. Trees, you had me so worried," Johanna said, as she placed the magazine back on the rack. She sat on the floor next to him. "Are you sure you're all right?"

"Johanna, we've known each other for almost a year now, and I think it would be appropriate for you to call me by my given name."

"Malcolm?"

"Yes. But all my friends call me Mal. You can call me Mal."

"Your friends?" She felt flustered. "Of course you would have friends," she babbled. "I don't know what would make me think you didn't have any friends. It's just that it seems like you always have your hands full, working here and all, and I didn't realize you had time for socializing."

"Oh yes, I have friends, and soon they will become your friends, too."

"Did you hit your head, Mr. Trees?"

"Mal."

"Did you hit your head, Mal?"

"I know why you're saying that, Johanna. You don't believe I've made any friends, nor that you'll ever meet them. But you will, you know."

"Are you having a party then, a little get-together with your friends? Are you inviting me?" She hated herself for sounding so condescending, but she really believed he might be hallucinating.

"You'll meet them here in the library. William Shakespeare. Rudyard Kipling. Mary Shelley. And their characters: Hamlet, Mowgli, and Frankenstein."

"You're friends with Frankenstein?"

"Of course. You'll befriend him and many other illustrious personages as you take on your role as the new *Curator of Illumination.*"

"But that's your job."

"And it has been for centuries, but I'm tired, Johanna. It's time for me to go. I've been grooming you, you know, and you're more than ready to take my place."

"But I can't do this, Mr. ... Mal. I have a job, a very demanding one, and the commute would be horrendous." She stopped, realizing she had no job and no home. "I guess I *could* move closer, since I have to give up my flat. Maybe I could even find a job nearby." She paused for just a second. "No, it would never work. Taking care of this library takes a lot of time and commitment."

"Johanna, Johanna, Johanna, this would be your job—your career. And you've already demonstrated the passion it takes to get the job done. Besides, who do you think owns the company that employed you? LOI Book Services is a subsidiary of the library. Someone has to do the grunt work, making sure the scholars who use our tomes to keep literature alive get books when they need them.

"But not you, Johanna. Your devotion to the printed word is too finely honed. Your calling is to *illuminate*. It will be very rewarding, I assure you. And there's a lovely apartment upstairs for you to live in. You'll make ten times the salary you're making now, but you won't need it. Everything you could possibly want will be right here."

"I have to eat, Mal. I have to go out and buy food. Who takes care of the place when I'm gone?"

"If you need food, find *The Art of French Cooking*. Julia Child would be happy to whip up a batch of coq au vin. Or if you feel the need to get out—although, I never did—just go into the children's section and open up *Mary Poppins*. She's very good about watching the place. And always singing." Mal started humming and then broke into song about how helpful a little sugar can be.

"You know, Mal, I don't think they mentioned any such song in the P. L. Travers's book."

He smiled at her. "Maybe not, but we've got the manuscript for the Disney screenplay here somewhere, and that's the text you should use. Disney's Mary Poppins has a much better disposition than the original Poppins, who was quite a Tartar."

"We're getting off topic. What about a boyfriend, Mal? How would I ever explain this place to him?"

"Haven't you ever fallen in love with the protagonist in a book, or the antagonist, for that matter? Just open up *Gone with the Wind*. I'm sure Rhett Butler would love to have dinner with you. Or perhaps you would prefer Jay Gatsby?"

"I mean a real boyfriend. A living, breathing person with whom I can share my thoughts and ideas."

"Invite him here. I'm sure he'll love the place." He paused. "You may want to hide Oscar Wilde's *Salome* and Nabokov's *Lolita* in the beginning, but it should all turn out all right."

The idea of it all boggled her mind, but not for long, as she looked beyond her own concerns. "Where will *you* go? Will you be moving in with relatives, or into an assisted-living facility? Do you have a little retirement cottage waiting for you someplace?"

"You don't seem to understand, dear. I'll be going to a higher plane."

Tears started rolling down Johanna's cheeks. "You can't go, Mal. I'm not ready to do this."

"But you are, dear. I've read your diary. You've had appropriate reactions to every unanticipated experience you've faced in the library, and you've handled every one of them in the correct way. You also learned how to handle the day-to-day duties along the way. Help me up." He offered her his arm.

Johanna helped him stand up, all the while wondering how he got hold of her diary. She couldn't picture Mal on his hands and knees, routing behind the toilet tissue in her bathroom cupboard.

"Come with me." Mal slowly climbed the spiral

stairs to the balcony on the second level, and Johanna followed. He pushed a crystal lever on the end of one of the shelves.

The bookcase swung open, revealing the entrance to a charming living room lit by clusters of hurricane lamps in all different shapes and sizes. A fire sprang to life in the fireplace, and in the corner, a perfectly proportioned Christmas tree glowed with the flicker of candles. Jewel-like ornaments and sprigs of fresh herbs adorned it, filling the room with the aroma of balsam and lavender.

Johanna followed Mal into a kitchen, where a freshly baked apple pie sat cooling on a creamy marble counter. Gleaming brass pots and pans hung from a rack above a large enamel stove. And she would swear she could smell the enticing scent of lemon chicken roasting in the oven.

Mal led Johanna into a bedroom highlighted by a huge four-poster bed covered with a thick, down mattress and a fluffy duvet. On top, she saw beautiful decorative pillows, and tall windows played host to billowy, white curtains that invited any breeze to make them flutter. Tables flanking the bed contained bright reading lamps and stacks of books.

Johanna stared at the books, straining to read the titles. She wanted to know just what went on in there at night.

Mal laughed when he saw the look on her face. "You don't have to worry, Johanna. This room is a safe haven. The only thing that will jump off the page in here is your imagination." A tiny white kitten leapt onto the bed and became almost invisible as it sank into the duvet. "And maybe that kitten."

"What's her name?"

"Ophelia."

"That's exactly the name I would have chosen. And this room is exactly how I envisioned my dream bedroom. The kitchen is my vision of the perfect kitchen. And the same is true in the living room. How is it that your home is the very home I've always dreamed of owning?"

"It's like the books we love to read. No two people see the same thing. The story is shaped by our individual imaginations. I've always felt bad for people who don't enjoy reading. They must have no imagination at all. But you, Johanna, have been blessed. I've seen glimpses of your imagination every time you opened a book in the library.

"I assure you, when I first opened *Noah's Ark*, it was the giraffes that sprang from the page. And they were nudging a pair of slow tortoises onto the ramp of the ark. We all see what we want to see. That's the miracle of reading. The way it stimulates the human mind to create its own story."

"You haven't answered my question. I still don't know how this could look like my dream home if it isn't bewitched in some way."

"While the library's books may be bewitched, these living quarters are merely enchanted, and I mean that in a good way. I can assure you, nothing treacherous will ever befall you within these walls."

"You also said you read my diary. How did you find it?"

Mal seemed to withdraw into himself. After a moment, he looked at her. "I can now see why it's taking you time to adjust. I just thought you knew ... that you figured it out ... like you did with the button in the vestibule."

"I don't understand."

He led her back into the library and spread his arms to indicate all of their surroundings. "This is the greatest library ever created, a virtual fountain of knowledge. Every book *emanates* from here, Johanna. This is the home of every text ever written. Even your diary, for once you wrote down your thoughts on the page, they miraculously appeared in an identical diary here. That way, if any journal, book, or manuscript is ever lost or destroyed, it will only be lost in the physical sense. The essence of its written words will live on in the universe. The only reason why anyone writes anything down is because they want to share it with someone. To write is to illuminate. This is the depository of all illumination, and you have been chosen to guide it into the future."

Mal walked over to a shelf and removed *Hawaii* by James A. Michener. He opened the cover, and the vast space in the center of the library instantly transformed into a golden beach at sunset. A wave crashed to the shore, sending up a spray of droplets that sparkled like diamonds in the last rays of the sun. Johanna could feel the mist as it touched her skin. Mal handed the book to her and smiled. "This will be my retreat."

She felt overwhelmed. She blinked back tears as she grabbed a tissue from her pocket to wipe her eyes. "What if I can't do the job?"

"You can and you will."

The tears seemed to be obstructing her vision. "Mal, you're fading away."

"My time here is over."

"But what if I need your help?"

"I read your diary. It's only fair that you read mine. It's on my desk. *Your desk.* Everything you could possibly need to know is in there." He had half vanished with the sunlight.

"Please, Mal. I don't want to lose you."

"You'll never lose me. We're born of the same cloth. Books are in our blood. Literature lives in our souls. I'll live on in this library, through the words in my diary. And you will, too.

"You're the curator now, Johanna. Go forth and illuminate."

The vision of Hawaii disappeared, and Mal with it. Johanna closed the book, replacing it on the shelf. She turned and looked out over the library, expecting to feel bereft; but instead, a sense of serenity washed over her, and she knew she had found more than a new calling and a new home. She had found nirvana.

—LOI—

C:L ❖ I

CHAPTER ONE

Doubloons

BLACK DOG GRABBED a wench and threw her over his shoulder. The pirate's ghostly pallor and missing fingers may have frightened some people, but they never stopped him from enjoying a little fun. *Yo-ho-ho, and a bottle of rum* was his personal anthem.

As he spun her around, the sweet scent of alcoholic spirits, along with the stench of human perspiration and sun-parched seaweed, filled the air. Underfoot, empty liquor bottles and gold doubloons littered the Persian carpet. Pirates had taken over the Library of Illumination.

The wanton partying stunned Johanna, the library's young curator, as she entered through the venerable institution's double front doors. "Jackson!" she yelled.

Sixteen-year-old Jackson Roth froze for a millisecond before closing the cover of *Treasure Island* by Robert Louis Stevenson. The pirates disappeared, but the odor lingered.

"Low tide," Johanna muttered as she cranked open a window. "Pick up those bottles and debris and clean up this mess," she scolded. "Then we need to have a little chat. This is the Library of Illumination, a repository for literature—not a theme park."

She stormed down the hall and into an antechamber. Johanna took a deep breath and exhaled very slowly. Gently, she set down an old book in need of a new binding that had just arrived from overseas. She had placed the library in Jackson's care while she ran to the local freight office, and now she regretted that decision. He apparently was not mature enough to deal with the unique ability of many of the library's books to come to life when opened. Johanna hoped she could turn the pirate party into a teaching moment by refusing to help Jackson clean up. He had to learn to deal with the consequences of his actions.

It took a while for the boy to get rid of the pirates' mess, and when he finally knocked on the antechamber door, his eyes had lost their sparkle and his usual grin was grim. He pushed his hair off his forehead.

Johanna knew he expected the worst. She had hired Jackson to work at the library because she desperately needed assistance after the position of curator was thrust upon her just six months earlier. Before that defining moment, she had sunk to a low point in her life. She had no family and had just lost her home, her job, and, she believed, her tenuous connection to the Library of Illumination. It was the only place that made her feel welcomed. Malcolm Trees, the library's former curator, literally handed Johanna his job and a diary detailing the history of the library under his command—a precious gift. She would do everything in her power to protect the library and the wonders it held.

She was barely older than Jackson, but seemed to be light years ahead of him in maturity. And the library was a big responsibility, a little too much work to handle by herself.

Exeter High School had referred Jackson, saying his father had walked out on the family and his mother could use the money to keep food on the table for Jackson's younger brother and sister. Johanna had grown up poor and felt empathy for the family. She identified with Jackson more than she cared to admit, but she didn't know how to corral his youthful enthusiasm. She tried to put herself in his place and wondered what she could say that would make the young man realize he had to act more responsibly.

"Please don't fire me," he croaked, barely above a whisper. His face looked calm, but she saw the tiniest flare of his nostrils—the kind of intrinsic movement that inner turmoil foists upon people who are trying to maintain their composure.

"I'm not going to fire you"—she saw his shoulders relax—"this time. But if you ever pull another stunt like that, you'll be out of here faster than a vacuum cleaner sucks up dust bunnies. I've already demonstrated what happens when one of the library's books is opened and how the results can sometimes be disastrous. As much as I'd like to believe *Treasure Island* opened by accident, the sheer amount of debris and the lingering odor tells me that the book was allowed to remain open for quite some time. And since you were singing along with the pirates when I arrived, I sensed you weren't being diligent about maintaining order in the library."

"I'm sorry, Johanna. I swear, it won't happen again."

She hadn't expected him to sound as penitent as he did. Any further reprimand died in her throat. Instead, she walked to her desk drawer and removed his paycheck. "Here." She handed it to him. "It's quitting time."

"Do you still want me to come in tomorrow?"

"Ten a.m.," she answered. "Don't be late."

Jackson smiled. "Don't worry. I'll be right on time."

JACKSON'S BIKE STOOD perched against a dumpster in the rear yard of the library. As he swung his leg over the battered frame, he heard the jingle of coins in his pocket. He reached in and removed them. Even though the sun barely penetrated the secluded area, the gold doubloons in his hand almost sparkled. Jackson's heartbeat quickened. He jammed the doubloons back into his pocket and wheeled his bike down the long alley that linked the yard to the street.

JOHANNA ROSE EARLY Saturday morning. She tranquilly repaired the binding on the book she had picked up the previous day. When she finished, she carefully removed the magnifying goggles she had inherited from Mal. They made her look like a mad professor in an old-fashioned science-fiction movie. The lenses were inset in brass frames that had been fitted into an old brown leather mask, similar to one an early aviator might have worn. Each lens could be adjusted by twisting the outer brass ring to increase or decrease the depth of field. Additional lenses on movable arms could be flipped down over the eyepieces to increase magnification. She studied the goggles and smiled. Mal had been very possessive of them, but when Johanna found them, they'd had a note attached, written in cramped script upon a tiny piece of vellum:

Johanna,
Use them well. They will give you vast insight.
Warm regards,
Mal

He had released his goggles into her custody, and she did her best to take good care of them. She polished them with a soft cloth before placing them in their protective leather box. The goggles were precious; however, no more precious than any book, armillary, or fountain pen found inside the library. Johanna treated every little bit and bob with the utmost respect.

The ancient grandfather clock in the corner struck ten. She wondered if Jackson had already arrived, or would be late as usual.

JACKSON STOOD BEHIND the circulation desk, staring into space. He had hurried to get there a few minutes early, and waited patiently for Johanna to appear. He thought about the ruckus the pirates had caused the day before and what had happened once he shut and shelved the book. Almost everything had gone away. Almost. He could see the gold doubloons in his mind's eye. *Why didn't they disappear with the pirates?* At the moment, they sat in a jar of change he kept on his dresser at home. He wondered if the pirates would contact Johanna somehow, demanding the return of their money. The thought made him uncomfortable.

He unconsciously played with a large gong sitting on the corner of the desk. It was quite old, with a dark patina on the outer rim, although the center remained bright. He picked up the mallet that lay beside it and, without thinking, banged it against the gong. The rich sound reverberated throughout the library.

He felt a hand grip his shoulder. *Oh my God, Long John Silver!* He whirled about, a sheen of fear-induced perspiration oozing onto his face.

"What are you doing?" Johanna asked, with an edge to her voice.

Jackson felt his terror evaporate, only to find it immediately replaced by a different kind of fear. "Waiting for you?"

"Did you read the sign below the gong that says, 'Please do not handle'?"

"I thought that was for visitors."

Johanna noticed the beads of sweat on Jackson's upper lip. "Are you all right?"

The teen took a deep breath. "Fine."

She continued to stare at him.

"Really, Johanna, I'm fine. I wasn't thinking straight. It's my little brother—he's sick, you know? My mom's taking him to Saint Thomas Hospital this morning, to see if she can get some medicine for him."

"I didn't realize he was that ill. Do you need to go home and watch your sister?"

"No, that's okay. Mrs. Caruthers, our next-door neighbor, is watching her so Mom doesn't have to pay a babysitter."

Johanna removed the mallet from Jackson's hand and placed it back in its rightful place. "All right then, let's get to it."

For several hours, Johanna and Jackson pored over long lists of book titles, retrieving them from the stacks and packing them for delivery. Jackson did most of the grunt work, climbing the ladder and carrying piles of books. Johanna handled the administrative work, filling out invoices and making sure boxes were labeled correctly. They worked quietly, stacking completed orders one next to the other, until they had built a wall of cartons nearly four feet high and twenty feet long. They finished late in the afternoon.

"I'm sorry, Jackson. I didn't mean to keep you so long." Johanna pulled out a one-hundred-dollar bill. Jackson's eyes widened when she handed it to him. "This is for today's work. It's more than I usually pay you, but you deserve a little extra for working on a Saturday and missing your lunch. Normally, I'd make you wait until payday, but it doesn't seem fair to make you wait a whole week." She prayed he wouldn't spend the cash on something frivolous like sneakers or beer.

"Thanks, Johanna." He shoved the bill into his pocket. "See you Monday afternoon."

JACKSON WALKED OUT the back door feeling funny about taking the money when he had a fistful of doubloons at home. He grappled with the idea of returning the doubloons to the library and telling Johanna he had forgotten to give them to her when he had cleaned up after the pirates. Would she even believe him, or would she call him a thief? He didn't know if they could actually be considered stolen property, because they had come from the pirates and not from the library. He shook his head, making a face. *Of course they're stolen, you dimwit! The pirates stole them!*

Jackson knew his friends would be playing ball in the park by the train station, but bypassed them and peddled straight home. If he showed them the hundred-dollar bill, he would feel really cool. But someone might try to steal it, and that wouldn't be cool at all.

He dropped his bike in the driveway next to his house and walked into the wood-frame cottage with its peeling white paint. He had offered to re-paint it, but his mother had no money for paint. He wondered how much a gold doubloon was worth, and if it would cover the cost.

He found his mother at the kitchen table with her head in her hands. Nearby, his younger brother slept on a battered, old sofa, wheezing with every breath.

"How is he, Ma?"

She looked up at her eldest son, her face puffy and her eyes bloodshot. "He's got pneumonia. The doctor gave me some pills for him, but not enough. I've got prescriptions for more pills, but he needs antibiotics and steroids and cough medicine and inhalers ..." The tears began pooling under her eyes.

"It's okay, Ma. Look what Johanna paid me." He stuffed the hundred-dollar bill in her hand.

"Why would she give you so much? You're not doing anything illegal, are you?" His mother stared at him.

He thought of the doubloons and felt the heat build as his face reddened.

"Oh no, Jackson. Please don't tell me you're stealing." She paused. "Or dealing."

"No, Ma, no," he blurted, shocked that she implied he might sell drugs. "Johanna paid me this for working all day on a Saturday to pack up a shipment of books. I didn't get to eat lunch, so she paid me extra."

His mother eyed the hundred-dollar bill. "We do need the money." She pushed herself up from the table. "If you'll watch your brother, I can run to the store and get more medicine and maybe buy some groceries."

"Sure, Ma, you go. I'll make sure he's okay."

JACKSON'S MOTHER RETURNED an hour later, looking as depressed as ever. "How's Chris?"

"He's fine, Ma. He woke up and started coughing, but I gave him some cough medicine and told him a story about pirates. He fell back asleep. Why? What's wrong?"

"I always thought a hundred dollars was a lot of money, but it was barely enough to pay for the prescriptions. So instead of completely filling the order, Mr. Meyer gave me less medication so I'd have some money left for food. I bought bread and soup and eggs, and I found some halfway decent fruit and vegetables in the half-price bin, but by then I had spent it all. I don't know what we're going to do when this runs out."

A vision of doubloons danced in Jackson's head. "Don't worry, Ma, something will turn up."

JACKSON SPENT THE weekend thinking long and hard about the pirate gold. He hadn't really meant to take the doubloons. He'd stuffed them in his pocket because he didn't know what else to do with them. Now, he'd had them for three days. He knew Johanna would question why he didn't return them to her immediately. She might even claim he was untrustworthy and fire him. He could not afford to lose this job. What would he tell his mother if he did? It would break her heart. He had to hold onto the doubloons and keep his mouth shut about them to avoid getting fired.

He cut out of school early on Monday, taking one of the doubloons to the village pawnshop. He didn't know what it would be worth, but if it was made out of gold, it had to be worth something.

"WHERE DID YOU GET this, kid?" Larry Farmer, the owner of Once A-Pawn A Time, was short and squat and had long, grey fringe surrounding his shiny domed head. He inspected the coin carefully, then took a knife and scored the edge. He tried to hide his smile, certain it was gold. It had all the markings of a Spanish doubloon. Still, it should look several hundred years old, and this coin looked like only a few years had passed since it was minted.

"I found it," Jackson answered, avoiding the man's eyes.

"Sure you did, kid. Now why don't you tell me where you found it?"

"Near the Library of Illumination. You know, the building that looks so old it's a wonder it's still standing? I found it behind the library, in the dirt by the dumpster. I don't know, maybe someone dropped it? Is it worth anything?"

The pawnbroker thought the kid might be lying, because Jackson wouldn't look him in the eye. Still, the kid's story had enough detail for the pawnbroker to recognize the place where he said he found it. Larry borrowed books from the library when he had to appraise old coins and jewelry. Wouldn't it be something if a coin he needed to research actually came from there? *It's an old building in the oldest part of town. What if someone buried doubloons there centuries ago, and they're just showing up now because of last month's rainstorm?*

"So what do you want to do with this, kid, pawn it or sell it?"

"What's it worth?"

"I don't know, a few hundred dollars maybe?"

"That's all?"

"Yeah, kid. Who knows if it's real? All I can go by is the weight of the metal, and I can't tell if it's gold all the way through without cutting into it. I'll give you two hundred dollars for it."

"You said 'a few hundred dollars.' Two is just a couple. A few means three or more. I want three hundred for it."

The pawnbroker eyed the kid. He looked like the stubborn type, like he'd be annoyed unless he got what he felt he deserved. Truth be told, if the coin was genuine, it would be worth more than hundreds—it would be worth thousands. "Why you need this money so bad, kid?"

"Because my little brother needs medicine. He's got pneumonia. Are you going to pay me or not?"

Finally, the kid's answer had a ring of truth to it. The pawnbroker had nieces and nephews. His sister always complained about how doctor bills piled up when they were sick. "Okay, kid, three hundred dollars." He counted out a pile of twenty-dollar bills and placed them on the counter. "This is a sale, not a pawn. Once you accept this, you can't get your coin back."

"Fine." Jackson picked up the money. "Is that it?"

Normally there would have been paperwork, but

the pawnbroker decided not to document the sale. "Yeah, kid, that's it."

JACKSON ARRIVED TEN minutes late for work. When he rushed into the library, Johanna just shook her head. It had looked like he would turn over a new leaf after their confrontation on Friday; indeed, he had worked like a trooper on Saturday. But here it was Monday, and he was late as usual.

"Held up at school?"

"Yeah," he mumbled.

She didn't believe him, but she let it slide. There was only so much she could do.

After he finished dusting the stacks in the main reading room, Johanna called him over. "We're going to do something that I don't think has ever been done before at this library. We're holding a book reading for a small audience. An actor who performs at the community theater is going to read aloud from one of the classics. I'd like you to help me move these tables to the executive boardroom. We have to make space for folding chairs."

"Where are the folding chairs?"

"Downstairs." Johanna walked over to the back wall and twisted a wooden rosette that decorated part of the paneling. A section of wall slid open, revealing the stairs to the basement. She started down the steps with Jackson, but the phone began ringing. "They're in the first room on the left," she said, pointing before sprinting for the telephone. As she ran across the room, something shiny caught her eye. She quickly scooped it up along the way and managed to answer the phone by the third ring.

"I need some research material about Spanish

doubloons," said the disembodied voice on the other end of the line. "Do you have anything like that?"

Johanna didn't answer. Instead, she found herself mesmerized by a gold doubloon of her own.

—LOI—

C:L⬢I

CHAPTER TWO

"Hello? Is anyone there?" The caller on the other end of the phone raised his voice.

"Where do you want these?" Jackson asked. He stood not too far from Johanna, holding two folding chairs.

Johanna raised her eyes to meet Jackson's gaze, but instead of looking at her, he stared at the doubloon in her hand. "Did you say you want to research Spanish doubloons?" she asked the caller.

"Yeah. It's Larry Farmer over at *Once A-Pawn A Time.* I've been borrowing research materials from your library for years."

'Where did you get a gold doubloon in this day and age?" She hoped her voice sounded non-committal.

Larry paused a second too long before answering, "An archeologist. At least she called herself an archeologist. She left it here a year ago and never came back to claim it. Now I want to determine its value and sell it, so

I can make my money back."

Johanna thought it very coincidental that someone called her about a doubloon at the exact same moment that one appeared in the library. "Will you be picking the books up, or would you like us to deliver the materials to you? I should inform you that some of the information you want is currently on loan, so we won't be able to send it all out until the weekend."

"But I need it right away," he whined.

Fancy that. He supposedly had the coin for more than a year, but now he wants information about it—right this minute. "I can inquire if the current borrower has finished using those books," she hedged. "I could let you know, tomorrow."

"Yeah. Sure. Thanks. I'll talk to you then."

She hung up the phone. "Do you know anything about this?" she handed the doubloon to Jackson.

"Uh... it looks like a doubloon."

"Yes," she murmured.

"I guess one of those pirates dropped it last week when they were here." He handed it back to her.

"I wonder if there are any more?"

"I don't know," Jackson mumbled. "I'll look." He gave the surrounding area a cursory glance, but nothing caught his eye. "I don't see anything. I doubt any more of them will turn up."

"I wonder," Johanna said quietly.

AFTER THEY SET the last chair in place, Johanna handed Jackson a list of chores to do around the library. She turned away and then turned back, "There's one more thing. I noticed the back door sometimes squeaks when you come in. There's a small can of lubricating oil in the cupboard. Please oil the hinges."

She disappeared into her office and closed the door. It had been six months since she had taken over the duties as library curator from Mal, and in all that time she had never used his diary to access information. He had promised her before he died that she would find everything she needed to know about running the library in the compact book. Now, she hoped it would help her determine the authenticity of the doubloon and what to do with it. She studied the pages, looking for insight.

Jackson's knock on the door interrupted her. "Hey, I've done all the stuff on the list and it's after 6:00. Is it okay if I go home now?"

"Sure."

"See you tomorrow?" It sounded more like a question than a commitment.

"Yes." She watched him leave and locked the back door behind him. Then she returned to her reading. She hadn't found anything about doubloons, or money of any kind that had been left behind by characters from a book. However, Mal had recorded an incredible number of interesting incidents in his diary. She learned H. G. Well's Time Machine had once sat right in front of the Circulation Desk. She read Mal's description of the incident three times, trying to conjure up an image of it.

The apparatus is magnificent! An ornate brass frame—creating a canopy of sorts—sits upon a hammered metal base, barely a meter and a half in diameter. It's fitted with delicate pieces of ivory, inset in a sunburst pattern. Settled beneath it, a burnished leather saddle awaits man or beast. And under the saddle, a large cylinder containing a crystalline substance slowly rotates. The

*controls are in front, where a three-foot
high podium of hammered brass and nickel
has ivory levers coming out of each side.
The podium houses three asymmetrical
clock-like devices, one in front of the other,
with the furthest one being the largest.
Only one displays the hours of the day.
The middle one is separated into twelve
sections, with small indentations marking
each day of the month, while the largest
clock is divided into the years making up
several millennia. The timepieces are set
for the current date and tick quite loudly.
Indeed, the entire contraption hums, and
the twisted quartz frame that fences in the
time traveller, has a softly glowing aura. It
is a wonder to behold.*

The next paragraph nearly took Johanna's breath away.

*I used the Time Machine to visit my family.
Upon my arrival, I faced a great deal of
difficulty in trying to keep the machine
hidden from curious onlookers. I found
little in the way of bushes to hide the device.
I finally dragged over a canvas tarpaulin
and did my best to cover the machine with
it. It invited scrutiny, so I piled some buoys
and fishing nets around it to complete my
sleight of hand. I chewed my nails for the
next few hours, fretting about what would
happen if someone discovered the machine*

and figured out how to use it, before I could return. My mother finally scolded me for being so distracted. I wished her and my father well, telling them I had just remembered urgent business that I needed to attend to, and I departed. Saying goodbye broke my heart, knowing they would both die of consumption the following month. In the future, I must remember not to treat treasures—like the Time Machine—so cavalierly.

Johanna carried the diary upstairs to her apartment. She hastily made dinner, but remained so engrossed in Mal's observations, she barely touched her food. When she next glanced at the clock, it was nearly 3:00 a.m. She put the book down and yawned. "Where am I going to find something that tells me if the doubloons are real?" she asked aloud.

The pages of the diary began fluttering, and she watched wide-eyed as they fell open to a specific entry. All thoughts of sleep evaporated. Johanna grabbed the book and began to read. Mal wrote about a file of newspaper clippings that he dropped one day while straightening out the archives. It contained articles on John Dillinger, a notorious bank robber who had died in a hail of bullets outside a Chicago theater in 1934. The dropped file opened up to a story about a daring robbery. Mal said he saw one of Dillinger's men running in his direction and without thinking, he tripped the gangster. The man dropped a moneybag before Mal scooped up the file, and although everything else disappeared, the bag of cash remained.

Mal deliberated on what to do with the money, but had a quandary on his hands. He did not know how to return the money to the bank. He did not want to return the money to the bank robbers. And if he spent the money, he risked being arrested if authorities connected the bills to the robbery.

The entry ended.

"That's it?" Johanna complained. The passage didn't tell her what happened to the money, and the next entry detailed some mischief caused by Mark Twain's character, *Huckleberry Finn*.

"Mal, what did you do with the money?" The pages in the diary shuffled once more to a much later date.

> *As I stretched to replace a war novel on a high shelf, I lost my grip and the book toppled to the floor. It opened up to one of the last pages, and instantaneously an explosion blew away part of the roof. Luckily, no other buildings sustained damaged, but that didn't stop neighbors from calling the authorities, who came nosing around the library asking questions. I managed to convince them a faulty gas stove caused the explosion. However, the inspectors turned out to be the least of my problems. What could be worse than a library without a roof during rainy season? I needed it repaired quickly, but didn't know where I would get the money to do so. I asked construction workers from Eric Hodgin's book, "Mr. Blandings Builds His Dream House," to help out. Unfortunately, they needed slate tiles to complete the job,*

which Mr. Blandings hadn't used. I took a risk and deposited the Dillinger money in a local bank. Surprisingly, they didn't ask where the old bills came from. Instead, the assistant manager teased me saying, "What've you been saving this in your mattress?" He laughed at his own joke and I laughed too, if only out of nervous relief. I used the bank heist money to buy roofing supplies, and completed the job before the weather turned against us.

Mal's answer made Johanna feel a little better, but did not ease all her fears. Sure she could invest the doubloon in the library; maybe even use some of the money to pay for refreshments for the public reading they planned to hold. But what about the doubloon at the pawn shop? Its existence worried her. She got out of bed and went down to her office, where she had locked the gold piece inside a secret compartment in her desk. She took it out and studied it, before looking for a book on the valuation of old currency.

When she opened the book, an expert in a three-piece suit appeared. He blanched when he saw Johanna and turned his back to her. "Madame, I'm not sure what I'm doing here, or why you are clothed in such a provocative way, but if you think you can sully my reputation by compromising me, you'll be sadly mistaken."

Johanna shut the book and checked the publication date. The book was old, but not *that old*. The thought of a coin dealer who sounded like a throwback to the previous century made her laugh. She went upstairs to dress, before returning to her office to try again.

William Pierpont Davidson reappeared and looked Johanna up and down. "Well, that's better," he huffed.

"Sir, I would like your expert opinion on the value of this coin." She handed him the doubloon.

He looked at it carefully. "Is this a commemorative coin of some sort?"

"Why do you say that?"

"It's a beauty," he replied. "Right down to the detail of its slightly irregular shape."

"Why do you question its authenticity?"

"If it's a commemorative coin, then I'm not questioning anything. However, this coin looks much too newly minted to be authentic. It is styled like doubloons from the 18th century, but it is not discolored at all. Even though gold doesn't oxidize, a coin such as this one would still show some kind of patina and wear, unless completely sealed from the elements shortly after being struck. Considering that you just handed it to me without any type of protective covering and without using gloves to shield it from the oils or dirt on your hands, tells me you don't particularly value this coin."

"Oh! But that never occurred to me."

"Where did you get his?"

"I guess you could say I found it under the sofa. I don't know how long it was there. I only found it after we moved the furniture."

"I don't suppose the sofa is two-hundred fifty years old?"

"No. At least I don't think so."

"You don't know how old your sofa is?" he asked with a touch of sarcasm.

"The sofa arrived here long before I did," she answered impatiently.

"If this proves real, it would be worth a pretty penny.

But as I said, it's a tough sell, because its condition appears to be way too good for it to be authentic."

"That doesn't help me at all."

"That's the best assessment I can make outside my office."

Johanna picked up the book and closed it. William Pierpont Davidson disappeared. She bundled a similar (but un-enchanted) book with some coin auction catalogues and blue books. She planned to have Jackson babysit the library while she delivered them to the pawnbroker. She wanted to get a look at Larry Farmer's doubloon and learn a little more about it. She shuddered when she realized that leaving Jackson in charge of the library was probably what got her into this predicament in the first place.

Once-A-Pawn-A-Time appeared poorly lit, even though its corner location allowed it to have windows on two sides. A sign proclaiming the shop's name hung from a cantilever arm protruding from the corner entrance, with the requisite three gold spheres suspended at the bottom. In one window, a tarnished tuba dangled from the ceiling along with other musical instruments. Beneath it, a child's train on an oval track sat motionless amid miniature plastic houses and rubber shrubbery. The window on the other side sported a set of golf clubs, a number of hand tools, and a kayak floating in midair with the help of some ceiling chains.

Bells above the door jingled when Johanna entered the shop. The proprietor stood to greet his customer. "Can I help you?"

Johanna looked around. Her eyes settled on a man's face peering at her over a high counter. "Larry Farmer?"

"Yes," he said warily.

"I'm from the Library of Illumination. I brought the books you requested to research a gold doubloon. I can't tell you how exciting that sounds. Imagine a gold doubloon in this day and age. Why, it must be worth a fortune!"

"Yes, yes," he smiled at her against his better judgment. He didn't want anyone to know he might have something valuable, but he got caught up in her enthusiasm.

"I'm Johanna Charette, the curator of the library. I know I must sound like a gushing schoolgirl, but do you think I could have a peek at the doubloon? I've never seen anything like that before."

She was young and pretty, and he fell for her spiel. "I'm not sure what I've got, Johanna. It may be a trinket from a recent Mardi Gras, or a game token. But it won't hurt anything to let you have a look, on one condition."

"What's that?"

"In case it does have some value, I don't want to end up getting burglarized. So you have to promise me you'll keep it a secret."

She nodded her head. "Sure. I understand."

Larry disappeared into the back room and unlocked the safe. He returned with the doubloon, wrapped in a bit of flannel. He held it up for Johanna to see, but far enough away so she could not reach out and touch it.

"Wow," she said, "It's beautiful, and so shiny. Something that shiny has to be real."

The pawnbroker shuddered. The doubloon's shiny, new appearance was the exact reason why he questioned its legitimacy. "Remember our agreement, Johanna."

"Mums the word," she said. "Should I come back on Saturday for the books?"

"Hmmmmm..." Larry paused. This woman claimed to be the curator of the library where the kid found the coin. She seemed kind of young to be a curator, but what did that matter? If he wanted to see the source of the doubloon, he would have to come up with a good excuse to get a look at the library's rear yard. "Tell you what, Johanna. Since you were nice enough to bring these books to me, let me return the favor and deliver them back to you on Saturday."

"Okay, Larry. I'll see you then." She smiled at him and left.

JOHANNA FELT DIRTY. She winced at the thought of flirting with the pawnbroker, just to get him to show her the doubloon. It worked, but she ridiculed herself for sinking so low.

His doubloon had been identical to the one she now held in her hand. She could only surmise that Jackson had found one when he cleaned up after the pirates and had hocked it. Her ethical dilemma returned. *Who is the rightful owner of the doubloons?* Surely neither Johanna, nor the pirates could claim that right. The true owners were long dead and the doubloons' provenance could not be proved. Is it a case of finders-keepers? Under old maritime law, the first person to lay claim to an abandoned object, became the treasure's owner.

Her main problem would be keeping it a secret. She imagined people breaking into the library and opening books to reap the rich rewards they might hold. She could imagine them destroying Carl Wheat's *Books of the California Gold Rush* in their lust for loose nuggets, or volumes of Greek Mythology recounting the tales of Midas and his ability to turn everything he touched into gold. The thought of such mayhem made her tremble. But she calmed down knowing intruders would have to figure out how to gain entrance to the library, which could be tricky.

She had a duty to protect the library at all costs, and the first step was to find out how much the pawnbroker knew about the origin of the doubloon. That meant grilling Jackson.

All weekend, Johanna labored over how she would approach the teen. She planned to be direct. She would not accuse him of anything; indeed, she could blame him for nothing, other than a sin of omission. She wanted him to work with her, not against her, and planned to tell him that if he found any more doubloons at the library, he could keep them. She paused. *What am I saying?* She certainly didn't want to give him a reason to re-open *Treasure Island*, or books like it, in her absence. *That would never do.* There had to be another way.

—LOI—

C:L ✦ I

CHAPTER THREE

On Monday, Johanna received a message saying Jackson had been sent home sick and he would not be able to fulfill his work commitment. She called the school, asking for more details, but the secretary told her they could not release personal information about their students. The only way she could learn more would be to visit Jackson at home.

She recalled a conversation she had once had with Mal about how easy it would be to find someone to watch the library. All she had to do was open a book and ask the protagonist for a favor. He had suggested Mary Poppins; however, Johanna felt she would prefer leaving the library under the watchful eye of someone else. She opened the P. G. Wodehouse book *My Man Jeeves*, and when the valet appeared, Johanna explained her dilemma. Jeeves agreed to take care of the library until she returned.

A LOCAL COIN shop with a good reputation was more than happy to pay Johanna cash for gold. She did not say she had a doubloon, just an "old gold token my grandfather gave me before he died." That stopped the proprietor from questioning her about where it came from and told him she did not seek any profit above the value of the metal. She slipped the money into her wallet and caught a cab to Jackson's house.

Johanna stood for a moment on the sidewalk outside the teen's home. She envisioned what the dilapidated cottage might look like with a few repairs, a fresh coat of paint, and some rose bushes planted out front. The sound of a dog barking brought her back to reality. She walked up to the front door and, seeing no bell, knocked firmly.

Mrs. Roth opened the door. Her hair had escaped from a clip loosely secured to the top of her head. She had fine lines around her eyes, and unconsciously clamped her lips together in a frown. Fuzz balls matted her pink sweater, which had a stain on the front. Her feet were bare, her toenails plain, and her hands looked rough and red, as if continually immersed in detergent and water.

Johanna stuck out her hand. "Hi, Mrs. Roth. I'm Johanna Charette, from the Library of Illumination. Jackson's school nurse told me he didn't feel well, and I came to see if there's anything I could do."

Jackson's mother's composure crumpled, and she sniffed back the threat of tears. "He's so sick. His brother has pneumonia, and I think Jackson has it too. But I have no money for medicine, and I don't know what to do."

Johanna thought about the cash she had just

received from the coin dealer. If it weren't for Jackson, she wouldn't have that money. "I think I can help out. Has he seen a doctor?"

"I wanted to take him to the walk-in clinic, but I can't leave my other son alone, especially now that he's just starting to feel better. If I take him with us, I'm afraid he'll have a relapse ..." Her voice trailed off as she tried to hold back more tears.

"You take Jackson to the clinic. I'll watch your younger son while you're away."

"It's no use. I have no money."

Johanna opened her bag and removed several bills. She handed them to Jackson's mother. "See how far this goes."

The woman stared at the cash for nearly a minute. "I can't take this."

"Yes, you can. Think of it as a loan. I'll give Jackson some extra work when he's feeling better to pay it off."

Ten minutes later, Johanna watched as Jackson's mother led him out of the house. His face had lost all color, his eyes looked dull, and his hair hung limply. He coughed a phlegmy, rumbling sound that seemed to originate deep within his lungs. He did not acknowledge Johanna's presence.

While she waited, Johanna wondered what Jackson had done with the money from the doubloon he had pawned. Surely he would have given at least some of the proceeds to his mother. Then again, who knew what a poor teen with a sudden windfall would do?

A couple of hours passed before Jackson and his mother returned. He walked straight to his room and closed the door. "You have to excuse him," his mother apologized. "He's really sick."

"Does he have pneumonia?"

"No. The doctor said it's good that I brought him in before it got that bad. I used your money to pay the doctor and fill his prescriptions on our way home. I'm sorry, I don't have any change for you."

"Don't worry about it," Johanna replied. "I'd better be getting back to work. Tell Jackson I hope he feels better soon."

BACK AT THE library, Jeeves gave Johanna an inquisitive look. "Is the Royal Family coming for a visit?" he asked in a clipped British accent.

"What makes you say that?"

"While you were gone, some men delivered these." He pointed to a number of metal stands and a pile of red velvet ropes that Johanna had rented. She wanted to prevent people attending the library's public reading from getting close enough to the shelves to open any books.

"I had a devil of a time letting them in," Jeeves continued. "I could hear them banging on the door, and sometimes they sounded like they were right in the room, screaming something about the buzzer not working. Then one of them used rather coarse language involving something to do with illumination, and a big opening appeared out of nowhere. The less gifted of the two grumbled the entire time they were here, because he apparently had to do all the work. The other one insisted on standing guard to make sure the door didn't close. Then they acted like I should pay them something for making the delivery, but the invoice they gave me clearly indicated the order had been paid in full, and I told them as much.

"They stomped out of here like a couple of delin-quent school boys. I'm sure I don't know what this world is coming to."

Johanna couldn't hide her smile. "You handled it just right, Jeeves. These ropes are to cordon off the library shelves, to keep visitors from reading the books."

Jeeves didn't miss a beat. "Yes. I can see how that would be a brilliant tack for a library to take—keeping readers away from books. It would certainly eliminate wear and tear."

Rather than explain, Johanna thanked Jeeves as she walked over to the novel bearing his name and closed the cover.

She almost regretted not asking the valet to help her set up the stanchions. Almost. Instead, she took her time moving each one in place and attaching the velvet ropes. They couldn't ensure that no one would open a book, but they would send the signal that getting too close to the shelves was frowned upon. As a safeguard, Johanna had also ordered mass-produced leather-bound books that she knew would not come to life within the library walls, and placed them within easy reach of people attending the reading. That way, they would have something to divert their attention from the library's cherished and enchanted hoard of books. She spent the rest of the day moving any book that might look interesting out of sight.

JACKSON DID NOT return to work the following day, so when another shipment of un-enchanted books arrived, Johanna took on the task of spreading them around. She scattered a pile of them not too neatly on the refectory table. She put a few on the reception desk. And some others on a rolling cart. She made sure they were the only books within reach on any shelf positioned close to the velvet ropes. She would also advise guests not to stray when she greeted them at the door.

Their speaker would bring his own annotated book to the library to read. She had ordered a selection of hard and soft-covered copies of the classic he had selected, for anyone who wished to purchase or borrow one. She had taken every precaution she could think of to avoid disaster. She hoped her perseverance would pay off.

THE FOLLOWING AFTERNOON, last-minute preparations kept Johanna busy. She didn't know if Jackson would return to work, and she could not afford to depend on him.

Just when it looked like she had everything under control, the phone rang.

"Is this Johanna? It's Larry Farmer from Once A-Pawn A Time."

"What can I do for you, Mr. Farmer?"

"Mr. Farmer? Why so formal all of a sudden? I like to think of us as friends."

"Yes, of course, Larry, how can I help you? Do you need some other coin catalogues?"

"No, nothing like that. I just heard my favorite thespian is doing a reading at the library. We're actually old school chums. I admire him a lot, so I just called to tell you to make room for one more guest tonight."

"I'm sorry, Larry, I don't think I can do that. Members of the library board put the guest list together, and it's by invitation only. We have a finite amount of space here, and a long waiting list in case anyone cancels."

"Oh, come on, Johanna. I'll stand if I have to. It's just that I already told him I'm attending. He'll never forgive me if I stiff him. Please ... do a guy a favor."

She really wanted to say no but thought better of it. Maybe she could pump him for more information about the doubloon. "Okay, Larry, but don't tell anyone about this. It's another one of our little secrets."

"Don't worry, Johanna. My lips are sealed."

LARRY FARMER DID a little jig around his pawnshop. He needed a reason to be on the library grounds, and with so many people there for the reading, nobody would notice him snooping around.

He was fired up, especially after the kid had returned that morning with another doubloon. Larry had taken it to a coin dealer he knew and asked him for an appraisal. The dealer told him it would take a couple of days. When he asked the dealer to rush, the man said he couldn't because he had to quit work early to take his wife to a reading at the Library of Illumination.

The pawnbroker had immediately felt his excitement build, and now that he was on the guest list, nothing could stop him from doing a little prospecting.

He put the Closed sign in the window and lowered the lights. He opened the drawer under the cash register and removed a small Smith & Wesson handgun. A man had pawned it years before, and when he never reappeared to claim it, Larry loaded it and put it in the drawer behind the front counter. You never knew when there was going to be trouble. He slipped the gun into his waistband. If he found any doubloons, he might be forced to protect them. Besides, there was nothing like a little heat to make you feel warm all over.

THAT AFTERNOON, JACKSON knocked on Johanna's office door. His complexion appeared mottled, and his red nose rivaled one belonging to a certain holiday reindeer, but Jackson said he felt better and wanted to work. Then he stepped forward and put a fistful of ten and twenty-dollar bills on her desk.

"What's this?"

"It's the money you lent my mother to take me to the doctor. I'm paying you back."

Her eyes unconsciously narrowed. "Where'd you get the money to pay me back?"

Jackson's face went totally red. He looked down at his feet. "I found a doubloon in the library," he said softly. "I cashed it."

"At Once A-Pawn A Time?"

His head snapped up. "How did you know that?"

Before she could answer, the phone rang. Then the door buzzer sounded. Everything started to happen all at once. People called for directions, the caterer arrived to set up coffee and dessert, and a return shipment of books came in from a borrower.

Their conversation would have to wait.

JOHANNA MANAGED TO shower and change before guests started to arrive. She had just propped open the interior door when the head of the library board walked in. The public reading had been his idea, and he grinned from ear to ear. Johanna shared her concern about guests not straying beyond the velvet ropes, and considering the blank look he gave her, she wondered if he actually knew about the library's charms. A group of patrons entered, and as Johanna checked off their names on her guest list, the administrator wandered off.

When Larry Farmer arrived, he reached for her hand. She realized too late that his hands were filthy.

"Sorry about that. Flat tire. Do you have a men's room?"

She pointed it out, and he wandered off in that direction.

Finally, the star of the show made his grand entrance. As people took their seats, Johanna realized she had forgotten to set up an extra chair for Larry Farmer. She saw him comfortably ensconced in the front row, while an elderly woman remained standing. She went to her office to find Jackson. "I need you to run downstairs and get one more chair. We had a last-minute addition to our guest list, and I forgot to bring up an extra one."

"Sure."

THE PAWNBROKER DID a double take when he saw Jackson walk past the self-absorbed group and activate the entrance to the basement.

Larry abandoned his seat and walked behind the crowd. When he felt sure no one was paying attention to him, he slipped down the stairs and headed toward the spill of light coming out of the storage room.

"I've got it," Jackson said as he turned around. His eyes nearly bugged out of his head at the sight of the pawnbroker. "What are you doing here?"

"I came to ask you the same thing, kid. You never mentioned that you worked here. I want to know where you're getting all those gold doubloons."

"I told you, I found them out back."

"Well then, let's you and me take a walk out back, so you can show me where those shiny golden coins are coming from."

"I can't. I've got work to do." Jackson picked up the folding chair.

"Now, kid," demanded the pawnbroker.

JACKSON STILL HAD a fever and felt pretty lousy. He had shown up for work only because he had a crush on Johanna and wanted to impress her. He knew she would have her hands full. But that didn't mean he had to put up with the pawnbroker. He turned to look Larry in the eye and lay down the law, but instead, he found himself looking down the barrel of a gun. He could no longer think of a thing to say.

"Is there a way out back from here?" Larry asked.

"No."

The pawnbroker snarled, "You'd better not be lying to me, kid."

"I'm not. I always use the back door by the utility closet."

Larry stuffed the gun in his jacket pocket. "Okay, kid, here's what we're going to do. You're going to carry that chair upstairs and set it up. Then you're going to walk straight to the utility closet. I'm going to watch you every step of the way. When I'm sure no one is looking, I'm going to meet you at the utility closet, and you and me are going to take a little trip out back." He thrust the barrel of the gun forward, so it was clearly outlined in his pocket.

Jackson merely nodded. He didn't have much of a choice.

—LOI—

C:L I

CHAPTER FOUR

UPSTAIRS, JOHANNA INTRODUCED the speaker to the audience, unaware that anything was amiss. She watched as Jackson placed the folding chair at the end of the back row. Her words of introduction faltered, however, when she saw him walk behind the velvet rope by the stacks. Her eyes widened when he grabbed a graphic novel off one of the shelves. Before she had a chance to yell "No," the superhero known as Impervio the Indestructible landed in front of the podium. The audience looked startled at first, but after a moment they broke into applause. They obviously thought it was some form of entertainment.

Jackson dove under the velvet rope, rolled across the floor, and jumped up behind Impervio, shouting "That man has a gun!" as he pointed to the pawnbroker. Jackson moved so gracefully that it looked like it had been rehearsed. Impervio took a step toward Larry Farmer, who fired several bullets at him. Just like in the comics, the bullets could not penetrate Impervio's force field; but before he could reach Larry, the pawnbroker threw his gun at the superhero and rushed out of the library. Impervio followed closely on his tail.

Jackson walked over to the graphic novel, closed the cover, and re-shelved it. Impervio, wherever he might be, disappeared as quickly as he had arrived. Jackson calmly walked over to the podium, where Johanna stood speechless. He smiled at her and said to the audience, "And that, ladies and gentlemen, illustrates the power of the written word and demonstrates how reading can be so richly rewarding. But you already know that, which is why you're here. So let's give a warm welcome to a man we all know and admire, who will entertain us with a reading from his favorite book."

The audience clapped. Jackson took Johanna's arm and led her to the circulation desk, so the evening could continue without further interruption.

"What is going on?" she whispered not so calmly in his ear.

"I'll explain everything when everyone is gone. I swear."

The rest of the evening progressed smoothly, although the local thespian later complained that he should have been informed about the Impervio skit. Everyone else loved it, and patrons chatted happily as they departed. The public reading was a huge success.

"I WANT AN explanation. Now," Johanna said as they locked the door to the library.

Jackson's calm, cool demeanor evaporated. "It all

started with the pirates from *Treasure Island*. The book really did open by accident. I had re-shelved a bunch of them and needed to insert one next to *Treasure Island*, but the linen on the front cover was loose and bunched up every time I tried to slide it into place. I didn't want to damage it, and I figured if I pulled out *Treasure Island* and placed the linen book next to it and pushed them both in together, it would work. Except I pulled *Treasure Island* out a little too fast, and it fell open. Before I could do anything, one of the pirates grabbed the book and handed me a mug of rum. I was so surprised, I guess I got carried away.

"Anyway, when you came in, I closed the book. But when I cleaned up, I found a bunch of doubloons on the floor and ..."

"A bunch?" she interrupted.

"About a half dozen. I was going to give them to you then and there, but you were pretty angry and had locked yourself in the back room. So I stuck them in my pocket until I could talk to you. But by then, I was so scared you would fire me that I forgot all about them.

"Then when I left, I found them in my pocket. I was afraid you would think I had tried to steal them, because I didn't give them back right away. I didn't know what to do. Plus, my brother has pneumonia, and my mom said the hundred dollars I gave her last Saturday didn't go very far, so I took a doubloon to the pawnshop so I could give her more money."

"Where are the others?"

"Uh ... well ... I took a second one to the pawnshop today. And that guy who owns the place must have gone bonkers, because he showed up tonight with a gun."

"You told him the doubloons came out of the book?"

"No! I would never do that. I told him I found them out back under the dumpster."

"It's a wonder he's not back there right now with a shovel." She thought of Larry's dirty hands.

"I think Impervio scared him away."

Johanna cringed. Just for a moment she had forgotten about the superhero known as the *avid activist*. "I only hope everyone in the audience believes it was a theatrical performance for their entertainment."

"C'mon, Johanna. No one's going to think he's anything but an actor. Do you know how crazy people would sound if they said Impervio landed in the library, and acted like they actually believed it?"

Johanna stared at Jackson but didn't respond. He made sense, and his observations, for the most part, seemed sound. She thought of the impromptu speech he had given after Impervio landed in front of the room full of guests. Jackson had effectively provided instant damage control.

The teenager dug deep into his pocket and took out the remaining doubloons. "Here."

She took one. "This is for the library, to cover the costs of tonight's event."

"What about these?"

"I don't want you to get any bright ideas about using library books for personal gain. However, I think you should use those to help your family. Just be careful about cashing them."

"I'll be careful. I swear."

"There you go swearing again. It's becoming a habit

with you."

"It's pretty late. Can I go home now?"

"Yes, but be careful. You never know if that crazy pawnbroker is going to suddenly appear."

ACROSS TOWN, LARRY Farmer fumed. He could not understand how he had lost control of what should have been a simple situation. All he wanted the kid to do was show him where he had found the doubloons. But the kid was greedy. He had no respect for his elders and made Larry look like a fool. Plus, Larry had lost his gun in the process. No matter. He had plenty of firepower in the back.

He pawed through a box of handguns until he found a Saturday night special. Someone had to put that young hoodlum in his place. He regretted that he never asked the kid to fill out paperwork. That meant he had no address for him. But now that he knew the kid worked at the library, he figured he could find him there.

ANYONE WHO PLANNED to hock something at Once A-Pawn A Time the following day would be out of luck. At 7:00 a.m. Larry parked an old car someone had abandoned at his shop years before on a side street across from the library. He had a direct view of the front door. He picked up the steaming cup of coffee he had purchased at a local convenience store and gulped the liquid down, cursing because the hot coffee burned his tongue and throat. Some spilled on him, burning his hands, and he threw the cup on the floor. The coffee slowly seeped into the vehicle's carpeting, making the car stink. *It's the kid's fault, but he'll get his due.*

Hours passed, but no one entered or exited the library. Larry's eyelids felt like lead weights had been built into them. He had been up all night planning his revenge, and now Morpheus had come a-calling. The pawnbroker struggled to remain awake, but without coffee, he fought a losing battle. His lids slammed shut, and he slept for hours.

The sky had darkened to a deep navy by the time Larry woke up. He saw the light go out in the vestibule of the library and figured he had awakened just in time, but no one exited the building. Exhausted, Larry eventually gave up and drove home.

IT TOOK LARRY an additional hour to find the Library of Illumination on Friday morning. He thought he knew how to get there and was angry that he arrived after nine. He parked his car in the same spot that he had parked in the previous day. He had another cup of coffee with him, but it had sufficiently cooled before he got around to drinking it. Someone had to eventually show up at the door of the library. When he or she did, Larry would make his move.

THAT SAME DAY, Exeter High School held its Parent-Teacher Conferences and had suspended all classes.

Jackson had big plans for the day. As soon as his mother left, he went to a home-improvement store and bought several gallons of paint as well as the supplies he would need to fix up the exterior of the house. When he returned, his best friend, Logan, and two of their buddies were already waiting to help. He had promised to pay them for their work and figured, if they could each paint one side of the small house, they could finish the job before his mother returned.

Jackson placed a ladder against the facade and started scraping away the worst of the old paint. His friends removed the shutters that were still attached and sanded them down. It took them most of the morning just to prepare everything, and a few hours more to paint the exterior and replace the trim.

"The house looks great," the mailman called out.

Jackson smiled. He happily paid each of his friends and then sat on the front steps, waiting to see the look on his mother's face when she returned. He was glad he had told Johanna what he planned to do and asked for the day off. He felt really good inside, something he hadn't felt since his father walked out.

MRS. ROTH STARED at the house. She looked around to make sure she was on the right block. She spotted her son sitting on the front stoop, smiling at her. Tears prickled her nose. Overcome with emotion, she began to cry.

Jackson ran over and threw his arms around his mother. "Don't cry. If I knew you wouldn't like it, I would never have done it."

That made her laugh and cry at the same time. "Not like it? I love it. But the money."

"It's money I made at the library."

She shook her head slightly, looking confused. "But you've given me most of the money you made at the library."

"Right, this was another ... uh ... bonus that I made from cleaning up after a party."

"I guess you're the man of the house now, Jackson."

More tears rolled down her face. "And you're doing a very good job," she added as she hugged him.

LARRY JIGGLED HIS knee. It kept bumping up against the steering wheel, which made the whole car shake. How could these people run a library if they never showed up for work?

The kid had said he found the doubloons behind the building. Larry got out of the car and looked for an alley next to the building. When he couldn't find one, he walked around the block, looking for an entrance to one. He arrived back at the front of the building without seeing a back alley. *It's too dark to see anything. I'll look again tomorrow.*

HEAVY CLOUDS DRIFTED so low in the sky on Saturday morning that even though the sun was up, it looked like the middle of the night. That might have explained why Jackson overslept. Or it could have been the exhaustion he felt from all the work he had done the day before. Either way, when he saw the time, he jumped out of bed and grabbed his clothes. He wanted to get to the library as early as possible to make up for not working the previous afternoon.

WITH EACH PASSING day, the Library of Illumination became more and more difficult for the pawnbroker to find. The lack of sunshine and constant drizzle obscuring his vision didn't help. By the time he finally pulled into his parking space, he could spit bullets. *I better not be wasting another day.*

He remembered the kid saying he parked his bike

behind the library. Larry hit himself in the forehead three times with the palm of his hand. *That's why I never see them enter and leave. They must use the back alley.*

He got out of his car and went for another walk around the block. He made a full revolution and still did not see a driveway that opened onto the back of the library, just a narrow, metal gate attached to a townhouse on the opposite side of the block. He retraced his steps to get a better look at it. The gate had a latch instead of a lock, with a tiny brass plaque above it, engraved with the words *Library of Illumination*. Larry grinned. *Pay dirt!*

THE LIBRARY HAD always appeared to be cheery and bright inside, regardless of the weather outdoors, but on this particular day, the usual warm glow from the windows was subdued. Johanna lit the fireplace to remove the chill from the air. When that failed to work, she put on a sweater and vowed to call a heating specialist first thing Monday morning.

She wished she had a little heater in the antechamber where she repaired bindings. Restoring damaged books to their former glory was Johanna's favorite job. She loved the feel of fine leather, the variety of intricate patterns on marbleized end papers, and the deep sense of satisfaction that washed over her whenever she finished a project. She put on her goggles and gently inspected the damage on a centuries-old copy of the *Nuremberg Chronicle*. Some of the book's signatures had come loose and needed to be hand-sewn. She inhaled the musty scent of the aging cotton bond. The illustrated book of world history had been printed in 1493, and her inspection showed it had previously been repaired, perhaps centuries ago.

Her concentration was broken by the distant sound of metal crashing. *Jackson.* He probably had just arrived, and his bike must have fallen against the dumpster. She reluctantly took off her goggles and got up to unlock the back door.

JACKSON HATED BEING late for work again, so he pedaled as fast as he could. But he was already behind schedule, and he still had a half mile to go. He hated himself for oversleeping. He knew Johanna had pegged him as immature and lazy, and he wanted to do everything in his power to prove that wasn't true.

She had complimented his speech after the superhero incident, and that made him feel good. But he had unleashed a cartoon character in front of a roomful of people, which upset her. He sighed, annoyed that he hadn't come up with a better plan to scare off the pawnbroker.

JOHANNA UNLATCHED THE back door and poked her head outside. "Jackson?"

"So that's the kid's name."

Larry appeared from behind the door, and Johanna found herself staring at the gun in his hand.

"I sure hope you have a shovel handy," he continued, "because you're going to do a little digging for me."

"I'm going to what?"

"Don't play dumb with me. The kid already told me this is where he found the doubloons. And if there are any more of them out here, you're going to find them for me."

"What makes you think I have a shovel? The only

person who ever comes back here is Jackson."

"Suit yourself, Johanna. It's okay with me if you want to dig with your bare hands. The rain is making the ground soft. It'll be just like digging up mud pies."

Her shoulders sagged.

"Or you can use the shovel I saw in the basement the other night, when I followed the kid down there."

"I'll get it," she said.

Larry shoved his foot in the door to keep her from locking him out. "Not without me you won't." He waved his gun toward the wall containing the panel that led to the basement.

JACKSON EYED THE open gate, certain that he had latched it the last time he was there. *Johanna will kill me if she thinks I left the gate open.* He looked down the alley and saw movement. The pawnbroker. He watched Larry push Johanna inside the library.

Jackson carefully walked to the building, his footsteps muffled by the rain. He quietly laid his bike down next to the dumpster and hoped Johanna and Larry were not standing near the back door when he gently pulled it open.

Eeeeeeeee. He had never gotten around to oiling the door hinge like Johanna had asked. He prayed the pawnbroker was deaf.

LARRY'S HEAD JERKED. "Did you hear something?"

"No," Johanna lied.

"Maybe it's the kid?"

"He's not working today." She couldn't believe how easily she had lied again. *Must be self-preservation.*

"Yeah? Then why'd you say 'Jackson' before when you stuck your head out the back door?"

"I heard a noise and didn't know who else it could be."

Larry walked to the stairs. "Jackson," he shouted, "if you don't want me to put a bullet through the pretty little librarian's head, you'll come down here now, with your hands up. You've got five seconds ... four ... three ... two ... one. Come out, come out, wherever you are," he finished in a singsong voice.

There wasn't as much as a squeak.

"He's not here," Johanna repeated as she stared at the gun.

"Find me that shovel. I know it's down here somewhere. I saw it with my own eyes."

"If you know where it is, why don't you find it?"

"Because, sweetheart, this isn't my library. It's yours. So move your pretty little ass."

JACKSON SLOWLY EXHALED. He tiptoed behind a stack, so he wouldn't be seen if Larry came upstairs. As he listened for further movement from below, his eyes settled on the screenplay for the film *Dirty Dirk Daily.*

He wondered if he could reason with Dirk, quietly, before the pawnbroker came back up. *Stop thinking and start doing!* He opened the cover.

Dirk appeared with his gun drawn. Jackson made the universal sign for quiet by putting his finger over his lips. Dirk scowled but said nothing.

Jackson whispered, "Look, this has nothing to do with the Thriller Killer. You're in the Library of Illumination, and a man is holding the curator at gunpoint. He wants her to dig for doubloons that don't exist, and when he doesn't find any, he may go nuts and kill her."

—LOI—

C:L◉I

CHAPTER FIVE

DIRTY DIRK DAILY scratched his chin. "How do you know this has nothing to do with my current case?" he asked evenly.

Jackson handed him the screenplay. "Because you're a character from a film, and she's not in there."

Dirk looked at the title page. "'Dirty' implies I'm a dirty cop. I'm not, you know. I just do whatever it takes to get the bad guys off the streets."

"And I'm hoping that's what you do right now. Just subdue this guy, and then you can return to your case in this script."

Dirk stared at the open pages. "I guess that explains it."

"Explains what?"

"My whole world begins and ends with the Thriller Killer. I have some knowledge of what came before, but no real memories or feelings. And I can't seem to get beyond the big shootout. I often wonder if maybe I'm really the one who dies in the end ..."

Dirk turned at the sound of Larry and Johanna coming up the stairs.

THE PAWNBROKER'S VOICE carried. "If the kid is hiding out up here, I'm going to shoot you, and then I'm going after him. So you'd better tell him to show himself now, or else."

"Jackson?" Johanna shouted, even though her voice quaked. "Don't come out. If anything happens to me, find Mal's diary. It'll explain everything."

Larry grabbed her shoulder and spun her around to face him. She could see him turning purple. "Lady, what are you doing?" he screamed.

Whoosh. Ping. Clatter! Dirk shot the pistol out of the pawnbroker's hand.

Larry turned, surprised.

"I'll just bet you're wondering ..." Dirk began.

Johanna slowly edged away.

"Dirty Dirk Daily?" Larry stared in disbelief as the fictional detective spouted the most memorable dialogue of his movie.

Jackson snuck around Larry and grabbed the pawnbroker's pistol off the floor.

Larry got a look at the film cop's heavy-duty firearm and started to sweat.

Dirk continued his monologue.

Johanna snuck up behind the pawnbroker and brought the big, brass gong down on his head.

Larry crumpled to the ground, unconscious.

Dirk looked quizzically at Johanna. "I wasn't done. I'm supposed to save the day."

"Don't worry, you did," she said. "Jackson, grab some plastic cable ties from the utility closet and bind Larry's hands and legs."

The teen wasted no time making sure the pawnbroker stayed immobilized.

"Thank you, Dirk." Johanna smiled as she picked up the script and closed it. The detective disappeared. "I'd better call the police."

"How are we going to explain the doubloons to them?" Jackson asked Johanna.

"The ones we found outside in the dirt?" There was a hint of conspiracy in her voice.

"Right." He dug his hand into his pocket and removed the three remaining doubloons. "What about these?"

"I suggest you wait a while before trying to cash them."

"I don't want them."

"They helped you fix up your mother's house and buy medicine."

"They also nearly got you killed."

"Jackson. It's okay if you keep them."

"Johanna. I don't want them."

"Come with me, then." She walked over to the shelf containing *Treasure Island*. She looked at the pawnbroker to make sure he was still out cold. "We have to work fast. As soon as I open the cover, place the doubloons on the page."

They each did their respective task, and Johanna

snapped the book shut before any pirates could take shape. She held it up, and they inspected it. There was no telltale bulge where the doubloons should have been.

"Where are they?" Jackson asked.

"Back where they belong."

Someone began banging on the walls of the vestibule.

"That must be the police," she said. "You'd better let them in."

WHEN JOHANNA SPOKE to the responding officers, she used the word *lunatic* more than once. By the time she finished recounting how Larry had disturbed a private book reading and tried to hold someone hostage and how the "lunatic" forced his way into the library at gunpoint earlier that day, the pawnbroker regained consciousness. He began defending his actions to the police, telling them about pirate doubloons, Impervio the Indestructible, and Dirty Dirk Daily.

One of the cops rolled his eyes. "We'll probably have to take this guy for a psychiatric evaluation at County Hospital. He's not making a whole lot of sense."

"Does that mean you're not going to lock him up?" Johanna asked.

"Don't worry. The locks at County are just as strong as the ones in our jail."

When the police finally left, Johanna's knees turned to rubber, and she collapsed on the sofa.

"Why didn't you mention me by name?" Jackson asked.

"So you wouldn't have to lie to them."

"You did a great job explaining everything. It

sounded totally reasonable, even though you left out a few things. And then the pawnbroker told them all the stuff you left out. And now they think he's nuts."

"I was so afraid they would start opening books ..."

"I didn't even think of that."

"We got off lucky."

"Yeah. It was a learning experience," Jackson replied, "for me at least. But it looks like there are some things *you'll* never learn."

"What's that supposed to mean?"

He picked up the gong and placed it back on the circulation desk. "Didn't you read the sign?" he asked as he turned toward her and smiled. "It says, 'Please do not handle.'"

—LOI—

C:L ❂ I

CHAPTER SIX

The Orb

LATE-MORNING SUNLIGHT filtered through the soaring windows of the Library of Illumination. The leaded panes cast a glowing grid upon the intricate design of the Persian carpet. Suddenly, something more ominous obscured the pattern—a pulsating blue light that seemingly appeared out of nowhere.

"EVEN THOUGH THE gold highlights on the richly illuminated text have faded with age, the impact of their beauty is no less powerful," Johanna said, as she gave Jackson a lesson on restoring illuminated manuscripts.

"Look at the delicacy of the acanthus leaves surrounding the main letter," she continued. "They're only a small part of the whole, yet their intricate beauty lends depth to the illustration."

As she sighed, in awe of the beauty of the artwork, Jackson sighed inwardly over the beauty of Johanna.

He had been working with her for several months, and when school went on summer break, he had jumped at the chance to work additional hours at the library, so he could be near her. He didn't know if she knew how he felt about her. Nor how she felt about him. For now, the job gave him an excuse to be by her side, five days a week. So here he sat—a hairsbreadth away from her, inhaling her scent and becoming intoxicated by the tone of her voice.

Johanna was older than Jackson, but he had no idea how much older because she refused to tell him. He looked mature for his age and was at least eight inches taller than her, making them look like contemporaries. He knew she had an active social life, because he'd once seen her having dinner with some guy when he and his pals had walked home from the movies. Johanna and her date sat at a window seat in Le Chat, Exeter's excuse for a French bistro.

"... the ink isn't absorbed by the parchment. So the pigment merely lies on the surface of the page, which is why it's unstable and has a tendency to fade." Johanna pulled out the Swiss Army knife attached to her key chain and lightly scraped the top of a letter. She turned toward Jackson to show him the dusty residue. In doing so, her thigh brushed against his bare leg. It was the middle of summer, and they both wore shorts to stay cool in the heat.

Jackson felt every nerve ending in his body jump to attention. His face reddened.

"It's too hot back here, isn't it?" Johanna asked, not waiting for him to answer. "I can tell you're uncomfortable just by looking at your face. I'd better read Mal's diary tonight to see if he mentions whether the library has air conditioning. If this heat keeps up much longer, the books are going to melt." She opened her desk drawer and dropped her keys inside.

"Yeah," was the extent of Jackson's reply.

"Why don't you go get something to eat? The luncheonette has air conditioning. The pizza place has fans, but with those big ovens going, you couldn't pay me enough to eat there."

Was she asking him to have lunch with her? "Sure. Wherever you want to go."

"Oh, I can't go. I'm expecting a call from Book Services about a delivery. You go. I think you need to cool off."

Did he ever, but not for the reason she thought.

They walked out of the library antechamber.

"When you come back, we've got to finish setting up the display for the Gutenberg Bible. We don't want the board of directors to get their hands on it during their meeting here on Thursday. They may decide to read part of it, and we don't need Moses parting the Red Sea in the middle of the library. I know it's hard to believe, but even though they're the governing board of the Library of Illumination, they have no clue that these books can come to life. And I think it's best if it remains that way. Mal, the former curator, wrote in his diary that some of the directors just want the prestige and power that comes with being on the library board. Like the saying goes, 'power corrupts.'"

Johanna often spoke reverently about Mal. Jackson had never met him. *You would think Mal is a god the way Johanna refers to him.* Jackson stared at her, wondering if she felt about Mal the way he felt about her.

"Don't stand there scrutinizing me. Go to lunch."

Jackson felt his face grow hot. He tried to change the subject. "Do the books come to life even when they're loaned out?"

"There are a few, select scholars and universities that have been approved to receive the enchanted books. I usually have to borrow books from other libraries for people who aren't on my master list."

"Who approves them?"

"Well ... Mal approved them, I guess, and then when someone who's on the list retires, he or she usually recommends someone they trust to be added to the list. So I guess it's self-perpetuating."

"So when they open the cover, stuff happens, even though they're not here in the library?"

"Yes, but they know how to handle it."

As they walked down the hallway, Jackson noticed something blinking in the main reading room. "What's that funky blue light?"

They stopped in their tracks when they spotted a large sphere in the middle of the room. It was about three feet in diameter and appeared to be studded with smooth silver disks. On closer inspection, they saw the metal disks were attached to internal spikes, aimed at a smaller black globe suspended in the center of the orb. An iridescent blue-and-purple gelatinous substance surrounded the globe and pulsated, emitting the dull blue light.

Jackson reached out to touch the sphere. The teenager's hand never made contact. Instead he felt a buzzing sensation that propelled his hand away from the orb, like a mild electric shock. "It won't let me touch it."

"What do you think it is?"

"I don't know, but it doesn't look good."

"Why?"

"Because it looks like something from a science-fiction movie. Think about it. It came out of nowhere; it's got its own defense shield; and it's pulsating."

"Like it's alive?"

"Like it's ticking."

Johanna paced nervously. "Let's be logical about this. Where do you think the device *might* have come from?"

Jackson shook his head. "You're the curator. You tell me."

She nudged a piece of lint with her toe and then bent down to pick it up. "Do you think someone could have broken in while we were in the antechamber?"

He looked at her in disbelief. "I doubt it. You know how hard it is to find this place, much less get inside."

"Maybe they *knew* to ask for illumination," she said.

"Maybe the sphere came out of a book," he answered.

"Spontaneously?"

"Why not?"

"Because a book wouldn't just fly open."

"Are you sure?"

"Right now"—she sighed—"I'm not sure about anything."

Jackson tried again to touch the orb. This time the shock was not as mild. "Maybe we should call the police."

Johanna shuddered. "The police will ask too many questions. They might poke around and start opening books. It could be a disaster. And after what happened with the pawnbroker, I'd rather not call them."

"If it's dangerous ..." Jackson could not fathom her reluctance, but stopped short, realizing he sounded confrontational. "Maybe it's from Mal," he speculated in a quieter voice.

"Like a fount of knowledge?" she asked wistfully. She reached out to touch the orb, but Jackson grabbed her hand.

"I would think a fount of knowledge would be ... I don't know ... friendlier?" He realized he was still holding her hand, and blushed as he dropped it. "You don't want to touch that thing."

"Knowing you, you probably think it came from another planet."

He made a face at her. "You mean like Krypton?"

"Something like that." She paused. "It could be a communications device."

"Or maybe H. G. Wells visited the library again in his time machine. You told me that once happened here, right? So maybe he dropped it off while we were in the back."

Johanna narrowed her eyes at him.

"You look sexy when you do that."

"Jackson!"

He grimaced. "I didn't mean to say that out loud." He had the good sense to look embarrassed. "Sorry."

She took a deep breath. "The first thing we have to do is determine if it's dangerous. I just don't know how to do that without getting any authorities involved."

"Why don't you just open a book about Albert Einstein?"

Her face lit up. "Oh my God, you're a genius!" She walked over to the science stacks. "Of course, you should take that with a grain of salt, because if you really were a genius, we wouldn't need Einstein."

"Thanks."

Johanna found a manuscript of Einstein's *Relativity: The Special and General Theory* and opened it. A man with dark, wiry hair who looked like he had just stuck his finger in a live electric socket materialized in front of her. He had a bushy mustache that matched his hair, and wore a shapeless oatmeal-colored cardigan.

Einstein stared at Johanna for a moment before breaking into a warm smile. "I'm Albert Einstein. What is this place? I don't remember traveling here."

"Dr. Einstein, we'd like your opinion about an unusual object that, as far as we can tell, appeared out of nowhere. It's giving us cause for concern." She led Einstein to the blue orb.

He studied it for several minutes before trying to touch it. The orb repelled his hand. "It contains a great deal of energy."

"Yes, but what is it?"

"Do you have notes or drawings outlining the construction of this device?"

Johanna shook her head.

"Formulas?" Einstein continued. "Schematics? Without those, I can only theorize that what I see before me is extremely powerful."

"Is it a bomb?"

"Perhaps."

"Perhaps?" Jackson shouted. "Is that the best you can do? You're Albert freakin' Einstein!"

Einstein looked at Johanna. "Who is this young man?"

"Jackson." She lowered her voice to a whisper. "He works here."

Einstein turned to the boy. "Everyone should be respected as an individual, but no one idolized."

Jackson wiped the sweat from his brow. "What does that mean?"

"Why do you think I, more than you, should know what this is?"

"Because you're a genius."

"The difference between stupidity and genius is that genius has its limits."

The rebuke left Jackson speechless.

Johanna closed the manuscript about relativity.

Einstein vanished. She removed a later work by the physicist.

A white-haired version of Einstein appeared almost immediately. He looked at the blue orb and smiled. "I remember this from earlier in my career. It's still here." He studied Johanna and Jackson. "You, too, remain and have not aged."

"We're trying to determine if the sphere is dangerous," Johanna continued.

"Where did it come from?" Einstein asked.

"We don't know," she said.

"This technology, while intriguing, is not within my field of expertise. If you believe it to be a bomb, then may I suggest J. Robert Oppenheimer as a suitable expert? He is a theoretical physicist with a great deal of knowledge in the area of explosive devices." He paused. "How long has it been since I was here last?"

"Just a few minutes," Jackson said.

"Then it's true." Einstein smiled. "The distinction between the past, present, and future is only a stubbornly persistent illusion."

He disappeared when Johanna re-shelved the second manuscript.

Jackson's curiosity was piqued. "Who is this Oppenheimer guy?"

"The director of the Manhattan Project, or as he's better known, the father of the A-bomb."

"So you agree, it's a bomb?"

"*You're* the one who said it was ticking."

"So where would I find a book on Oppenheimer?"

"I'll get it," Johanna said, taking the stairs to the second story. "You look around to make sure no one got in here while we were in the back room."

It took several minutes to find the right book.

Jackson waited patiently until Johanna returned. "This place is locked tighter than a drum."

"I thought so. Anyway, here goes nothing." She opened the book to a page at random.

INSTANTLY, A SMALL group of scientists, engineers, and mathematicians appeared. They were deep in conversation and scarcely noticed that their surroundings had changed, except for one man. He looked at Johanna and Jackson through intelligent blue eyes. He took a deep drag on the pipe he held clenched between his teeth before speaking.

"I won't even hazard to guess how we got here, when mere moments ago we were sitting in my office at Project Y. What I do wish to know is, what do you want with us?"

"Are you J. Robert Oppenheimer?"

"I am."

"Albert Einstein told us you might be able to help us. We need to know what you think this is." Johanna pointed to the blue orb. The others had already noticed it and gathered around it.

"Where did it come from?" Oppenheimer asked, mesmerized by the pulsating blue light. The hypnotic strobe cast a ghostly pallor on the faces of the people who had accompanied him. Oppenheimer reached out to touch it. He felt the energy of the force field, but not the sphere itself.

"Spooky, huh?" Jackson stated. "I tried that, too. There's a force field around it."

"It would seem our esteemed director has been warned off," one of the scientists joked. The others began talking excitedly about what could create such an energy shield.

"It just appeared," Johanna told Oppenheimer. "There was nothing here an hour ago when we went into a back room to work on an illuminated manuscript. We found the orb sitting here when we returned. The thing is, the library is a locked facility and there are no signs of a break-in."

As Oppenheimer listened, he surveyed his surroundings. The words *library* and *illuminated manuscript* piqued his curiosity. "What is this place?"

"It's the Library of Illumination," Johanna answered. She turned when a scientist who touched the orb for the third time cried out in pain. She moved closer to the injured man and looked at his hand.

The distraction didn't faze Oppenheimer. He walked over to the nearest shelf to see what treasures it might hold. On it lay the Gutenberg Bible, which had not yet been locked in the display case. He gently ran his finger across the tooled calf cover that carried the scars of more than five centuries of use. He slowly opened the book, recognizing its history and value, and he carefully turned the pages to the book of Genesis. Instantaneously, Adam and Eve sprang to life, standing naked before him.

—LOI—

C:L◉I

CHAPTER SEVEN

ADAM STOOD AT least a foot shorter than Oppenheimer, who was six feet tall. Eve was even smaller. The first couple was surprisingly bald, with no facial or body hair. Instead, they had the soft, downy skin of newborns. They had not been exposed to the elements long enough to be either tanned or hirsute. They neither cowered in fear nor tried to cover their naked bodies, but stood as still as statues, their skin so pale they could be mistaken for alabaster figurines. Their muscles were clenched and their eyes wide. They seemed to be on high alert, monitoring every sound and movement around them.

The scientists slowly turned away from the orb, their attention now focused on the naked couple who miraculously materialized.

They all stared at each other, not knowing where the others had come from. No one besides Johanna and Jackson had any knowledge of the unique peculiarities of the Library of Illumination, nor had they seen the physicist open the Bible.

Oppenheimer slowly looked from Adam to Eve, and then to Johanna, whose eyes were fixed on the book. The physicist looked down at the Bible, then closed his eyes for a second as he processed the information at hand. When he opened his eyes, he smiled at the first couple and closed the cover on the Gutenberg Bible. Adam and Eve disappeared as quickly as they had arrived. The scientists gasped and immediately began speculating about what had just happened. The disappearing couple was, to them, just as astounding as the strange blue orb with a force field.

Johanna took the Bible out of the scientist's hands. "Please, Dr. Oppenheimer, we need to discuss that pulsating sphere."

One mathematician refused to be put off. "Where did they go?"

"Back to their own reality," Oppenheimer replied. "Just as we will return to ours. Is that not right, miss?"

"Is that one of your random hypothetical suppositions, Oppie?" a scientist asked.

"There is nothing random about it, gentlemen. We've been brought here to discuss this device." He gestured toward the orb. "Care to share your opinions?"

"It's very powerful, and the field around it is becoming exponentially more dangerous," a mathematician stated.

"It gives off light, but doesn't appear to generate heat," noted an engineer.

"The interior protrusions are aimed at what appears to be a carbon ball in the center. If the protrusions have been engineered to act as a fission trigger and the central ball contains an adequate amount of uranium and plutonium, or even chemicals unknown to us at this juncture, then this could be a powerful explosive that needs to be immediately disarmed," another scientist concluded.

Oppenheimer walked around the orb, noting what his colleagues had said. "Gentlemen, if devices like this are possible and there are people who have access to them, then we have a big job ahead of us."

"Can you disarm it?" Jackson asked.

"No," Oppenheimer answered, "not without more information on who created it and why. Or how it was put together." He looked at Johanna. "What year is this?"

A colleague berated him. "How can you ask such a ridiculous question? You know very well it's 1943."

Johanna locked eyes with Oppenheimer and imperceptibly shook her head. "This is the twenty-*first* century," she said quietly.

Oppenheimer nodded. "Then there is nothing we can do for you." He paused. "There must be so much to observe outside these walls. I don't suppose you would take us on a tour?"

"What a wonderful idea," one of the scientists exclaimed. "And I would love the opportunity to explore this library." He swung his arms in a wide arc to illustrate the breadth of what he wished to take in. As he twirled around, he lost his balance and fell into the blue orb. He immediately disappeared.

"Where did he go?" The missing man's colleagues looked around.

"This device is obviously much more dangerous than it appears!" the mathematician claimed.

"We must commence an immediate search," Oppenheimer demanded.

"That's out of the question," Johanna replied,

still holding the book that had produced him and his colleagues. She closed it, and the group disappeared.

JACKSON TUGGED ON the book. "Why did you do that? We need their help to find out what happened to that guy."

Johanna refused to let go. "Hopefully, he's now back in his own time period, and has been reunited with the others."

"What if he isn't there? What if his disappearance changes history?"

Johanna pulled the book away from Jackson and returned it to the upper level. She brought down a later book about the Manhattan Project and began searching through pictures of the team members. She found the missing scientist in a picture taken after the gadget—a code name for the A-bomb—had been tested near Alamogordo, New Mexico.

"Look. That's him." She pointed at the picture. "I don't know what happened to him, but his disappearance could not have been permanent. If it were, all these books would have changed automatically, and he wouldn't be in this picture."

Jackson ran his hands through his hair, pushing it straight back off his forehead. "So now what?" He picked up a pencil and shook it rapidly between his thumb and his index finger, watching the movement. He lost his grasp and the pencil flew into the orb, but instead of disappearing like the scientist, it ricocheted off the force field at an accelerated rate of speed. The mustard-yellow Dixon Ticonderoga #2 pencil pierced the spine of a 1773 *Samuel Johnson English Dictionary*, embedding itself between the signatures.

Johanna walked over and inspected the damage

as she struggled to control her anger over her protégé's careless behavior.

JACKSON SENSED HE was in trouble. His thoughts all tumbled out at once. "Johanna, I'm sorry. I didn't realize what I was doing. Is the book badly damaged? Do you want to dock my pay so you can buy the materials to fix it? You can, you know." His tone sounded earnest.

Johanna inhaled sharply. "Do you realize how lucky we are that this pencil only pierced a book? What if it had careened in a different direction, and embedded itself in my eye? Or your heart?"

The sixteen-year-old paled. "I didn't know that might happen. How could I? I didn't expect to lose my grip on the pencil."

"Whatever that thing is"—she tilted her head toward the orb—"it's very dynamic." Her shoulders slumped and her voice quieted. "I think we have to call in the authorities."

"That's what I was thinking." Jackson grabbed the phone off the circulation desk.

She snatched it away from him. "But first, we have to move as many of these books as possible into storage." She placed the phone back on the desk. "I think we need to buy a couple hundred regular books for the shelves down here, so if someone happens to open one, nothing will pop out."

"Isn't that going to take a lot of time and money?"

"I cashed in the last doubloon from your impromptu party with the pirates of *Treasure Island* and put the money into the library account. I can use that to pay for the books. Maybe we can find a used-book store that will sell us their contents at a good price."

"What if we can't?"

She sighed. "We'll cross that bridge when we come to it."

Jackson's childhood came straight out of a fairy tale, not the sanitized retelling of a children's story with a happily-ever-after ending, but an older, medieval fairy tale with dark tendencies and, usually, an unhappy conclusion. The source of Jackson's misery was his father.

Sean Roth should never have married— he wasn't faithful, he drank too much, and he hated little children. It didn't take him long to tire of Naimh Fitzpatrick, a girl he had impregnated at the age of sixteen. His lack of interest, however, hadn't stopped him from getting her pregnant again and again.

Somewhere along the way, he actually put a ring on Naimh's finger, but you would never know it by the way Sean lived his life. The more his babies cried, the less time he spent at home. The less time he spent at home, the more money he gambled away. Needless to say, the family lived in squalor. After years of an empty marriage, Sean abandoned his wife and three kids, leaving them with a pile of bills, no income or insurance, and a house that was falling apart.

His eldest son, Jackson, fully expected Sean to return, but after a year had gone by without one word from his father, the teen's hope was replaced by anger. He found himself yelling at his mother and brother as if it were their fault, and then punching holes in the wall to release some of his rage, because he knew they weren't to blame. Only his little sister escaped his wrath. His fury soon gave way to depression, and Jackson couldn't help crying whenever he was alone. Eventually, he accepted the fact that his father was never coming back. Somehow, he managed to pull himself together and get a part-time job at the Library of Illumination, so he could contribute a little money to the family coffers.

Even though he worked at the library, Jackson knew he could never borrow its enchanted books. He loved reading science-fiction and fantasy novels, but could not afford to buy new ones. That forced him to find used-book stores so he could feed his habit for space-ships and zombies. In his estimation, Bebe's Bibliothèque on High Street was the best place to get a lot of books for a little money, and he shared his insight with Johanna. "I promise you, we can get a good deal there."

"Okay. I'll call them," she replied. "In the meantime, could you lock the Gutenberg Bible in the display case? We don't need another appearance by Adam and Eve."

"Did they look a little like space aliens to you?"

Johanna didn't answer. She just shook her head and walked away. She had enough on her mind without having to think about the human race being the spawn of E.T.

THE OWNERS OF Bebe's Bibliothèque agreed to sell the library a thousand used books for $1,000 and arranged to deliver them the following morning. Johanna knew they would send her their shabbiest hardcovers, but that would be fine for her purposes. She had also ordered several cases of new books about the Gutenberg Bible for the shelves immediately surrounding the display case. They would be the first things anyone walking into the library would see, and since they were there to complement a special exhibit, no one would question why all the central stacks were filled with similar titles. If Johanna and Jackson stocked the remaining shelves only half to three-quarters full, the used books would go a long way.

She refused to contact the authorities until they had everything in place, and whether that call would be made to the police or the FBI, she did not yet know.

The pair spent the rest of the day and most of the evening moving books from the main level into a storage room in the basement.

"What do you call this thing again?" Jackson slid a pile of books into a square cupboard on a pulley system.

"A dumbwaiter."

"I love that."

"You would."

"Why didn't they just call it a mini-elevator?"

"Because it was created to move food from basement kitchens to upper-level dining rooms like a waiter would do, but a dumbwaiter never complains because it can't speak. I'm hoping you'll follow its example."

He made a face. "Right."

THE SUN HAD nearly set by the time Jackson got home. He still had a lot of pent-up energy, so he invited his brother, Chris, to shoot hoops.

Chris was a year younger than Jackson, but almost as tall, and just as athletic. He sensed that something bothered his older brother by the way Jackson slam-dunked the ball. "Hey, Jax, what are you trying to do, bust the rim?"

Jackson dribbled the ball for a moment, and then tossed it across the driveway.

Chris lunged for it. "Giving up so soon? I guess my game's too much for you."

The older teen walked to the far side of the garage and sank down on the grass.

"It's Johanna, isn't it?" Chris guessed. "She's not responding to your wit and charm, is she?"

Jackson smirked at his brother but shook his head. "I wish it were only that."

"What do you mean?"

"I can't tell you."

"Ohhh ... the secret world of the library," Chris mocked him. "What happened? Did her boyfriend show up?"

Jackson sighed. "I can't tell you."

"Okay. Hold it in till you explode."

Jackson leapt to his feet and shoulder-rammed his brother, knocking him off balance.

"What—is—your—problem?" Chris demanded.

"You've got to promise not to tell anybody."

"I promise."

"No, Chris, really, really promise—cross your heart and hope to die promise."

"What have you gotten yourself into now?"

"Do you promise?"

"I already said I promise."

Jackson took a deep breath before blurting, "There's some kind of *thing* in the library, and nobody knows what it is."

"You mean like a giant prehistoric turd?"

"You're not being serious."

"Or like a dumpster that's really a doomsday

device?"

Jackson froze.

"Wait. You mean I'm right?"

Jackson pushed his brother down onto the grass. "Keep your voice down. We don't want to start a panic."

"A panic. If there's a bomb in the library, don't you think people should, you know, *get out of town*?"

"Shut up!" Jackson whispered fiercely. "It's not that easy. We don't really know what it is, or where it came from. Johanna is going to call someone tomorrow to come take a look."

"And what if it explodes tonight?" Chris demanded.

"Then I guess it doesn't matter, does it?"

"I want to see it."

"No."

"I have a right to see what's going to bring my short, precious life to an end before I ever get a chance to squeeze Brittany Chelvie's boobs."

"Forget it. If that's all that's bothering you, go to Brittany's house right now and ask her to come out and play."

"You think that would work?"

"Yeah."

"What about the bomb?"

"Forget I even mentioned it."

"No way. How am I supposed to forget something like that?"

"Go call Brittany and invite her over to study."

"That might work, if I don't *die* first."

They heard the screen door on their house scrape open and their sister Ava call out, "Jackson, Chris, Mom says it's time to come inside."

"Remember," Jackson warned Chris, "you can't tell anybody."

* * *

JACKSON ARRIVED AT the library the following morning at the same time as the shipment of used books. He directed the truck to the back alley and helped the driver carry in piles of old hardcovers.

The temperature had already risen to the upper eighties, and the humidity was just as high. Sweat dripped from the driver's face, which had turned bright red after a few trips down the alley. Jackson looked only slightly better. Johanna had asked them to stack all the boxes just inside the back door—not to lighten their load in the heat but to prevent the driver from seeing the pulsating blue orb. She had extended the pull-up screens for the Gutenberg Bible exhibit to block any view of the mysterious sphere, but off in the corners, telltale flashes of blue light reflected off the polished wood.

When he finally brought in the last book, the driver handed Johanna an invoice. She handed him a check and a tip and pushed him out the door.

Jackson walked the driver back to his truck. After the pawnbroker incident, a new lock had been installed on the back gate to prevent people from entering through the alley, and it was Jackson's responsibility to make sure it remained secured at all times. Johanna had given him a key to the gate so he could leave his bike behind the building, but she wouldn't give him a key to the back door, citing security issues.

He kicked a piece of trash lying in the alley. If she trusted him enough to make sure the back gate was locked, why didn't she trust him enough to give him a key to the back door? It meant he always had to borrow her key, or bang on the door for her to let him in.

Not that it mattered. A few weeks ago he had forgotten to return the key to her, and when he realized he had it in his possession, he had a copy made—in case of an emergency. He needed to tell Johanna he had it, but now, with the orb pulsating in the library, he was afraid to. Still, he knew he had to come clean soon if he wanted her to trust him.

—LOI—

C:L ⬡ I

CHAPTER EIGHT

Johanna untied a bundle of used books. They were worn and dog-eared, but the titles encompassed a good selection of politics, travel, and art, as well as several hundred novels and anthologies covering different genres. She and Jackson spent the rest of the day shelving them all.

"What's this? Jackson asked, picking up a book that sat by itself on a bottom shelf. A thick layer of dust obscured the cover. "Did you leave this book down here?"

"What book?"

He opened the book to a random page to see what it was about. Dracula suddenly loomed over him, blood dripping from his mouth. "Uhhh ...!" Jackson's scream did not get past his throat.

Dracula moved in for the kill. The teen managed to slam the book shut just as the vampire's teeth made contact with his skin.

"What are you doing?" Johanna poked her head around the corner of the shelf and spotted the blood on Jackson's neck. She looked down and recognized the volume of *Dracula* by Bram Stoker and winced. "We must have missed that one. Are you all right?"

Jackson swiped at his neck.

"Come with me." Johanna led him to the circulation desk. She took out a first-aid kit and cleaned away the blood with an antiseptic wipe.

"Am I ...?"

"It's just a surface wound." She wrapped the bloody wipe in a tissue and threw it in the wastebasket. "You're going to live ... but not forever."

Jackson sighed with relief. "You know, when my mother used to patch me up, she would kiss it to make it better." He raised his eyebrows and grinned at her.

"If you got hurt working for Larry at Once A-Pawn A Time, would you ask him to kiss it to make it better?"

"You really know how to hurt me."

Johanna laughed. She leaned in and lightly kissed Jackson's neck.

He could feel the hairs along his nape tingle.

"All better?" she asked.

He merely nodded, too stunned to answer.

THEY RAN OUT of books before reaching the rear stacks, so Johanna taped signs across the shelves that read, "Maintenance Required," hoping the signs would be enough to keep authorities from questioning why shelves were empty.

The evening shadows lengthened, making the pulsating light from the orb appear more pronounced. Johanna said a silent prayer that the object's purpose would remain a mystery for at least a few more days, to give them time to deal with it.

The next morning, she waited for Jackson to arrive before calling the authorities. She wanted to make sure they had their stories straight, and instructed Jackson to say, "I don't really remember, you'd better ask Johanna," if questioned about anything they hadn't gone over. Finally, she took a deep breath and called police.

The teens propped open the library's front door and waited for cops to arrive. Johanna sighed in relief when she realized the responding officers were not the same ones who had handled the previous call from the library. She showed them the device, and they stood and stared at it for several minutes, before asking the inevitable, "What is it?"

Before Johanna could say a word, Jackson jumped in. "It's pulsating, you know, which made us think it might be a bomb. That's why we called you."

"It's a bomb?"

Johanna took control of the conversation. "We don't know that it's a bomb, but since we have no other ideas about what it could be, we thought it best to let you handle it."

"Where did you get it?"

"We were in a meeting in the back. It wasn't here before the meeting. It just—kind of appeared."

"This morning?"

"Uh ... Tuesday morning."

"You waited more than twenty-four hours to call us?"

"Because we were busy trying to figure out a logical explanation for it being here. We didn't want to bother you needlessly," she said, to placate them. "But after we exhausted all possibilities, we called you."

One of the officers tried touching the sphere, to ill

effect. "It's got something weird going on with it. Like one of those old novelty handshake buzzers that kids used to buy to zap their friends."

The other officer reached for the orb, with the same result. "I'd better call the precinct."

While he spoke on the phone, his partner started inspecting the books nearest him. "I'm surprised places like this exist. Isn't everyone reading e-books nowadays?"

"Not everyone," Johanna replied. "This library provides a lot of resource materials for people conducting research, and many of the books they request do not have digital versions."

"Yeah. My wife always says she likes to hold a paper book in her hands."

"And you?" Johanna asked.

"Anything that's worth my time is probably going to turn into a TV show or movie, and I'll see it when it hits the screen, or watch it on my computer."

"Philistine," she mumbled under her breath.

"What's that?"

"Like Wolverine," she substituted.

"You're an X-Men *fan*?" He grinned. "I love those comic books. But it proves my point. Even they're being made into movies."

The other officer walked back in. "The higher-ups decided to call in the FBI. This is more their turf. My partner and I will wait for them outside. If there's any change in that thing, let us know." The cops walked out, leaving the teens alone with the device.

Johanna sank down on the sofa. Jackson pulled a chair over and straddled it. "You originally planned to call the FBI. What made you change your mind and call police?"

"I don't know. I guess I thought the FBI would be

more responsive if the police called them, rather than us."

"So now we wait."

WITHIN THE HOUR, the cops returned with their chief of police and two agents from the Federal Bureau of Investigation. The officials eyed Johanna and Jackson, but ignored them and headed directly for the orb. Their conversation mimicked the discussion by the scientists who had preceded them. Additional attempts to touch the sphere were futile.

The older FBI agent was a muscular man named Mace. "We have to move it out of here."

"If we can't even touch it, how's that going to be possible?" a cop asked.

Salisbury, the younger FBI agent, caught his eye. "Backhoe."

"What if it blows up?" the police chief conjectured.

"How did it even get in here?" Mace asked. "Somewhere, someone knows just what this thing is, and how to move it."

"Maybe Scotty can beam it up?" Jackson said dryly.

Johanna unobtrusively kicked him in the ankle.

"Hey, the kid's a Trekkie," one of the cops said.

"*Star Trek* is not going to help us here," Mace replied as he slowly circled the orb.

"I still think a backhoe is the way to go," Salisbury said. "It might be a little tough getting it in here, but it should be able to handle the payload."

"What if the driver fries on contact?" the police chief asked.

"There doesn't have to be a driver," Salisbury answered. "We can use a robotic backhoe, that way nobody gets hurt."

"Yeah, unless the freakin' thing explodes," Jackson

added. He felt Johanna's shoe connect with his ankle again. "Hey," he whispered. "I'm too young to die, and I don't want these guys doing something stupid."

"If you're scared, leave, or else shut up," she hissed under her breath.

Jackson clamped his jaw shut, fisted his hands, and stared at the floor. Johanna's reprimand surprised him. *Aren't we in this together?* he wondered, but didn't say out loud, not wanting to upset her further.

"All right, young lady, who's in charge here?" Salisbury asked.

Johanna bristled at the agent's tone. "I am."

"No. I mean, who's your boss?"

"I am the curator of this library."

"There's no CEO? No board of directors?"

"The library board has little to do with the day-to-day operation of the library."

"Just get the top guy down here, now. This is a matter of national security. Go on. Get on the phone!"

Johanna had no other choice. She called the head of the library board and told him he needed to come down right away. He tried to put her off, until she said, "The FBI is here." He arrived twenty minutes later.

She could see his annoyance turn to fear as he stared at the pulsing blue orb.

"Johanna," he called out. "Where did this device come from?"

"I don't know. We found it sitting here when Jackson and I returned from working in the antechamber."

"Where's your loading dock?" Salisbury asked the head of the library board.

He shrugged. "Johanna, where's the loading dock?"

"We don't have one."

"What do you mean, 'we don't have one'?" the

director said. "We have to have one. All this stuff didn't get in here through the front door."

"As far as I know, it did. There is a narrow alley in the back, but it's too small for a large vehicle. And there's no ramp, just concrete steps up to the back door. So, as far as I know, there's no loading dock."

"A backhoe could fit through the double doors out front, as long as we can get it up the steps," Salisbury speculated. "Maybe we could lay some planks across them and drive the backhoe up the incline."

The older agent nodded. "That seems like our best plan." He lowered his voice. "Just make sure we're not going to all this trouble for nothing. Take a walk around the building and check whether what she's saying is true. She's just a kid, and how she ever got to be curator of this place, I'll never know."

"Would anybody mind if I went out and got some lunch?" Jackson looked from face to face. Nobody seemed to care, so he left.

Before long, more agents arrived. They measured the width of the front door and nailed planks together to form a ramp. Officials were intent on driving a backhoe through the main entrance.

Johanna felt the sting of tears. How could this happen? How could she have let Mal down? He entrusted her with the library, and now it looked like the entire place would blow apart as soon as the backhoe made contact with the blue orb.

She slipped away from the main room and went into her office to retrieve Mal's diary. As she opened the book, she heard Jackson call her name. She placed the diary on her desk and walked out front.

"I got you a chicken-salad sandwich and a latte."

"Thanks." She picked up a cellophane bag filled

with foil-wrapped chocolates. "What's this?"

"I thought we could share a few kisses."

Johanna smiled in spite of herself. She had to admit, Jackson had a certain amount of boyish charm.

THE HEAD OF the library walked over to them. "I'm glad to see you two enjoying yourselves while the rest of us scramble to avert a catastrophe that could cut the future of this library short."

"If there's a catastrophe, at least I will have had a last meal," Jackson replied, "because if that thing blows up, I get the feeling that a lot more than just the library will be affected."

The head of the library board remained speechless for a moment before rushing off to the FBI agents, with whom he initiated a spirited conversation. A short time later, he climbed into a shiny, black, high-performance sports car. It was his pride and joy—the ultimate status symbol—something that made women notice him and men envy him.

He dialed his wife from his mobile phone and insisted that she grab the children and immediately drive to their country home up the coast. He told her she didn't have time to ask questions or pack.

She argued with him, but he raised his voice. "Just grab the children and go. It's a matter of life and death. I'll meet you there and explain everything."

"What's happening?" she cried.

"Just do it." He peeled away from the curb. He couldn't care less if the library blew up, as long as he wasn't anywhere near it when it did.

JOHANNA UNWRAPPED HER first kiss to the rumble of the backhoe making its way up the hastily built ramp. By the time she swallowed the chocolate, the machine had reached the outer lobby door. "No!" she said, choking.

Dax, the backhoe operator, let go of the joystick on the remote control as Johanna pulled at one of the Persian carpets.

"Jackson, help me get this rug out of the way before it gets ruined." The two of them dragged the cumbersome carpet into a corner.

"Lady," Dax shouted, "if that thing is what we think it is, the carpet is the least of your worries."

Johanna blushed, but didn't care. Until they were all blown to kingdom come, she would do whatever she could to protect the library and everything in it.

"Get everyone out of here," the backhoe operator told officials. "The last thing I need is another ridiculous interruption."

Mace walked over to Johanna and Jackson and yanked his thumb toward the door, hitchhiker style. "Out."

"I need my bag," Johanna said, rushing toward the antechamber. She saw Mal's diary and stuffed it in her purse. Jackson waited for her, and they walked out together.

The temperature outside the library was stifling. Johanna thought she could fry eggs on the sidewalk. The entire week had been unseasonably hot and humid, but she had forgotten all about the heat once the big, blue orb appeared. Now, with the sun beating down on her, she could feel the sweat on her upper lip.

Jackson took her hand.

"What are you doing?"

"If I'm going to die, like I said before, I want to die happy." He leaned in and brushed her lips with his own. When Johanna didn't pull away from him, he wrapped his arm around her, and pulled her closer.

"Hey, library curator, hot lips, we need you."

Agent Salisbury's sarcasm brought her back to reality. She pushed Jackson away. "What is it?"

"How do you open that door? Our man inside removed the chair propping it open, to get it out of the way of the backhoe, and the wall slid shut. Now we can't get inside. And apparently he can't get out."

Johanna tried to enter the lobby. All she needed to do was push a button and say, "Illumination," but the backhoe blocked her way. She tried to climb over it, but it effectively blocked her path. "You've got to move that thing out of the way."

"Call Dax and tell him to reverse the backhoe, so the little lady can get into the lobby," Mace ordered.

"I can't reach him. He's not responding," another agent replied.

"What do you mean you can't reach him? He's just on the other side of the door."

"He's not answering on the two-way radio or his mobile. Do you think the orb is causing interference?"

"How the hell do I know?" The increasing humidity and tension had eroded the professional demeanor of the older FBI agent.

"I can let you in the back." Johanna opened her bag and searched for her keys, but they weren't there. She envisioned the last time she had used them, and remembered dropping them in her desk drawer. "Except I don't have my keys."

"Right. National security is thwarted, all because some little girl who somehow got to be a library curator forgot her keys." The agent's voice mixed scorn with frustration.

Jackson studied Johanna for a moment before

replying. "I have a key to the back."

"But you can only get him inside the gate," she reasoned. "How are you going to get him inside the library?"

Jackson took a deep breath. "I have a key to the back door." He avoided looking at her, shifting his gaze to Salisbury. "Follow me."

The agent trailed Jackson around the block and through the alley. At the back door, Jackson pulled out a brand-new key and unlocked it.

"Your girlfriend didn't know about that key, did she?"

Jackson shrugged. "She does now."

Inside, the frustrated robotics operator banged his fist against the front door. He turned when he heard their voices. "Thank God. I thought I'd never get out of here. My radio doesn't work, and neither does my mobile. I thought I was going to be trapped in here with that thing until the end."

"You've got to reverse the backhoe, so the girl can open the front door."

Jackson spoke up. "I can open the door from in here. Illumination."

The door slid open to cheers from the people outside.

"Now for this—" Salisbury began. He stopped mid-sentence as the large blue sphere rose ten feet off the floor, and floated in midair above the circulation desk.

"Are you going to move this backhoe or what?" Mace grumbled before noticing that the status quo had changed. He followed his partner's gaze. A guttural noise escaped his throat when he spotted the orb hovering overhead.

* * *

OUTSIDE, JOHANNA SAT on the curb, despondent over the fate of the library she held so dear. It was her life—literally. She dug through her bag and found Mal's diary. After she made sure no one was watching her, she nonchalantly walked into the lobby. Her heart nearly stopped when she saw the sphere floating above everyone's heads. She claimed a corner of the vestibule not blocked by the backhoe and sat down. She held Mal's diary open in her hands and whispered, "Nuclear device." It brought her to Mal's recollection of the Trinity Project and nuclear testing in White Sands, New Mexico. It outlined the devastation following the use of atomic weapons against Hiroshima and Nagasaki. It included the meltdowns at nuclear power plants in Chernobyl, Russia, and Fukushima, Japan. But aside from a few Cold War and Middle East references, there was nothing else.

Johanna leaned her head against the wall and closed her eyes. "Mal, why aren't you here to tell me what the big blue ball is?"

The pages shuffled. She looked down at the diary, which now appeared to be an inch thicker. It lay open on one of the last pages.

—LOI—

C:L 🟤 I

CHAPTER NINE

Johanna felt her pulse quicken when she noticed a picture of the blue orb. She devoured the words written below the image. The device was a special reactor, independent of the electrical grid that provided energy for homes and businesses in the area. The orb supplied power for only the library and nothing else. It had been that way since before Mal arrived, but the former curator had noted that the reactor showed signs of failing and that he needed to do something about it.

Suddenly, the handwriting in the diary changed to printed instructions. Item number three advised against touching the device because a force field protected it. *No kidding.* Number six indicated the sphere would rise as it lost power. *It's getting weaker?* Suddenly, she didn't feel so bad. Number eight instructed curators to move the reactor into direct sunlight every half millennium to recharge it. *How do I do that if there's a force field?* She found her answer in number ten, which indicated that the word *illumination*—spoken only by the curator—would give that person voice control to move the object. And number twelve said, once the object was charged, the word *delumination* would remove the reactor from sight. Number thirteen, however, chilled Johanna to the bone. It said under no circumstances should force be used against the generator, or a nuclear chain reaction could occur.

Johanna scrambled to her feet, and climbed over the backhoe. It was easier now that the inner door was open. Inside, she found everyone gathered around Salisbury, who outlined his plan to catch the orb in a net.

"Gentlemen," Johanna cried out, "false alarm. We don't need your assistance anymore. You can go."

Mace spun around and glared at her. "I'm calling the shots here, and this is not a false alarm. I'm not leaving without that thing."

Johanna tensed. *How am I supposed to get out of this?* When the group turned back to observe the orb, she walked to the antechamber and opened the diary again. "Mal," she whispered, "you've got to tell me, is there any way to make them forget why they're here?" She waited for the pages to flutter, but they remained still.

"You okay?" Jackson had followed Johanna to the antechamber.

"It's not a bomb," she whispered. "It's a nuclear power generator that supplies energy to the library. It has to be charged every five hundred years, and now is the time. Except, how am I going to charge it without the authorities going all crazy on me?"

"Do you know what you're saying?"

"Of course."

"That five hundred years ago, shortly after Gutenberg came out with the Bible in the display case inside, a nuclear generator existed *here on earth* to supply power to this library."

"Yes."

"I can't wait to hear you explain that"—he nodded toward the agents—"to those guys."

"I guess ... I'll just have to make something up."

Jackson picked up a lock of her hair. "What can I do to help?" He looked at her and saw her eyes riveted to the strand of hair that he held. He dropped it. Now that they weren't going to die, she seemed a little more standoffish.

Johanna remained quiet for so long that Jackson thought she hadn't heard him. Finally, she looked at him and smiled. "You've got to get them out of the main reading room. Lure them down to the basement with the promise of showing them something odd that may be connected to the device."

"What am I supposed to show them?"

"I don't know. Improvise."

"This isn't some pawnbroker. These guys are feds. They can lock us up. I need to show them *something*."

She pictured an old, clunky instrument gathering dust in a corner. "The Graphophone! Show them the Graphophone."

"That thing that you showed me the other day?"

"Yeah."

"That thing's as old as the hills. Only an idiot would think it's connected to the orb."

"Jackson, the orb is older than the Graphophone. I need you to do this for me. Besides, they already think we're incompetent." She grabbed each of his hands in hers and looked him in the eyes. "They can't expect you to know what that thing is. It's way before your time. It would be an honest mistake. And even if they do think you're an idiot, I would know you're a hero." She stretched up and kissed him.

Jackson felt an electric current, almost as strong as the one he had felt the last time he tried to touch the orb. "Okay," he sighed. "I'll be your idiot."

Johanna gave him a big smile. "Sooner is better."

They walked together to the circulation desk, but their smiles faded when they saw the orb spinning wildly. The younger FBI agent smothered a smoldering paper on the reference desk.

"Oh my God, what did you do to it?" She spotted what looked like a fishing net lying on the floor.

"We tried to catch it in the net, and it went ballistic, rotating like that and throwing off sparks."

She looked at Jackson. "Now what?"

"I'll bet you anything that it's being controlled by that thing I saw down in the basement," he said excitedly.

"You're crazy," she said.

Mace pushed past the other agent. "What thing in the basement?"

"Some kind of really odd thing that I've never seen before."

"Show us." The FBI agents, followed by the cops and Dax, paraded down the stairs.

As soon as they were out of sight, Johanna looked up at the orb and said, "Illumination." The spinning slowed, and the orb lowered. "This way." She walked to the back door, and said, "Outside." The orb slipped through the door and rose until it sparkled in the light of the sun.

In the basement, Jackson took officials to see an intricate piece of machinery made up of several brass and nickel rods connected to gears and a handle. A wax-coated tube covered one of the rods. An arm with a metal stylus swung freely from another. The contraption sat on a walnut box resting on a rusty, iron treadle frame, similar to the ones used on early sewing machines.

Mace's voice echoed off the gray stone walls. "What the hell is that? You brought us down here to look at that piece of junk?"

"How am I supposed to know what it is? I've never seen anything like it before. What if it's important?"

"It's an old recording device," Dax said, "used to capture the sound of music and voices on wax cylinders."

"My great-grandfather used to have one of those," a cop said, rubbing his finger over the brass gears. "My uncle made a mint selling it online."

"Forget this," Mace growled. "We'd better get back upstairs before that thing incinerates us all."

While the men were downstairs, Johanna let herself back into the building and quietly closed the door. She retreated into the antechamber to await the agents' return.

The FBI agents led the way up from the basement, but stopped short when they got to the reading room, causing the other officials to bump into them.

"What now?" Salisbury sighed.

"It's gone," Mace growled.

Jackson pushed past them. "Johanna," he yelled.

She rushed out of the antechamber. "Did you find something?"

"No. It was some old recording device. Are you okay?"

She nodded.

"Where's the orb?" Mace demanded.

Johanna looked up. "What did you do with it?" she asked, feigning ignorance.

"We were downstairs. You were the one up here with it."

"I ... I ... had to use the ... facilities."

"The facilities? You didn't see where it went?"

"No." She circled around the circulation desk. She felt as nervous as her voice sounded, but not for the obvious reason. The big blue generator floated in the sun right outside one of the library windows. If she could see it, so could everyone else.

"Maybe it's behind the stacks," she said, trying to throw them off.

The men split up and searched the interior of the library. "Check downstairs," Mace told Salisbury, "in case that thing followed us down and we missed it. I'll check the back offices." He headed toward the antechamber that Johanna had just vacated.

One of the cops searched the stacks to the left, while another searched the shelves on the right. Dax took the stairs to the second floor, while the police chief went out the front door to call for backup.

Johanna's nerves stretched to their limit. They hadn't taken any precautions with the books on the second level or in the antechamber. Those books were all enchanted, and she feared that Mace and Dax would either open a book, unleashing its power, or look out the window and see the orb floating behind the library.

She picked up the remote control for the backhoe and made sure she pushed the joystick in the process. The backhoe roared to life and rolled into the library. Even though Johanna had pressed the lever, the movement startled her and she dropped the controller. The joystick hit the floor, making the backhoe change direction. It headed straight for the stacks. "No!" Johanna screamed.

She scooped up the controller, but it was too late. The backhoe slammed into a stack, causing it to tip over, and each bank of shelves tumbled into the one behind it, toppling them like dominoes. Books crashed everywhere.

The cop investigating that section had just rounded the corner of the last stack and wasn't in direct range of being hit, but his color drained as he witnessed the chaos.

Jackson came running. "Johanna, are you all right?"

She nodded.

Dax rushed down from the second level, still holding one of the books he had found up there. He grabbed the controller away from her. "What are you, crazy?"

"I picked the controller up to put it by the backhoe. I accidentally dropped it, and the backhoe went berserk."

Everyone reunited to inspect the damage.

Johanna caught Jackson's eye and looked out the window. He followed her line of vision and returned her gaze with a half shrug.

Mace leaned over and picked up a few books. He placed them on the circulation desk, and as he turned away, his eyes came to rest on a blue blur on the other side of the window. "Outside." He pointed. "I see it."

He started for the front entrance, but Salisbury yelled, "Use the back door, it's closer."

Dax threw down the book he held as he ran after them. In an instant, an unshaven, ill-kempt man dressed in rumpled linen breeches and a checked shirt appeared. He stood outside an odd enclosure made up entirely of well-worn sea chests. The handsome trunks were reinforced with iron hardware and leather straps, and were stacked end to end to create a wall. The man stared at Johanna. "Do you speak English?"

Johanna ignored him. She turned toward the orb. "Delumination." Then she nodded her head at Daniel Defoe's most famous character, knowing the shipwrecked man's look of relief would be short-lived. She grabbed the book off the floor and slammed it shut, hiding it in a drawer behind the circulation desk.

OUTSIDE, OFFICERS FOUND nothing. "It must have been a trick of light. Or maybe an airplane passing by," Salisbury said. "There's nothing out here."

Still, the FBI and the police spent another hour inspecting the back yard and the surrounding area before finally admitting the orb had disappeared.

Dax returned for the remote control and maneuvered the backhoe onto a flatbed truck that blocked the street.

"Where do you think it went?" one of the cops asked.

"Hopefully, back where it came from," Mace answered.

They took one last look inside the library, but conceded the device had evaporated into thin air. The parade of government vehicles departed, and all the people who had gathered on the sidewalk hoping for a spectacle returned to their mundane lives.

Johanna secured the front door lock before plopping down on a sofa.

"Where do you think it went?" Jackson asked.

"Wherever it originally came from."

"This may be off topic, but I have to ask—who was that grungy-looking guy with all the trunks?"

"You saw that?"

"Yeah."

"Do you think the others did?"

"No. They were too focused on the orb."

Johanna relaxed. "Robinson Crusoe."

Jackson smirked. "Did he think you were there to rescue him?"

"We didn't get that well-acquainted. I was too concerned about the orb."

Jackson sat down next to her. "I sure hope its power cell had time to recharge."

"Of course it did, can't you tell?"

"No. How would I be able to tell?"

"Think about it."

"I'd rather think about you." He rubbed her arm and pointed out the goose bumps that puckered her skin. "I'm definitely having an effect on you."

She laughed. "I hate to disappoint you, but I have goose bumps because I'm freezing. The orb obviously controls the air conditioning. Better luck next time."

That was fine with Jackson. As long as there was a next time to look forward to, he was willing to keep trying.

—LOI—

C:L ⊛ I

CHAPTER TEN

Casanova

ANNO 1750. CARNIVAL. *It was Giacomo Casanova's favorite time of year. He dreamed of all the women waiting to be unmasked at the redoutes—or masked balls—being held all over Vienna. Beautiful women. Rich women. Vulnerable women. The uppermost echelons of society hosted the lavish balls for their friends in the aristocracy.*

Casanova was not a member of the nobility. Both his parents were actors, and he was considered something of a dandy. However, he had been educated in medicine and law and had a quick wit. He also possessed a fair amount of charm and had ingratiated himself to a rich patron who introduced him into society. Now, the young man looked dashing—dressed in the garb of a whimsical knight, complete with armor and a full-face mask. The costume provided a great deal of anonymity and would give him the opportunity he needed to win a wager. A nobleman had bet Casanova that he could not abscond with a valuable book that the challenger had seen in their host's possession. He gave Casanova explicit details about the book's location. All the errant knight had to do was borrow the precious tome for a little while.

Casanova stealthily made his way to the second story of the palazzo and into the library chamber. He found the book he'd been told to liberate, prominently displayed on an ornately carved podium. He ran his fingers over the dark mahogany wood richly burnished with gold leaf. It was beautiful, and he loved beautiful things, but he dared not linger. He grabbed the folio and hid it under the folds of his cloak before he quietly made his way out of the chamber. He had prepared a place where the book would remain secure until he won his bet and the wager was paid. Then he would happily return the collection of stories to his host, for it was not the treasure but the gamble that gave him the most pleasure.

His escapade, however, was not fated to proceed as planned, for he had failed to anticipate that his host might leave his guests at the masked ball. Casanova panicked when he unexpectedly encountered the man.

The owner of the palazzo looked just as stunned to see someone sneaking out of his library. "You there, what business have you in my private chambers?"

The naughty knight panicked and bolted in the opposite direction, heading for the servants' staircase. He hurtled down the steep steps, clutching the book beneath his cape, and ducked around the wait staff and food preparers who rushed about below. He careened into a servant who lost his grip on a tray of raw fish, and the lovely silver creatures flew in all directions. One of them landed right in Casanova's path. When his heel made contact with the slippery seafood, he yelped as he lost his footing and plunged toward the back door. He threw the book outside so his hands would be free to grab on to the door frame and break his fall. The folio landed on its spine with a resounding crack, the pages falling open to either side. Casanova landed just as hard after being tripped by the raised door saddle. He crashed onto the open book— and vanished into thin air.

THE PALAZZO OWNER entered the kitchen, huffing and puffing from the chase. As soon as he saw the book, he scooped it up and quickly closed it. He had borrowed it from the Library of Illumination, and knew it was enchanted. How irritating that the thief got away, he thought, but having the book back was all that mattered.

—LOI—

C:L ❖ I

CHAPTER ELEVEN

Early-morning birdsong crept through Jackson's bedroom window, waking him. He had no trouble shaking off the drowsy stupor he usually felt in the mornings. It was a brilliant October day, with plenty of sunshine and a clear blue sky—but better than that, it was Jackson's birthday. He toyed with the idea of skipping school and going straight to the Library of Illumination to see Johanna. However, on second thought, doing that might make him look like an overexcited child, and he wanted to impress her with his maturity now that he'd turned *seventeen*.

Instead of throwing on a tee shirt and jeans, Jackson took a sartorial risk and put on a collared shirt and khakis. He wanted to look more adult, just like the guy he saw Johanna having dinner with at Le Chat.

The day dragged. His physics lab had been pretty

interesting, and he was a wiz at English, but his economics class was the epitome of boring. He couldn't care less about somebody's "marginal propensity to consume," unless it was about him consuming fries at McDonald's. Thank God he had lunch next period.

Finally, his last class ended. Jackson jumped on his bike and headed to the library. The school day could not have ended soon enough for him, even though his friends *had* acknowledged his birthday by presenting him with a giant cupcake with a candle on it. Still, all he really wanted was to be with Johanna.

He found her standing behind the circulation desk, going through mail and package deliveries. "Hey," he greeted her.

"Hey, birthday boy."

He smiled as he watched her crumple up a piece of junk mail and toss it into the wastebasket at the other end of the long desk. She never missed, and it intrigued Jackson that her throw always hit the mark. He wondered if he could succeed in luring her out to the park to shoot hoops.

AFTER SORTING THE letters, Johanna started going through packages. Most of them contained single volumes of unenchanted books that she had requested for borrowers who were not on her "approved" list. Two cartons remained. She grabbed one and ripped it open. "Oh my God, I can't believe they're already here."

"What?" Jackson asked.

"I bought a couple of iPads for the library. I thought it would be a lot easier to search for books using these, rather than always running back to the main computer. And now that you're almost done updating our digital database with all the new catalog information, we can save it to the cloud and use these to keep track of everything."

"Cool."

She put the iPads in a drawer behind the circulation desk.

Jackson did a double take. "Why are you putting them away? Aren't we going to fire them up?"

"That can wait." She grabbed the last carton and ripped off the cover. The package contained a multitude of Styrofoam packing peanuts cradling a smaller box. Johanna lifted it out of the carton, spilling Styrofoam everywhere.

"I hate this stuff," Jackson complained, trying to corral the loose bits.

"Whatever this is, it's really well packed." Johanna ripped paper away from a wooden box and felt something inside subtly shift. The sender had paid extra postage to mail the contents in a wooden container. That meant it was probably special. She removed the top of the box and found a letter from a collector who had previously used the library for repairs. The note rested on top of a large, calfskin-covered book.

Her eyes widened while she read the missive. She grabbed the book and studied the cover as she let out a small gasp.

"What is it?"

She made eye contact with Jackson and held his gaze, as if to signal the importance of the book in her hands. After a moment, she reverently whispered, "*Shakespeare's First Folio.*"

"THAT BOOK SURE beats a bunch of fairy stories," Jackson said, pointing to the 1890 edition of *English Fairy Tales* that held a place of honor in the library's glass display case.

"Fairy tales have a long tradition of entertaining children while teaching them all things are possible—if they're resourceful," Johanna reasoned.

"I guess ..."

She shook her head as she lifted the cover of the folio. The spine pulled away from the interior. "Look. It's not even attached." She removed the text block and laid it on the circulation desk. "That's not the only problem," she said, picking at a loose cord. "These quires need to be re-stitched." She pulled over an old library lamp and raised its green glass shade to get a better look. "I'm pretty sure I have the right size cord in stock," she said, more to herself than to Jackson. She placed everything back inside the box and carried it to the antechamber that served as the library's bindery and repair room.

"Are we going to work on that now?"

"I'd rather wait till morning. There's more natural light, and besides, I want to start fresh."

"What do we need to do tonight?"

"All of those used books from Bebe's Bibliothèque are in the basement storage room taking up space. Now that we don't need them anymore, I think it's time to get rid of them."

"Do you just want me to throw them in the dumpster?"

"I'd like to think you meant to say 'recycle them.' And we may end up going that route, but first, I'd like to try to sell them back to Bebe's."

"Good luck with that," Jackson replied. "I was in there the other night, and the shelves are filled with books that are in better condition than the ones we have here."

"There's no harm in trying. The most she could

say is 'no.' Besides, maybe the idea of buying all those books back at only *half* the price will appeal to her."

"You give it your best shot." His tone was cynical.

"C'mon. I need your help with something. Upstairs."

Jackson followed her up the spiral staircase and watched curiously as she pushed a crystal lever at the end of one of the stacks. The bookshelf *whooshed* open, and Jackson followed Johanna into a part of the library that he'd never been in.

They stumbled through one room in the dark before Johanna flipped a light switch.

"SURPRISE!"

Jackson stared at a bunch of people crammed inside Johanna's kitchen: his mother; his sister, Ava; his brother, Chris, and some girl; and his best friend, Logan, who was with Cassie, the girl who had baked Jackson's birthday cupcake. Half-filled bowls of corn chips and pretzels as well as open soft drink cans littered the table. Platters of sandwiches and salads, wrapped in colorful cellophane, lined the kitchen counter. A large cake claimed a sizable amount of space in the corner.

"Hey, bro, bet you never expected to see me here." Chris punched his brother in the arm.

Jackson nodded at the girl standing at Chris's side. "And who's this?"

Chris put his hand on the girl's shoulder. "Brittany, I'd like you to meet my brother, Jackson."

Brittany smiled and her cheeks dimpled. "Hi, Jackson. Happy birthday."

"Brittany." He looked from her to his brother, who winked at him.

JOHANNA GOT BUSY setting out plates and napkins, while

Jackson made his way around the room greeting friends and family.

His mother put her arms around him and gave him a hug. "Wasn't it nice of Johanna to do this for you? I was stunned when she stopped by and suggested it. I know you don't like surprises, but this is such a sweet thing for her to want to do that I just couldn't say no."

"Yeah." The last thing he could tell his mother was how he would much rather have Johanna all to himself on his birthday. He had to admit that he was impressed by all the trouble she went through just for him. He would have to give her a special thank-you kiss, later. *She can't refuse—it's my birthday!*

His sister passed him the chips. "There's cheese dip on the table. I made it just for you. It's your favorite kind."

Jackson kissed the top of Ava's head. "Thanks."

"We meet again, Jax." Logan grinned. "We would never have beaten you here if your mom hadn't called the school and asked if I could be let out early to help with a surprise party for you. I told Old Man Benson that Cassie was part of the surprise and dragged her out with me. Your mom picked us up, and we've been here for the past hour, eating chips and decorating."

Jackson looked up and saw streamers crisscrossing the ceiling and small bunches of balloons in each of the corners. "How nice for me."

Johanna handed him a soda. "Time to eat. You get to go first, since it's your birthday."

He grabbed a plate and filled it with food while Chris helped Johanna carry in extra chairs. Once they were all settled, the conversation revolved around how everyone managed to keep the party a secret from Jackson for more than a week.

He recognized the irony of the situation. The entire time he had been planning to make a move on Johanna in celebration of his seventeenth birthday, everyone else was organizing a party—that would keep him from reaching that goal. He mentally slapped himself for not catching wind of it, but he had been much too involved in fantasizing about seducing the library curator. His delightful daydream was now destined to die. He surely couldn't hope for anything more than a chaste birthday kiss with his family crowded around him, and once his birthday ended, his argument that he deserved a kiss because it *was his birthday* would no longer be valid.

He looked at his brother. Chris's arm had migrated around Brittany Chelvie's shoulders, pulling the pretty, young girl up against him. His younger brother was apparently better at the art of seduction than he was. *Where did I go wrong?*

THERE WERE ONLY crumbs of food left by the time the party ended. Johanna had ordered double the amount of sandwiches and salads normally recommended for the number of people she had invited, and she had baked a huge cake. She thought she would be swimming in leftovers, but teenage boys—like human vacuum cleaners—had sucked up every bit of food she had. *What is it about red velvet cake that everybody loves so much?* The party lasted longer than expected, mostly because Cassie suggested a game of charades and Brittany seconded the choice. It turned out to be so much fun that the evening flew by. The females trounced the males, game after game, although the guys boasted that they *let* the girls win.

Finally, Mrs. Roth could no longer stifle her yawns and stood up. "Thank you, Johanna, for throwing this wonderful party for Jackson."

Clearly, the festivities were over.

JACKSON VOLUNTEERED TO stay behind and help Johanna straighten up, but Chris said it wouldn't be fair, considering it was his birthday. Instead, the girls cleaned up while Chris and Logan put away chairs, leaving Jackson with no excuse to stay and be alone with the object of his affection. *What do they care? They've each got a girl to walk home. What do I have, my mother and my little sister? Some birthday.*

Even after he got home, random thoughts of what might have been kept him awake for hours.

JOHANNA ALSO FOUND it difficult to fall right to sleep. She had anticipated spending a little more quality time with Jackson on his birthday. Instead, she had been too busy to kiss him goodnight. She tried to console herself. It would have been awkward with his family and friends around; after all, she was technically his boss and was older than him. Still, memories of the previous summer held a special place in her heart. Jackson had shamelessly pursued her, even while they dealt with the sudden appearance of the blue orb. She remembered how vulnerable she felt after the FBI had virtually taken over the library, and fondly recalled how Jackson had stuck by her, so she didn't have to face the craziness alone. She had stupidly distanced herself from him after that incident, afraid that she had allowed him to get too close, but now she missed the special bond they had shared.

Growing up, Johanna had surrounded herself with an imaginary wall to protect herself from being hurt. Over the years, it had become practically insurmountable. She *had* dated a few guys she met outside of the library, but they rarely cared about the same things that interested her. So while she had gone out on quite a few first dates, she had refused the prospects of any second ones. She rationalized those decisions by convincing herself that she did not mind being alone. But she *was* lonely. Now Jackson had breached her defenses, and she did not seem to mind at all.

THE GRANDFATHER CLOCK in the main reading room struck the quarter hour. Jackson usually arrived at the library before ten on a Saturday morning, but it was well past noon and he still hadn't walked in. She completed all the chores she normally would have given him before starting repair work on *Shakespeare's First Folio*.

She heard the crash of metal hitting the pavement behind the library. Jackson burst into the main reading room a few seconds later.

"You must have had quite an after-party last night," she commented.

"I wish. I went straight to bed, but couldn't fall asleep. I was so exhausted this morning I didn't hear my alarm go off. Everyone else was gone by then. Chris had a track meet, and Mom and Ava went to cheer him on."

"I already did all your work."

"Does that mean you don't want me to stay?" he asked, confused.

"That means you get another lesson in bookbinding."

JACKSON SMILED. *HAPPY birthday to me.* He thought of how they would be huddled together in close quarters as they worked on the book. "Lead the way."

THE INTERIOR OF *Shakespeare's First Folio* had yellowed with age. Johanna slowly removed the threads that held the sections together. "Once I remove these," she said, picking away another thread, "we'll re-sew the quires and then reattach the cover."

"We will?"

"Yes. I'll show you how."

"What if I make a mistake?"

"You won't, because I'll be right here to stop you if you make a wrong move. You're my apprentice now, just like I was Mal's apprentice."

He liked the sound of that. "Okay."

Johanna leaned over to inspect the original holes that had been made to bind the folio. She studied them so intently her nose practically touched the paper.

Jackson picked up a loose quire. "Did Shakespeare have a lisp?"

His question made her sit back and stare at him. "Should I even ask?"

"Look. It says, 'The moft excellent Hiftorie of the Merchant of Venice.' Now tell me that Shakespeare didn't have a speech impediment."

"That's the way they wrote the letter *S* back then."

"Ahhh ..." He opened the *Merchant of Venice* to a random page. A handsome young man wearing something that a medieval knight might wear suddenly appeared.

"Jackson," Johanna barked.

The teen closed the pages and pushed the quire away. The knight, however, remained.

Johanna stared at their unexpected visitor. He had long, dark-blond hair and the most beautiful gray eyes she had ever seen. She looked from him to the folio pages he had sprung from, and her brow wrinkled. *What is he still doing here?* "Can I help you?" She didn't know what else to say.

He gave her a dazzling smile. "Buongiorno, signorina. Sono Giacomo Casanova." He stared at her for a moment. "Non riconosco il tuo stile del vestire. Sono a Venezia?" *I do not recognize your style of dress. Am I in Venice?*

Johanna nudged Jackson. "Do you speak Italian?"

"No."

"Buongiorno is 'good morning.' That much I know. And he said something about Venice, so maybe that's where he's from." Johanna turned toward the knight. She tapped herself a couple of times and said, "Johanna." It had worked for Johnny Weissmuller in *Tarzan of the Apes*, so why shouldn't it work for her?

The knight gave her another dazzling smile. "Si, si, Johanna." Then he tapped his own chest. "Casanova."

Jackson narrowed his eyes. "Casanova, like the lover?"

"It can't be. Shakespeare didn't write about Casanova."

"Shakespeare." Casanova said the bard's name with an Italian accent as he shook his head. He saw the folio and pointed to it. "Non Shakespeare." He tapped himself again. "Casanova." He looked around and held out his hands. "Dove mi trovo?" *Where am I?*

Johanna didn't know what to say, because she didn't understand Italian.

Casanova tapped the section of the folio that he had sprouted from. He pointed to it. "Questa è Venezia. Venezia." *This is Venice.* He looked around the room, then tapped the worktable and shook his head. "Non Venezia."

Johanna shook her head as well. "No Venezia. Library of Illumination."

"Library? Ahhh. Biblioteca di Illuminazione." He

nodded and smiled. "Grazie.

—LOI—

C:L⊙I

CHAPTER TWELVE

CASANOVA'S STOMACH RUMBLED. He patted it as he said, "Ho Fame. Mangiamo. Si?" *I'm hungry. Let's eat.*

Jackson quizzed Johanna. "What do you think he's saying now?"

"I'm not sure, but I think he's hungry."

"Either that, or he's asking where do you keep the Ex-Lax."

"Not funny." She turned to Casanova and said one of the few Italian words she knew. "Mangia?"

Casanova nodded. "Si, mangia. Mangia!" He slipped his arm around her shoulder and gave her a one-armed hug.

She looked at Jackson. "I don't have any food in the house. I need you to run out and pick up some lunch."

"You mean like pizza?"

"I don't know if he's the pizza type, considering he just came out of a seventeenth-century folio. Get some

grilled vegetables. Spaghetti with meatballs and sausage."
She paused. "Get lasagna, too. And a salad. And whatever
you want for yourself. Make sure they throw in garlic
knots and Italian bread."

"What ... no risotto or tiramisu?"

"Risotto. I didn't think of that? They probably
had that back then. Get shrimp risotto. And an order of
chicken parmigiana."

"That's a heck of a lot of food. Are you sending
King Arthur with me to help carry it back?"

"What are you, crazy? You know I can't let him
leave this place." She went into her office and took a
one-hundred-dollar bill out of her bag, thought twice
about it, and grabbed a second bill. She gave the money
to Jackson. "Here, this should be enough."

"So what are you and lover boy going to do while
I'm gone?"

She made a face at him. "Oh, I don't know. Just let
your imagination run wild."

THE PROBLEM WAS, Jackson's imagination *did* run wild,
and he didn't want to give Casanova enough time to get
too friendly with Johanna. He knew he couldn't carry all
the food back on his bike, so he literally ran to Piccolo
Italia, a popular Italian restaurant in the village. It was
lunchtime, and he was forced to wait on line behind all
the people who had just stopped in for a slice and a soda,
before he could place his order. The longer he took to
get lunch, the more time Johanna would be alone with
Casanova. THE Casanova. Jackson hated the idea, and
couldn't wait to get back to the library.

UNDER NORMAL CIRCUMSTANCES, Johanna and Jackson
might share a pizza in her office, but it would be too

crowded in there for three. Besides, there would be way too much food to spread out. The only solution would be to eat in Johanna's apartment. She beckoned Casanova to follow her up the stairs, which he seemed more than happy to do.

CASANOVA WATCHED JOHANNA as she pressed the lever that led to a private suite of rooms. He followed her into the kitchen and stared at the stainless-steel appliances. Johanna set the table with plates and glasses, while he inspected his surroundings. Overcome with curiosity, he walked over to the refrigerator and pulled the door open, then slammed it shut when he felt the blast of cold air. Not knowing what else to do, Casanova sat down and picked up his fork.

"THAT'S HOW IT is where you come from, huh?" Johanna said aloud. "You're ready to be served? I guess the men rest comfortably while the women do all the work."

He shook his head. "Non capisco." *I don't understand.*

"Yeah, I bet you 'non capisco' because you don't want to 'capisco.'" That much she knew from hearing Carmine and Dante say it at Piccolo Italia whenever she asked for extra bread or more olives. She was pretty sure they understood her but pretended not to.

She paced herself, setting the table very slowly. She had no idea how long it would take Jackson to get back with their food, and she didn't know what to do with Casanova once she was done. She looked at the clock. Jackson had been gone a half-hour. *I should have phoned in the order rather than just sending him there. He could have stuck around here longer, and the pick-up order would have been given priority.*

Instead, she was alone in her apartment with a sexy, extremely cute guy who was watching her every move—practically undressing her with his eyes. At least that's what she *thought* he was doing.

Stop, she scolded herself. *You're letting your imagination run away with you. This guy probably couldn't care less about you.*

"Johanna." Casanova said her name out loud.

She smiled at him. "Yes."

He thought she was very pretty in an exotic and unusual way. Most of the women he knew had an artificial beauty. They wore wigs, and their faces were often painted white and heavily powdered. Some of them had adopted the conceit of adhering patches of decorative fabric to their faces. The patches were considered very fashionable, but Casanova suspected some women used them to hide pockmarks and scars. The women he seduced were always clothed in corsets, petticoats, and stomachers, with overskirts made of lace, ruffles, or elaborate fabrics worn over hoops and panniers. They reminded him of an onion with many layers that needed to be peeled away.

But Johanna was different. She wore her hair long and loose, and her face was natural, with neither powder nor paint covering it. She dressed more like a man than a woman. She wore a scarlet satin shirt, and Casanova was fairly certain she wore neither a corset nor anything else underneath it. When she'd leaned over the table to set utensils in front of him, he'd been treated to a fairly good view of her attributes, and he saw no stays or padding of any kind. She wore tight breeches that closely followed her form, and knee-high leather boots with very high, skinny heels. He found it exhilarating just to watch her move—his senses heightened by his attraction to her.

His usual modus operandi had always been to gain an attractive woman's trust, shower her with small favors, and be attentive yet standoffish, so that *she* would desire *him*. But he was clearly at a disadvantage here, because they spoke different languages, and he had no idea *where* he was or *who* she was.

Johanna dropped a knife and it clattered to the floor. Casanova rose in a flash, scooped up the knife and handed it to her.

Johanna smiled at him. "Thanks ... grazie."

He returned her smile. Maybe seducing the intriguing Johanna would not be so difficult, after all.

"Johanna?" Jackson shouted her name when he did not find her in the main reading room or antechamber.

"We're upstairs."

He stormed the steps as noisily as a herd of stampeding cattle, balancing various containers of food on top of two pizza boxes. He exhaled his relief when he saw Johanna's clothes and hair did not look messed up and a table separated her from Casanova. Jackson placed the food on the kitchen counter.

"You bought two pizzas?"

"No. One's bread and garlic knots, and I think they stuffed the container of salad in there. This is the lasagna and sausage and veggies and stuff." He pointed to each as he named them. "I brought back an entire pizza in case Don Juan over there wants some."

Casanova perked up. "Don Juan! Don Juan Casanova era il mio grande, grande nonno." *Don Juan Casanova was my great-great-grandfather.*

Dismay showed plainly on Jackson's face. "What's he saying, that he's Don Juan and Casanova all rolled into one?"

"I don't know," Johanna answered. "He's responding to what *you* said. So please, stop referring to him as 'Don Juan' and 'lover boy.' It seems to upset him when you call him by another name."

"What do you know about this guy, anyway?"

"Not much. Just that legends say he's a great lover. I guess we could do a little research. This *is* a library. *The* library."

"All right. But let's eat first. My pizza is getting cold."

JUST LIKE JACKSON's birthday party, it looked like Johanna had ordered too much food, but by the time they finished eating, all that remained was a slice of pizza and a meatball. Lunch had looked like a race between Jackson and Casanova to see who could pound down the most food. *At this rate,* Johanna thought, *I'll soon be broke.* It's not that she had a problem with money, because—as Mal had promised—her salary was very, *very* good, and she didn't have many expenses. But after shelling out several hundred dollars for just two meals, she had to find a way to make the *men* foot the bill for their own food. It wouldn't be easy. Jackson didn't have much money to begin with, and Casanova had no income at all—at least, not in Exeter in the twenty-first century. *Casanova came out of a book. Where does he get off eating that much food? How can he eat at all? He isn't real.*

CASANOVA WATCHED AS Jackson helped Johanna clean off the table. *This young man is playing my game, making this woman indebted to him. I'll let him help her for now. I need to find my own door into her heart.*

After cleaning the kitchen, Jackson asked Johanna where he could find a book about Casanova.

"Why are you in such a rush?" she asked.

"I'm not in a rush. You've got a famous, historical person here, who came out of the pages of a book and did *not* disappear when those pages were closed. He's not supposed to be here. That's a pretty big problem, if you ask me, because he's in the wrong time period, and if he does something he's not supposed to do here, it could change the future. That may not bother you now, but remember what Einstein said when we asked for his help with the blue orb, that the difference between the past, the present, and the future is just an illusion?"

"I think you're getting all worked up over nothing."

Casanova watched as Johanna and the boy called Jackson got into a spirited debate. He didn't know what they spoke about, but they were both passionate about what they said. This was good; not that they shared passion but that they did not see eye-to-eye on whatever it was that they talked about. He would make sure he and Johanna were *simpatico*, so he could win her favors for himself.

AFTER LUNCH, JOHANNA led Jackson and Casanova back to the main reading room and motioned for them to sit on the sofa, while she searched for Casanova's memoirs. Even though she had pretended otherwise, she was as anxious as Jackson to learn more about their visitor. Whenever he looked at her with his gorgeous gray eyes or spoke to her, she felt all tingly inside. She wondered what it would be like to be romanced by Casanova, and felt herself blush.

MEANWHILE, JACKSON WENT on a quest of his own. He retrieved one of the iPads that Johanna had purchased for the library and brought it back to where Casanova waited. The Venetian watched as Jackson powered up the iPad, wirelessly matched it up to the library's computer, and downloaded a translation app. The sudden images that appeared on the piece of black glass and the way Jackson manipulated them with just his fingers left Casanova wide-eyed.

Johanna rushed back with *The Memoirs of Jacques Casanova de Seingalt* but stopped short when she spotted Jackson with the iPad. "What are you doing with that?"

"I just downloaded an app for an Italian-English dictionary that converts text to speech, so that we can figure out what Romeo over here is saying."

"I can't believe you did that. I didn't want you touching the iPads yet, so I put them in the drawer. Yet you went behind my back and not only took one out but downloaded an app without my approval. Which I still wouldn't mind, because your decision to use a translation app is brilliant. Except you then had to go and ruin it all by calling him 'Romeo.' He has a name. Call him Casanova, or Giacomo, or don't call him anything at all."

Jackson thought Johanna might get annoyed with him for using the iPad, but he didn't expect her to berate him for referring to Casanova as "Romeo." To make matters worse, she did it in front of the guy. That was not Johanna's style. Still, the randy Italian probably couldn't understand her, so Jackson didn't mind that much.

Casanova poked him in the chest a moment later and said, "Jackson." He then pointed to himself: "Giacomo Casanova." He said it louder. "CASANOVA. Non Romeo." He resolutely folded his arms across his chest.

"See what I mean," Johanna continued. "What are you trying to do, start an international incident?"

Jackson immediately became defensive. "How can I start an international incident over a guy who doesn't exist? Doesn't he have to be real to be involved in an international incident?"

"No. He doesn't," Johanna argued. "What you said about him was insensitive and demeaning, and a lot of people would jump all over it for being politically incorrect."

"You mean the *protocol police* are going to come breaking down my door because I referred to a guy—who has an infamous reputation as a womanizer—as *Romeo*?"

"*NON ROMEO*," Casanova shouted emphatically.

Jackson sighed. "Are you going to look for an answer in that book, or should I?"

Flustered, Johanna opened the book without thinking. A gaming table appeared, and so did a replica of Casanova, with a considerable pile of ducats sitting by his left hand.

"Ah," Casanova said, jumping up to get a closer look at the gaming table. "Excellente." He picked up a ducat and unexpectedly locked eyes with *himself*. The shock proved to be too much. He immediately fainted.

One of the men jumped up from the table and squatted down next to Casanova's slumped form. "Ci sono due di lei, Casanova? Lui è il suo fratello?" *There are two of you, Casanova? You and your brother?*

"Close the book," Jackson whispered. "Maybe he'll disappear."

Johanna did what he asked. The others disappeared, but Casanova remained on the floor, unconscious.

"It didn't work."

"Yeah, but at least we now know that if we meet ourselves in another time period, the world as we know it won't end. Do you have any idea what that guy said to him?"

"No."

His fingers flew over the virtual keyboard. "He said something that reminded me of the film *Goonies*. The bad guys were called the Fratellis. Remember that?"

"He didn't say 'Fratelli.' It sounded more like 'fratello.'"

Jackson's fingers danced across the keys. "'Fratello' is brother. That's got to be it. He called him the guy's *brother.*"

"What does it matter? It doesn't help us."

"Yeah, but at least it shows that the translator I downloaded works."

"Whoopee," she said quietly.

Casanova started to moan. "Looks like lover boy is coming back to life."

Johanna glared at Jackson for a second before brushing Casanova's hair away from his face.

Their Italian visitor opened his eyes. He blinked a few times and smiled. "Johanna," he said softly.

"Jackson, help me move him to the sofa."

As they lifted Casanova to a standing position, the ducat dropped to the floor. Jackson kicked it across the room without a second thought.

Johanna pouted but otherwise ignored what Jackson had done. "Get him a glass of water."

"Please?" Jackson chided her.

She ignored him.

He grudgingly left her alone with his rival while he fetched a glass of water. *Maybe I should throw some arsenic in it.* That made him wonder if he could be prosecuted for killing a man who died more than two hundred years ago.

Johanna took the glass. She sat next to Casanova

and held it to his lips. Casanova placed both his hands over Johanna's, as if to keep her from getting away.

The gesture did not get past Jackson, whose eyes were riveted on their hands. He didn't know what he felt more, jealousy or hatred.

JOHANNA FELT A warm flush when Casanova placed his hands over hers. She watched him sip the water, and then looked up to see his pale gray eyes drinking her in. She suddenly felt flustered, but didn't pull her hand away. She didn't want him to think she was rude, or uninterested.

"Is he actually drinking that stuff, or does he just like the feel of glass between his lips?"

Johanna stiffened. Jackson acted like they were married or something. *Has he forgotten I'm his boss?* She turned to Casanova. "Are you feeling better?"

He smiled at her.

"Okay, Jackson. Make the iPad ask him if he feels any better."

Jackson typed the question, and when the Italian version popped up, he clicked the icon that would allow them to hear the translation.

"Ti senti meglio?" came out of the iPad.

Casanova's mouth dropped open, and then he threw back his head and laughed. "Si, si," he finally uttered, "mi sento bene."

Jackson typed in Casanova's answer and hit the speaker. "Yes, yes, I feel good," the iPad translated in unaccented English.

Johanna broke into a wide smile. "Good job." The words were for Jackson, but her eyes never left Casanova's face.

THIS IS WORKING out nicely, Casanova thought as he

held Johanna's gaze. He picked up one of her hands and held it to his lips. The kiss was gentle—neither forceful nor needy. He believed in the premise that women had delicate natures and had to be treated carefully.

She did not try to pull her hand away. Instead, she curled *her* fingers around his.

She's mine.

—LOI—

C:L✹I

CHAPTER THIRTEEN

It took every ounce of composure that Jackson could dredge up to keep him from flinging the iPad across the room. Johanna kept sending him mixed signals, and it drove him crazy. Last night she hosted a birthday party for him. His mother told him Johanna had paid for everything. *That would indicate some kind of attachment, wouldn't it?*

Now, she made gooey eyes at a guy dressed in a weird costume. It looked like knight's armor, but on closer inspection he saw it was made out of a rough, red, knit material that mimicked the appearance of chain mail, completely covered with overlapping thin scales of rhinoceros horn that would not provide much protection. It looked flashier than it did authentic—just like Casanova. Sure, some girls might consider him handsome—the ones who went in for unkempt, smiley types with two-day-old stubble on their chins. *It's a look.*

But if you had asked Jackson if Johanna would ever fall for that type, he would have said no. The guys he had seen her with were clean-cut and polite—nice, normal guys (although he hadn't thought so when he first saw them with her). What was she doing falling for this Latin lover? It was so against type! Besides, the guy *fainted* when he saw himself at the gaming table. *Why couldn't he just die?*

BY THE TIME the grandfather clock struck six, the skies had turned to pitch. The only other sound in the library was the rumble of Casanova's stomach.

Johanna realized she needed more food. She had been tempted to open a cookbook and let Giada De Laurentiis whip up an evening meal for them, but decided against it. Giada was kind of pretty, and Johanna didn't want any competition.

"What should I feed him?" she asked Jackson.

Jackson looked over, surprised. She had pretty much ignored him, except to criticize him, for most of the afternoon. Now she wanted his advice.

He said the first thing that popped into his head. "Bouillabaisse?"

"Bouillabaisse." Casanova jumped off the sofa. He picked up each of Johanna's hands in his own. "Amo bouillabaisse!"

Jackson picked up the iPad. "Amo. That means love. Was he talking about the bouillabaisse or you?"

"Jackson." The reprimand was clear.

"Where are we supposed to get bouillabaisse?" the teen asked.

"Le Chat. Could you look up their phone number on that thing?"

"Only if you're going to invite me to stay for dinner."

The look on Johanna's face revealed how torn she was by Jackson's request. Part of her wanted to say yes without reservation, but another part did not want Jackson to get in the way of her chance to be alone with Casanova. "You can stay for dinner, but you're off the clock. I'm not footing the bill for dinner and then paying you a salary on top of that."

"I'm not asking you to," he said quietly.

"Fine."

CASANOVA STUDIED THEIR body language and tone. They were not *sympatico*, which was bound to work in his favor. He did not doubt the lad sought Johanna's affection, but Jackson was merely a boy who had no sense of *finesse* in the ways of women.

Casanova's stomach rumbled again. He looked over to see if Jackson would go out to get food, but the teen sat there, silently playing with the magic screen. The Venetian had never seen anything like it. He wondered if some sort of alchemy or wizardry was involved in its creation. Certainly nothing like it existed in Venice, although he would easily wager he no longer remained within the city of his birth. Maybe *this* was a magical place. He would have to poke around and see what promises it held for him, but later. For now, he was content to sit quietly and observe the dynamics between the young woman and her would-be suitor. *Hah!* The idea that Johanna would ever prefer Jackson over him was laughable.

A buzzer broke the silence.

He watched as Johanna walked to the other side of the room and said, "Illumination." The polished wall rumbled slightly before sliding to one side. A scruffy young man stood on the other side, holding a large brown bag. Johanna handed the messenger green papers in exchange for the package.

"I'll go up and set the table," she said aloud, heading for the circular stairs, carrying the aromatic bag.

Casanova trailed right behind her.

Jackson followed, close on his heels.

JACKSON SULKED AS he ate dinner in silence. Johanna made a few pleasant remarks to Casanova, but practically ignored her assistant. Casanova had a few comments of his own, but they remained untranslated, because Jackson had purposely left the iPad downstairs.

The teen sensed neither of them wanted him there, but he couldn't bear to leave. *Johanna is being ridiculous.* What was supposed to happen after he left? Would they spend the night together? It's not like she could just tell Casanova to go home. He had no home to go to, at least not in this century. Jackson had seen a little of Johanna's apartment over the past twenty-four hours. He knew she had a living room, dining room, and kitchen. He had seen the bathroom. There was only one other room that he knew of, and he guessed that was her bedroom. As far as he knew, there was no guest room, so that left one of the sofas. She had two of them that faced each other, but they were not that long, and Casanova had to be at least six foot three. The thought made Jackson smile. *Lover Boy is going to be awfully uncomfortable*—unless Johanna invited Casanova into her bed. Jackson's stomach turned to Jell-O. *She wouldn't dare.* But he could sense by the way she looked at Casanova that she very well might.

After dinner, Jackson offered to help with the dishes. He didn't want to give Casanova a chance to get Johanna alone. His suggestion backfired, however, when Johanna accepted the offer and put him to work—while she showed Casanova around her apartment.

Jackson strained to eavesdrop on their conversation. Most of it was muffled, but Johanna had apparently retrieved the iPad, because he caught bits and pieces of the electronic voice translating phrases in English and Italian. Obviously, they weren't having any trouble at all communicating with each other. *And I'm the idiot who made it possible.* He felt the grief of having lost something dear. There was nothing left for him to do but leave; after all, he was just the hired help. A third wheel. *Persona non grata.*

He threw the dishtowel on the counter and found Johanna and Casanova standing by one of the bookshelves that flanked her fireplace. "I'm going."

She turned to face him. Over her shoulder, he watched as Casanova pulled a book off the shelf and opened it. Jackson's eyes nearly bugged out of his head.

Johanna turned quickly and saw Casanova paging through the book. She took a deep breath and smiled at Jackson. "It's not enchanted. Nothing's going to happen here, unless I want it to."

Was that a double entendre? He didn't know if she meant the books or Casanova. "I'll see you Monday," he mumbled. "Have a nice weekend." He tried to keep the disappointment out of his voice, but didn't think he was successful. *Screw this.*

JOHANNA HAD WANTED a chance to be alone with Casanova all afternoon. Their mutual attraction was unmistakable, and the butterflies in her stomach increased with every tick of the clock. But after Jackson left, she felt another emotion she couldn't quite figure out. It made her ill at ease.

Casanova took a large picture book of Italy off the

shelf and sat down on the sofa, where he paged through it. He looked up at Johanna and patted the seat beside him.

She unexpectedly froze. She was alone with an older man (she estimated a difference of seven years between them) who was very good-looking (so many of the women she knew would *kill* for this opportunity) and happened to be known *everywhere* as the world's greatest lover.

Casanova held out the book, showing her a picture of the Grand Canal in Venice. "Guarda, mia casa è vicina questo posto." He looked for the iPad and typed in what he'd said. The iPad translated what he wrote. "Look, my house is near here." He smiled and waved the iPad, obviously proud of himself for having figured out how to use it.

What have I done? she wondered. *He's not even real—at least, not in this century. Now he's using technology that didn't exist in his own time.* She suddenly wished Jackson had stayed.

Casanova patted the sofa again.

Johanna stared at the cushion.

"Vieni qui," he coaxed gently. *Come here.*

Johanna sat down, leaving several inches of open space between them.

"Mia casa."

"Your house." She held her arms out with her palms facing up, then pointed to herself. "Mia casa."

Casanova laughed. He held up the book. "Libro."

Johanna smiled. "Book."

He picked up her hand and touched each of her fingers. "Dita."

She pulled her hand away and wiggled them. "Fingers."

He touched her ear. "Orecchio."

"Ear."

He tapped the tip of her nose. "Naso."

"Nose."

He gently traced the outline of her lips. "Labbra."

Their gazes locked. Johanna trembled as Casanova tilted his head and lightly kissed her. When she did not pull away, he kissed her again, giving her tiny butterfly kisses all over her face. Johanna was beguiled by his gentleness. Casanova slid closer until their bodies touched. It seemed natural when he slipped his tongue into her mouth, and she reciprocated. She scarcely felt him unbutton her blouse and cup her breast with his hand. But when he pushed her down on the sofa and set his full weight on top of her, the spell was broken. Johanna struggled, pushing him away. He landed on the floor with a dull thud.

CASANOVA HAD NOT anticipated that Johanna would reject him. "Qual è il problema?" *What is the problem?*

She jumped up off the sofa and buttoned her shirt, all the while shaking her head from side to side. "This can't happen," she said. She disappeared from the room as he got up off the floor. She returned with a blanket and a pillow. "You." She pointed to him, and then she pointed to the sofa, throwing the blanket and pillow on it. "Me." She pointed to herself, and then she pointed to her door. "Goodnight." She scurried to her bedroom and slammed the door, locking it behind her.

"Che cosa ho fatto?" he said aloud.

What have I done? Most women did not treat him this way. Most women were *very* receptive. *Johanna* had been very receptive. All the signs were there. Casanova did not handle rejection well, and his unspent passion raged within him. He picked up a glass candleholder from the end table and threw it against the wall. It shattered as it fell to the floor. "Donne." *Women.* "Non è una donna, è una bambino," he yelled. *No. Not a woman, a child.* He picked up the iPad, about to throw that as well, but decided to take it with him instead.

He left the residence and descended the spiral stairs to the main floor of the library. He wanted to leave, but couldn't find a door that would open. He remembered how the wall slid open for Johanna, but couldn't remember what she had done to make it move. *I'm a prisoner!* The sudden realization added insult to injury, and his aggravation continued to build. He threw the iPad at the sofa. It landed on the soft cushion without breaking. When that did not help ease his frustration, he grabbed a book from one of the library stacks and flung it at the circulation desk, watching it crash to the floor.

Suddenly a huge man—a *monster*—appeared. He was eight feet tall, with flowing black hair and an eerie yellowish pallor. His watery eyes appeared dead in his face, and his skin was pulled so tightly, it barely concealed the man's muscles and arteries.

"Nooooo," the brute roared. "How dare you steal me away from my moment of retribution. If someone cherished by Victor *Frankenstein* is not to perish, then surely you must die instead!"

—LOI—

C:L ● I

CHAPTER FOURTEEN

Jackson called Logan as soon as he got home. Maybe spending time with friends *outside the library* would make him feel better. But in the end, it only reminded him of what he desperately wanted to forget. Several members of the group had been at his birthday party, and they all met at Piccolo Italia, the restaurant where Jackson had picked up Casanova's lunch.

"You look like you got sucker-punched," Logan observed. "What gives?"

Jackson shrugged and clammed up.

"Here." Chris shoved a slice of pizza in front of him. "Pepperoni cures everything."

"I bet you and Johanna had a fight," Cassie guessed. "I hope it wasn't about last night."

Jackson took a quick bite and just shook his head, glad he had a mouth full of pizza, so he wouldn't have to talk.

Logan nudged him in the side. "What happened? Did Mr. French Restaurant show up at the library today?"

Jackson almost choked. He swallowed the pizza and grabbed on to the excuse. "Something like that."

"That sucks."

Jackson stuffed more pizza in his mouth so he wouldn't have to speak, and the conversation changed direction. He tried to look interested in what everyone else said, but his sense of loss kept him from engaging in the fun. The more they laughed, the worse he felt. He slipped away when everyone decided to head out to a movie.

He walked for a while, not paying attention to where he went, until he realized he'd been circling the block where the library stood.

He looked up at the light in Johanna's apartment. *What am I doing here?* Being near her just made him feel more miserable.

CASANOVA BACKED AWAY from the monster, moving behind the glass display case.

"You think you can protect yourself from me?" The giant easily flipped the case over, smashing it. The first-edition leather-bound volume of *English Fairy Tales* inside tumbled out and opened on the floor.

Both man and monster jerked back when a couple of talking pigs began banging on a small brick hut and shouted for their brother to let them in. The pigs had barely disappeared inside when a wolf began banging on the door. "Little pig, little pig, let me in."

"Aarrgghh!" the monster shouted, as he slammed his fist across the wolf's upper body, sending him crashing into the circulation desk.

An excited little voice from inside the hut

squealed, "He killed the wolf. HE KILLED THE WOLF!"

"Who killed the wolf?" a third pig asked.

"The monster."

"MONSTER!" the little pigs shrieked, their terror barely muffled by the hut's brick walls.

The monster lifted his well-muscled leg and used it to push over the miniature hut. The three little pigs squealed in horror at being exposed. Each one ran off in a different direction, but like pinballs, they continuously bumped into things and crisscrossed each other's paths, oinking at the tops of their little piggy lungs.

"WHAT IS GOING on here?" Johanna could barely contain her anger as she stood at the top of the circular stairs.

Everyone stared back at her in guilty silence for a few seconds before roaring, squealing, and complaining— in Italian—all at once. The monster picked up the sofa and heaved it across the room. The iPad fell to the floor. Frankenstein's demon crossed over to the shiny object, lifted his massive foot, and brought it down on the glass tablet, crushing it.

Johanna, in a well-rehearsed motion, slowly edged around the room, looking for open books, grateful she had wasted a moment putting shoes on. Broken glass covered the floor. She spotted *English Fairy Tales* nestled in the display-case rubble and used her foot to close it.

The sudden disappearance of the annoying little pigs and their brick hut distracted Casanova and the monster, but only for a moment. The monster used the diversion to rush Casanova, and lifted him up into the air.

"Aiutami! Aiutami! Devi fermarli." *Help me! Help me! You must stop him.*

Johanna found Mary Shelley's *Frankenstein, or*

The Modern Prometheus nestled among the debris, not too far from where she stood. She dove for it and slammed it shut. Casanova dropped from midair and crashed to the floor.

"La mia testa. Il mio braccio. Il mostro ..." *My head. My arm. That monster.* He sat stunned, looking at the disarray as blood dripped from his forehead onto the arm he clutched. "Dov'è il mostro?" *Where is the monster?*

Johanna was fit to be tied. She had no idea what he wanted, but knew the evening of pandemonium had been his fault. "You couldn't just go to sleep on the sofa." Her words were packed with scorn. "No. You had to go on a tear, destroying everything I love." With each word, her anger increased. "Look at this mess." She glanced up at the clock. It was shortly after four in the morning. "I wish Jackson were here."

The thought of Jackson made her cry. She suddenly realized she had pushed him away in favor of Casanova, and she remembered the frustration in Jackson's voice when he had said goodbye. "I can't even make you help me clean up this mess," she said to Casanova, "because your arm may be broken." Her sobbing became more pronounced, and the Venetian looked as helpless in alleviating her pain as she felt in lessening his.

She left him sitting on the floor doing nothing, as she cried her heart out while sweeping away debris and shoving the sofa back to where it belonged.

After she finished cleaning and had dragged the broken display case out to the trash, she pulled out the red metal first-aid case from behind the circulation desk and went to check on Casanova. She swabbed his forehead with an antiseptic wipe and hoped he would not have a permanent scar. She next focused her efforts on his shoulder. He shrieked when she touched it, but his protest did not stop her from thoroughly inspecting it. It did not seem to be dislocated or broken. More than likely, he had bruised it. At least she hoped so, because she couldn't take him to the emergency room at Exeter Hospital. He was from the eighteenth century, and she feared that if anyone in the emergency room understood Italian and heard his story, they'd insist on admitting him for psychiatric evaluation. She couldn't take the risk.

"Dov'è il mostro?" he asked again.

She shook her head. She didn't understand him, and the iPad with the translation app had died an ugly death.

He made grunting sounds and tried to imitate the demeanor of the monster. "Il mostro ..."

"The monster?" she guessed. She just shook her head. *No way I can explain that to him.* She helped him off the floor and led him to the sofa. "Sit," she demanded. He apparently figured out what she meant, because he wasted no time dropping onto the cushions. "Stay," she commanded, holding out her arm with her palm facing him, before disappearing up the spiral staircase.

She put on a pot of coffee and then carried the blanket and pillow downstairs. She doubted she would get any sleep, but maybe Casanova would take the hint. She needn't have worried. He had fallen asleep by the time she returned. She covered him with the blanket and put the pillow between his head and the arm of the sofa, in case he slumped over.

A small snore escaped him.

Satisfied that the library would be safe for the immediate future, Johanna went back upstairs to see if her coffee was ready. She got halfway up the steps when she heard someone banging on the front door. She peeked at the security system and saw two police officers standing outside. She recognized them immediately, having met them both the previous summer.

"Great," she grumbled, before proceeding to the door. "Illumination."

The wall slid open, and she smiled weakly at the two cops standing in the vestibule.

"Is there a problem, officers?"

"One of your neighbors called. Says he was out walking his dog and heard yelling and screaming coming from here. He said it sounded like you were slaughtering barnyard animals. I know it sounds far-fetched, but with *this place* you never know."

"As you can see, everything is fine."

"May we come in and look around?"

"Sure," she answered, glad that she had finished cleaning everything up. She prayed Casanova would stay asleep.

"That gentleman?" One of the officers nodded toward the sofa.

"Actually, he's probably responsible for the call you got. He had a little too much to drink last night and had trouble navigating the circular stairs when I told him it was time to leave. He fell, and he hit his head. He hurt his arm as well and began howling. I'm willing to bet that's what my neighbor heard.

"I already cleaned the cut over his eye and checked his arm to make sure it wasn't broken. Having broken my own arm, twice, I know the drill. By the time I finished, he had passed out. I covered him so he could sleep it off." *Thank God I covered him. He's dressed like a freaking knight.*

"Did he hurt you in any way?"

"No. If he did, I'd have called you *myself*. Trust me, everything here is fine."

The officer stared at her for a long, uncomfortable moment. Johanna knew he must have been thinking about the previous ruckus caused by the appearance, and sudden disappearance, of the blue orb.

"We'll patrol the area, just in case, and come back later to check on you."

"Thank you. I really appreciate it." She managed to dredge up a smile, but the last thing she wanted was another visit. She hoped they would get called away on some emergency.

Johanna yawned. She wanted to crawl into bed and get some sleep, but she was afraid of what Casanova might do when he awakened, so she sank into the overstuffed leather wingchair that had always been Mal's favorite. *Mal. I bet he'd know what to do. I'd better check his diary.* But she was too tired to go get it. *I'll just close my eyes for a second ...*

JACKSON YAWNED. HE had been out most of the night. He slept fitfully, dreaming of Johanna and Casanova cuddling together. To make matters worse, Casanova could speak English in his dreams, and Jackson had to listen to all their pillow talk.

"You are so beautiful, my love." Casanova stroked Johanna's face. "The most sensual woman in the world."

"Thanks," Johanna replied. "You're the hottest guy I've ever met. Your face is perfect." She ran her fingers through his long locks. "And you have awesome hair. But most of all, this suit of armor"—she flicked her fingers against the bits of rhinoceros horn—"it turns me on."

"I'm surprised. I thought you were attracted to the boy." Casanova nuzzled her neck, and Johanna closed her eyes—her face, a study in ecstasy.

"You mean Jackson?" she mumbled. "He's just a

child compared to you. What does he know about love? But you know a lot, don't you? You've been intimate with so many woman—governesses, maidens, their mothers, contessas ..."

"Umm ..." He smiled. "Several nuns, a royal highness or two, and quite a few ladies of the night. Ahhh ... and nurses. I love a sponge bath."

"I bet they all taught you a lot about what drives women wild." She yelped as he playfully pinched a part of her anatomy. "I want you to teach me everything," she gasped. "I want you to do to me everything you have ever done with another woman. And I want you to do it right now." She ripped open her shirt, the buttons flying in all directions ...

"Jackson," his mother called out. "We're leaving for church. Do you want to come with us?"

The amorous vision of Johanna and Casanova faded to black.

The closed door muffled his brother's voice. "I don't think he's into it, Mom."

"Why not?" she asked.

THEIR CONVERSATION AND footsteps faded away, as sleep reclaimed Jackson, and a new dream unfolded.

Jackson and Casanova stood facing each other on a grassy field not far from the library. Johanna walked up to them carrying a wooden box, similar to the one Shakespeare's First Folio *had arrived in. She wore a pale, silver eighteenth-century gown. A white wig topped her head, along with a slouchy hat festooned with feathers and birds. She opened the box. Inside were two books, each with a plain, black cover.*

"What books are these?" Jackson asked.

"Ah, that's for me to know and for you to find out. Choose wisely."

"I shall take this one," Casanova said confidently, as he reached between them, grabbing the book closest to Jackson. He gave Johanna a knowing wink.

Jackson's muscles tensed. He had no choice but to take the remaining book.

"I will count," Johanna explained, "as you walk ten paces away from each other. On the count of ten, turn and open your books. May the best man win."

Jackson's stomach tightened with each step. When Johanna called, "Ten," he turned and opened his book. Comic-strip characters appeared with word balloons floating above their heads. Jackson fiercely thumbed his way to the title page and found he had a bound edition of *Thimble Theater Comic Strips by Kings Features*. Sweat oozed from the teenager's pores. He looked over at Casanova, but Robin of Locksley blocked his view. "Oh my God," Jackson screamed, as Robin Hood aimed an arrow straight for him. He heard the snap of the bow, but not the arrow whizzing through the air, because it was blocked out by the sudden, oddly pitched laugh of a two-dimensional cartoon of Popeye.

"Arg-ug-ug-ug-ug-ug-ug-ug."

—LOI—

C:L ◈ I

CHAPTER FIFTEEN

Jackson shot straight up into a sitting position. He was drenched in sweat. He could feel his heart pumping in his throat as he tried to come to grips with his erratic breathing. There was no way he would even attempt to go back to sleep. He grabbed a change of clothes and headed for the shower.

He remembered his mother quizzing Chris about what might be bothering him. He did not want to be home when they got back from church. He jumped on his bike and pedaled as fast as he could until he reached the bay.

His stomach growled. He regretted not having stopped for breakfast, but he could eat after he left the beach. He needed its solitude to help him think. The gentle lap of the waves soothed him. He dropped his bike on the sand and looked for something to lean against. Finding a comfortable spot, he sat down and contemplated the surface of the water. He tried to make his mind go blank. If he could just stop thinking and dreaming for a little while, maybe he could regain his composure.

JOHANNA AWOKE WITH a start. The library's grandfather clock chimed eleven times. She shook away the last vestiges of sleep and saw Casanova snoozing on the sofa. There was something she wanted to do, but she couldn't remember what. She needed coffee. She remembered brewing a pot earlier that morning. By now, it was probably sludge. She wished she could run out to the local coffee shop, but she could hardly leave Casanova alone in the library. She had managed to keep the situation contained the day before only because Jackson had been there to help her. She felt a pang of melancholy. Jackson probably hated her for the way she had treated him. She was overwhelmed by sadness, but she couldn't stop to dwell on it. She needed to get the coffee going again, before "lover boy" woke up.

JACKSON SKIPPED STONES along the surface of the water, as birds fluttered about the shoreline. Their occasional squawks seemed to mock him. *Look at us playing together. We all get along. Why can't you?* The birds skittered along the water's edge. Afterward, some of them stretched out to bask in the sun, while others took flight to dry off.

  I wish I could be as carefree as these birds, taking each day as it comes. He used to think he was like that, before Casanova came along. He had to stop thinking of the Italian as a character. Like it or not, Casanova was a real person. Still, he was a man displaced in time, and he didn't belong here. Eventually, he would move on. No woman had ever owned Casanova, and that would probably include Johanna. Jackson didn't want to see her get hurt, especially by the Latin Lothario.

Why am I wasting time here? he thought, as he jumped on his bike.

JOHANNA BROUGHT HER coffee and Mal's diary into the main reading room and settled onto the big leather chair. Casanova still slept, so Johanna kept her voice down. "Mal, what happens if a character doesn't disappear when a book is closed?"

The pages shuffled to a hand-drawn chart entitled "Physical Properties of the Library of Illumination." It was a list of the various traits held by different *levels* of enchanted books.

The first book category was Level Zero. Most books in the physical world fell into this category. These books had no enchantments whatsoever, or as it was described on the chart, an "absence of presence." Nothing happened when you opened the book, or closed it.

Level One books had scenes that came to life when the reader touched the page, but all remnants of the scene disappeared when the book closed. Level Two books were the ones she was most familiar with: books in which characters from a particular page came to life, but disappeared when the book was closed or, at least, mostly disappeared. Detritus might be left behind. It reminded Johanna of the day when Jo from *Little Women* got her hair cut, and how the clippings littered the floor, even after Jo had returned to the written page. Level Three books were similar to Level Two, although the objects left behind were more valuable. *Ah, doubloons.* The description for Level Four books caught her attention right away. At that level, characters did not disappear when the book closed. *Shakespeare's First Folio* must have been a Level Four book. She continued to read about the higher levels, but they gave her no indication of how to solve her problem.

"Mal," she whispered, "you've got to help me."

The diary opened to the last page. One line of instruction was written across the top.

PLEASE LIST IN DETAIL WHAT NEEDS TO BE DONE.

She had forgotten to bring a pen. She gulped down some coffee before going over to the circulation desk to find one. She grabbed a fountain pen out of a cup decorated with the inscription *Librarians do it by the book.*

She nestled back in the chair and started to scribble, *Casanova needs to be—*

"Buongiorno!"

Johanna looked up. Casanova stared at her. He did not look happy—more like he was dazed and confused. He threw off the blanket that covered him and winced. The pain in his arm seemed to bring him back to alertness. He slowly looked around the library and continued to sit quietly.

"Would you like a cup of coffee?"

"Caffeè? Si." He nodded.

Johanna scrambled upstairs and grabbed a tray on her way into the kitchen. She grabbed the coffeepot, a cup, a spoon, sugar, milk—everything Casanova might need—and rushed back downstairs.

The heady aroma of the espresso gave her strength as she poured a steady stream of the hot liquid into his cup. She pointed to milk and sugar. He waved it away.

"Biscotto?"

It was a word she understood. "No," she answered, shaking her head. "No biscotti."

Casanova's sigh signaled his complete disillusionment with her.

Good girl, she thought. *You've driven away two men in less than twelve hours.* She reclaimed her chair and looked for the diary. She got up and checked the cushions. Had she taken it with her when she ran upstairs? She was about to retrace her steps when she saw Casanova turn a page. He had taken Mal's diary.

"Che cosa é questa? Questo libro non ha niente scritto in esso." *What is this? This book has nothing written in it.*

"My book, my *libro.* I'd like it back." She held out her hand.

"È vuoto." *It's blank.*

She shook her head. She had no idea what he meant. She looked down at the page to see what he had referred to, but nothing was written there. She watched him flip through the pages. All of them were as white as snow.

He slapped the book against her palm. She opened it, and the blank pages slowly filled with words. She realized, as curator of the library, Mal's diary was probably meant *only* for her, and no one else could learn its secrets. "Hmmm."

Suddenly, the back door flew open.

Johanna's eyes widened when she saw Jackson standing at the rear entrance holding a bakery bag. She blinked to hold back a tear.

"I didn't know if you planned to cook for lov— your friend," he ventured. "If not, I thought you both might appreciate some Italian pastries."

"You're a lifesaver," she said, accepting the bag.

JACKSON WISHED HE could wrap his arms around her and hold on to her forever. That probably wasn't a good idea, although she looked glad to see him.

Casanova also looked glad to see him. *Probably because I brought food,* Jackson thought. "Why is he just sitting there like that?"

"I'll tell you all about it, but not now. Let's just say a lot happened after you left."

Jackson felt his heart pound. "Are you okay?"

Johanna nodded. "I am now." She broke into a wide grin. "And I learned something interesting."

"What's that?"

"No one can read what's inside Mal's diary, except me."

Jackson looked at the book she held open. *He* could see words written on the page, but maybe that's not what she meant. "What are you looking up in his diary?"

"How to send my Italian friend back where he belongs."

"Then don't let me stop you."

"Please. I know it's Sunday, but can you stay? I'll pay you double."

His heart quickened. "You don't have to pay me." He was glad to be back in her good graces. "I'll be more than happy to make sure he doesn't bother you."

"That would help."

"Where's the iPad?"

"In about a hundred pieces in the trash."

"No," he wailed. He ran over to the trash bin and pulled it open. "Aarrgghh ..." He picked through the pieces to see if any of it was salvageable. It had been smashed beyond repair. "What happened?"

"Frankenstein."

"No way."

"His monster was here."

"I can't believe I missed that."

"Trust me, I wished you were here when it happened."

"Tell me ..."

"Later. Finding out how to book *Signor Casanova's* return trip is more important."

"I won't argue with that." He looked at them both for a moment and shook his head. "Too bad the library board rejected your request to install a sixty-inch TV in here. At least that would have entertained him."

"There's the other iPad. All I ask is that you try not to break it."

"Hey, I didn't break the first one."

"I know. Just take care of it."

WHILE CASANOVA WATCHED Jackson set up the other iPad, Johanna sequestered herself in her office, looking for guidance from Mal. She picked up a pen to detail what needed to be done. *Casanova needs to be returned to his own time,* she wrote. She looked at what she had written. The instructions said to list her request "in detail," but she did not know what details to include. She couldn't be any more specific than what she had written. After giving it a lot of thought, she added the words *as soon as possible.*

A new sentence appeared.

LIST IN DETAIL WHERE CHARACTER ORIGINATED.

Johanna was confused. Casanova had appeared when she opened *Shakespeare's First Folio*, but that wasn't where he originated. He came from Venice. He had shown her pictures of the Grand Canal and said his home was nearby. She wrote *18th Century Venice, via Shakespeare's First Folio*, but wasn't sure if that was the right answer.

PLEASE CLEAR MAIN READING ROOM FOR DELIVERY.

What the heck does that mean? She walked out and found Jackson and Casanova attempting a conversation in Italian. "Jackson, we need to clear this room for a delivery."

"What kind of delivery?"

"I don't know. It just said, 'clear main reading room.'"

Jackson pulled the leather chair into a corner and used the iPad to tell Casanova to move over to it. Johanna helped Jackson push the sofas and tables out of the way.

"Now what?" he asked.

"We wait."

Before long, the floor began to vibrate like an earthquake was imminent. Johanna kept her eyes on the shelves, praying the tremor would not send books tumbling to the floor.

Casanova shrunk back into the cushions of Mal's chair, with a look of terror on his face. A mechanical whining noise—like a helicopter engine roaring to life—blocked out all other sound until a giant glass-like bubble with a man inside materialized in the middle of the floor.

He appeared to be about twenty-five years of age, dressed in the style of the eighteenth century. His dark gray frock coat and matching breeches complemented his pale blue waistcoat and matching silk stockings. He wore a wig, but no hat, and his shoes were made of black kid with silver buckles. Suspended from a chain worn around his neck hung a pair of scissors-glasses, but the chain had caught on his cravat, ruining the perfect line of his outfit.

"Johanna," he said, taking her hands. "My older self told me all about you. Indeed, he made sure I read our *full* diary about how you came to replace us at the library!" He looked around, smiling. "It looks almost the same."

She stared, stunned. "Mal?"

"Yes. Isn't it amazing? Your dilemma gave me the opportunity to pull a few strings and finagle the use of this wonderful time machine from the twenty-second century. It looks fragile, but the turbulent passing through time didn't scar it in any way, although I'm sure my brains are quite scrambled."

"What are you doing here?"

"I've come to pick up Casanova, of course, and deposit him back in our time."

"'Our time'?"

"Yes, his and mine. As you know, I've lived a rather long life. I was more than four hundred years old when you met me. In Casanova's twenty-fifth year, which is the era I departed from, I am merely one hundred and forty. The easiest solution to your problem was for me to dispatch myself to help return him to his proper place."

He turned toward Casanova. "Buongiorno, Signor Casanova. Sei pronto a tornare a Venezia?" *Good morning, Mr. Casanova. Are you ready to return to Venice?*

Casanova jumped up. "Venezia. Si."

"So that's it?" Jackson asked. "You just hop into a time-traveling bubble, and poof?"

"It's not as simple as all that. Taking him home is considered the transport of human cargo, and as such, I had to declare the particulars of the trip to the members of Lloyd's of London on Lombard Street. And because of the *unusual* nature of the vessel we're using and the time period it originated in, the transaction required a lot of secret deal-making and under-the-table brokering. I dare say, it literally took months to accomplish."

"Months? But he's only been here since yesterday."

"The months dragged on during my wrinkle in

time, not yours. The past is past. But I must ask Signor Casanova how he got here." He turned toward the man. "Come sei arrivato qui?"

Casanova told Mal, in Italian, how he had "borrowed" *Shakespeare's First Folio* and, after falling, had become trapped inside of it. Apparently, it wasn't so bad, because he ended up inside the *Merchant of Venice*, so he felt right at home. But he could not travel outside of the parameters of the story, which he found very frustrating. Then, he showed up here, but once again, he could not escape this library. If he could return home to Venice, *his* Venice, or even Vienna, where he had been partying before he fell into the folio, he would be forever grateful.

Johanna hated not knowing what Casanova had told Mal. "What did he say?"

Mal winked at her. "I'm sure you'll read all about it in my diary. It's much too interesting a story to leave out." He put his hand on Casanova's shoulder and started pushing him into the bubble.

"Wait a minute," Jackson demanded. "You said this bubble came from the twenty-second century. If you're from the past, how did you get it?"

"Now that's an interesting story—but it probably won't appear in my diary for another two hundred years.

"Come, my good man." Mal grabbed Casanova and pulled him into the bubble. A moment later, they were gone.

"So that's it?" Jackson's tone expressed his disappointment.

"You want more?" Johanna raised her eyebrows, incredulous that he thought Casanova's departure in a time-traveling bubble was anticlimactic.

"It would have been nice to talk to Mal a little

longer. You always talk about him, but I never met him before. How could he be four hundred years old? I just wish he could have stayed awhile."

"And Casanova, too?"

"Not so much. Come to think of it, you've certainly cooled off toward him."

"I had a momentary lapse in judgment yesterday, but everything is fine now."

"So you don't hate me for the way I treated him?"

"I could never hate you."

"Oh. I guess I thought you did, because ... uh ... you never gave me a birthday kiss."

Johanna grinned. She walked across the room and picked up a coin from the floor. "Here. Maybe you'd like this better." She handed him the ducat.

"No. Old money can be more trouble than it's worth. I learned that the hard way. Anyway, you can use it to buy a new iPad for the library. Besides, I'd rather have the kiss."

"There's always next year."

"You're going to make me wait?"

"Okay. Just one birthday kiss."

"Fine." He pulled her into his arms, and he felt his spirits soar.

It's not the number of kisses that matter. It's how long they last.

—LOI—

C:L ⊛ I

CHAPTER SIXTEEN

Portals

JACKSON CARRIED AN armful of returned books to a dimly lit alcove in the Library of Illumination's cupola. It was a special area reserved for some of the library's quirkier offerings. The teen enjoyed reading the various titles, but after looking inside *The Pop-Up Book of Phobias*, he refrained from opening any of the others. Unleashing overpowering arachnophobia is not fun.

He hesitated as he shelved *Lamb: The Gospel According to Biff, Christ's Childhood Pal*. When he had some time, he would have to come back and take a closer look at that one. He wasn't sure what a few of the other books were about. *Prodigiorum Ac Ostentorums Chronicon* was Greek to him, and he had never heard of *The Codex Seraphinianus*. There was the *Egyptian Book of the Dead*, but there was no way he would ever open that one. And no library would be complete without *Ripley Scrowle* and *Prophecies* by M. Michel de Nostredame. *I wonder if Johanna has unenchanted versions of these.*

The recess appeared shadowy, which mystified Jackson because there was an octagonal window at the end of the alcove. It should have allowed light to flow into the library, but the aging etched glass looked frosted and did not permit a view of the outside.

Jackson shook his head. *Something's not right here.* After shelving the last book, he ran down the cupola stairs and shouted, "Illumination," as he took off out the front door. He looked up at the area where he thought the alcove should be located, but didn't see a window.

He tried circumnavigating the library, which wasn't an easy thing to do considering it had no side alleys, so he had to go around the entire block. Still, he couldn't find that particular octagonal window.

Johanna stood waiting by the door when he walked back in. "What's wrong?"

"Nothing, really."

"Where did you disappear to? I thought somebody died, the way you ran out of here."

"The thing is," Jackson mused, "there's a little window in the alcove where we keep the wacko books, which should be visible from outside, but there's no corresponding window out there."

"Repeat after me, there is no such thing as a wacko book. And there has to be a window. If there's one in here, you should be able to see it from out there."

He grabbed her arm and dragged her out the door. "Look up. If the cupola stairs are near the center of the building and the weirdo-book alcove is on the left, the window should be right there." He pointed. "But it's not."

"Wait. That doesn't make any sense. I've got to go back inside and get my bearings." Johanna went all the way up to the cupola, and then carefully traced her way back down and out the front entrance. "You're right. There should be a window there. I guess the one in the alcove is a fake."

"Why would anyone put a fake window in a library hundreds of years ago?"

"I don't know. It doesn't make sense."

"So I'm thinking, maybe it hides a safe and there are piles of gold in there."

Johanna covered her face with both her hands for a few seconds. When she finally looked up, she said, "That is so ... you."

"C'mon. Let's go look." Jackson grabbed her hand and dragged her back to the alcove window.

For several minutes, they stood and stared at the octagonal wooden frame filled with radiating triangles of leaded glass. "I never realized you couldn't see outside," she said. "I wonder what would happen if we cleaned it."

"Your wish is my command." Jackson practically flew down the cupola stairs to retrieve some rags and a spray bottle of glass cleaner from the utility room.

He returned before Johanna had a chance to miss him. He doused the fabric with cleanser and started rubbing the window. Grime came off on the rag, but the view remained obscured. "It's not a window, so no matter how much I clean it, we won't be able to see through it. I'm telling you, it's hiding something."

"Forget it. There's no way we're going to open it," Johanna said dismissively. "Besides, it looks like it's painted in place."

Jackson tried prying it with his fingers. "Wait ..."

He bolted down the stairs again, and returned a few minutes later with a box cutter. This time his breathing sounded a little more ragged. The cupola steps spiraled straight to the first floor—five stories below—with no exits along the way. Running up and down the staircase several times took a toll on the teen, but not enough to derail his overall enthusiasm. He used the box cutter to slice through the paint that sealed the window to the wall. Once he had cut through all eight sides, he tried to pry the window open again.

"I don't think it's going to open," Johanna said. "Let's quit before you hurt yourself."

"No. This is my mystery, and I want to solve it." He ran downstairs again, and returned with a crowbar.

"No." Johanna grabbed it away from him. "I can't allow you to destroy library property."

"I'll fix anything I destroy."

"Oh really?"

"Yeah. Ask my mother. I'm the one who fixes everything around the house. If I destroy this, I'll fix it and you can deduct the cost of materials from my salary."

"I don't know ..."

Before she had a chance to think it over, Jackson jammed the edge of the crowbar under the window frame and tried to pry it off.

"They must have screwed this thing in place, because it's not giving way. Nails would have pulled out by now." He inspected the wood, but it had been covered by so many centuries of paint and varnish, he couldn't determine where the screws would be. "I need to give this one more try." He grimaced as he shoved the crowbar against the window frame with all his strength. Little beads of sweat broke out on his brow, and a vein in his forehead became clearly visible. He stopped to rest for a moment.

"This is crazy," Johanna said. "It's not going to open. There is no safe behind it. Why are you wasting your energy?"

"It's my energy to waste. Besides, I think I can do it this time." Jackson took a deep breath before applying force against the crowbar. "Aarrgghh!" He grunted as he worked to remove the window frame. *Crack.* A one-inch chunk of wood broke away and dropped to the floor.

"At this rate, you should be done in less than a week."

"Not funny. The least you could do is help me. If we both pushed against the crowbar, I bet it would work."

Johanna sighed. "Okay. Whenever you're ready."

"On the count of three. One ... two ... three." They pushed as hard as they could, but nothing happened.

"Okay," he said reluctantly. "Forget it. I'm throwing in the towel."

"It's not like opening it is going to provide any illumination for this space."

As soon as Johanna uttered the word *illumination*, the octagonal window flew open, and the great outdoors did *not* appear on the other side.

Johanna and Jackson each held their breath for a few seconds.

"You said, 'illumination.'"

As soon as he repeated the word, the two of them were sucked through the portal to a place that was extremely strange, yet eerily familiar. It had the same proportions as the Library of Illumination, but instead of books, row upon row of crystal obelisks lined the narrow shelves. They walked out of the alcove and found the surrounding area laid out exactly like the cupola in their library.

"Where are we?" Johanna whispered.

"It looks like a mirror image of the library, but it's got all these tall, pointy things where the books should be."

"Let's get out of here."

"Wait. I want to see where we are."

Johanna shook her head. "I don't think that's a good idea."

"Where's your spirit of adventure? Where's your plucky, can-do attitude? Where's your imagination?"

"It's my imagination that's telling me to go back where we belong."

"Okay, see you later." Jackson said it breezily as he walked to the cupola steps. "Look." He pointed to a strange symbol embedded in the stair post. "This must be *their* equivalent of the number one. I'll never understand why this floor is considered the *first* level, while the main floor is called level five. It doesn't make any sense."

Johanna walked closer to look at the symbol. "I read about it in Mal's diary," she explained, as Jackson grabbed her hand and pulled her down the stairs. "The cupola is the highest level, so it's number one. Think of it like winning a prize. If you win first place, that's the highest you can go. It's *first*, not *fifth*. With that in mind, it makes sense that the window level right below it is the second level. Those massive arched windows were designed to flood the library with light, although the light in this library is sort of unearthly."

"Yeah, like they're lighting the place for a horror film."

"The third level," she continued, "is the halo. It's just a single layer of shelves on a narrow balcony that overlook the floors below. The fourth level is known as the residence level."

"That's a no-brainer, considering that's where your apartment is."

"And the main floor is the fifth level."

They had reached the main reading room. The circulation desk was the same familiar shape, but the shelves still held crystal obelisks.

JOHANNA REACHED FOR Jackson's hand and relaxed when his warm fingers curled around her own.

He pulled her toward the curator's staircase. It was right by the residence, and it was the staircase they used most often. There were also stone steps built into the foundation near the front door that linked the main reading room to the residence level, but that staircase was rarely used because the books closest to it were about obscure musical tonalities with archaic chord-scale relationships—not a trendy topic. The more popular books on music could be found closer to the curator's apartment.

Johanna studied the main floor as they walked across it. The reading room looked downright uncomfortable. The furniture, or what she supposed was furniture, included an assortment of oddly shaped surfaces dwarfed by the thousands of obelisks crowding the shelves. She looked up. The windows, opaque with grime, looked like they hadn't been cleaned in a millennium. It looked like their library, and yet it wasn't their library.

"Let's go up to the next floor," Jackson urged.

"I don't think that's such a good idea," she whispered.

"Why? I don't think there's anyone here."

"How can you be so sure?"

"Do you hear anybody?"

"Maybe they're in the antechamber, binding books."

"What books?"

"All right, they're polishing the crystal."

"One more level isn't going to hurt." He tried to pull her up the steps.

"No," Johanna said, wrenching her hand away from his. "That's the residence level, and I have no intention of finding out who lives there."

"I hadn't thought of that. Wouldn't it be cool to see how your other half lives?"

"My other half!"

"Shhh. They'll hear you," he whispered.

"Exactly." She turned to go back.

"I'm going without you." He quickly climbed to the next level.

Johanna couldn't help herself. Instead of returning to the cupola, she walked into the middle of the reading room, where she could keep an eye on him. The balconies on the residence level were fairly visible, and Johanna followed Jackson's progress until he stopped just outside the curator's apartment. She waved to get his attention, but either he didn't see her or he ignored her. *Why does he have to be so difficult? He's playing with fire.*

JACKSON BEGAN TO notice subtle differences in the obelisks, not just in their height and width but on their surfaces as well. At first he thought they were dusty, but on closer examination he saw that they had subtle etchings on them, like a design, or another language, or code. He looked down at Johanna and waved at her to come up.

She adamantly shook her head from side to side.

She's so stubborn. He felt sure they had discovered something monumental about this library, but he didn't know what it was. He wanted to discuss it with her, but knew if he walked back down the stairs, she would interpret that as a signal they could leave and would head back up to the cupola. *There has to be a way I can get her up here.*

Johanna's impatience grew. *Why tempt fate? Why can't he wait until I ask Mal about this?* She needed to know what to expect. She motioned for Jackson to return. He held up one finger, as if to say, *wait a minute.* She didn't want to waste another moment. *I should just leave, and if he wants to follow, fine.* She raised her arm to wave goodbye, but could not stop herself from shouting "No" when Jackson reached for the crystal lever that opened the bookcase-door to the residence. He looked down at her and waved.

She watched in horror as a dark tentacle shot out of the residence, wrapped itself around Jackson's neck, and dragged him inside. Her heart nearly stopped. Jackson had been caught trespassing, but by what? And who knew what kind of trouble he had gotten himself into? Her fear was for him rather than herself. She practically flew up the stairs to the residence. When she got there, the shelf that disguised the entrance had swung back into position and the crystal lever was gone. She began hammering on the wall behind the obelisks, hoping for Jackson's sake that there would be strength in numbers—hopefully, two against one. After not receiving any response to her pounding, she decided the best way to get attention would be to make some *real* noise. She picked up the closest obelisk and hurled it across the aisle, sending it crashing into a shelf crammed with more of the literary crystals.

Instantly, the balcony filled with swirling fog. An odd being that looked like he had been formed out of molten gold rose from the depths of the mist. A blue diamond band surrounded the entity's head, and lightning bolts shot out of it at varying intervals. It began communicating in a language Johanna could not understand. Even the translation app on the iPad would not have been able to help her. The words sounded more like grunts—"iks" and "ogs," "nnhs" and "utzs."

She shrank back against the shelf that had held the obelisk. She suddenly realized she couldn't calmly close a book and make the apparition go away. There was no book to close, and the obelisk that she had sent sailing through a sea of air had broken into tiny pieces. She thought about how she would feel if someone had trashed one of her precious books. Her shoulders sagged. She had done something childish, something to gain attention, although not the kind of attention she wanted. In the process she had destroyed something precious, if not to her, to someone else. Not to mention she could be electrocuted at any moment.

Before she could give it any more thought, something wrapped around her neck and dragged her into the residence. The sudden loss of oxygen coupled with surprise caused Johanna to black out. When she came to, she saw Jackson standing in the middle of the room.

"I knew you'd come," he said.

She struggled to her feet, choking on the oily mist that enveloped her. She looked around, but couldn't see much in the hazy darkness. "Where's ..."

"He went out after dragging you in."

"Come on, then, let's get out of here."

"I'd love to, but I can't move."

"What do you mean, you can't move?" She took a step toward him, afraid that she, too, might be unable to move, but if that were true, she would have never been able to get up off the floor. She reached for his hand. *Zap.* She felt electrified, in a bad way.

"Force field ..." they said in unison.

"I have to get you out of here." She thought of how they had handled the force field surrounding the blue orb. "Illumination."

"Uurrgg." Jackson gurgled and squirmed. He suddenly looked like he would choke to death.

"Delumination," she cried out.

He sucked in great gulps of air.

"Can you move?"

"No."

"I was hoping 'delumination' would work."

His body relaxed. He took another deep breath, then a step. "The second one worked, which is good, because for a moment I thought you might kill me."

"I guess it's like the little window. You have to say it twice for it to work. Anyway, we need to get out of here. But I did something stupid. I broke one of their obelisks ... on purpose, and it released an odd being with lightning coming out of its ... head. Since the obelisk is broken, I don't know what they're going to do to contain it. Whoever captured you may still be out there."

"Unless it took the obelisk to the antechamber to glue it back together," Jackson speculated.

"There must be something it can do to repair it. Anyway, just be prepared for anything when I open the door."

"Frit."

"Excuse me?"

"Just a family saying. My brother, Chris, once said 'friggan shit' in front of my mother, and she had a conniption. So he got into the habit of condensing it into 'frit,' and now we all say it, even my mother and my little sister."

"That's nice. Can we get back to the problem at hand?" She had no idea what kind of beings they were dealing with. "Do you think they're human?"

"My mother and my sister?"

"Don't joke. I'm talking about whatever captured you."

"I don't think so. I didn't get a chance to pay much attention to what captured me, but I can tell you, it had an iron grip."

"Just be prepared to run. But—and this is a big 'but'—if we can't outrun it, we shouldn't go back the way we came, because we don't want it following us back into *our library*."

"How are we supposed to stop it from doing that?"

"I don't know."

"I wonder if there are any more windows to nowhere, in any of the other alcoves."

"What good would that do us? We might just end up in a library that's scarier than this one."

"Yeah, but there's usually no one up in the cupola. We could just hide out until we think it's safe."

"Unless whatever is chasing us follows us there." She sighed. "Let's just make a run for it and try to get back home. Ready?"

They each took a deep breath. Jackson nodded to Johanna, and she hit the lever that opened the door to the residence. No one was there. They tiptoed down to the main level and across the floor, and then broke into a run—straight up the stairs to the cupola. They didn't slow down to see if anything was behind them. They couldn't afford to waste precious time.

"Illumination," Johanna cried as they ran into

the alcove. They hit the wall hard but remained in the same unfamiliar library. She could hear someone, or something, stomping up the cupola stairs.

"What are we going to do now?" Jackson asked.

Johanna thought about him being trapped behind the force field in the residence, and how she had said the wrong thing at first. "Delumination."

Nothing happened.

"Why did you say, 'Delumination'?" As soon as Jackson repeated her command, they felt themselves swoosh away to another place.

"Oh my God," Jackson exclaimed.

"What?" she cried, looking around in a panic.

"It's the *Pop-Up Book of Phobias*." He smiled at her, and in a singsong voice said, "Honey, we're ho-ome."

"Maybe not," Johanna whispered.

"What do you mean?"

She looked down.

Jackson immediately knew what she meant. The floors were as transparent as glass.

—LOI—

C:L ⊛ I

CHAPTER SEVENTEEN

"Do you see anyone?" Johanna whispered.

"No, but even if I did, how often does anybody look up at the cupola?"

A chime went off, followed by the whirring sound of the front wall sliding open four stories below. Johanna and Jackson stooped down to peer through the transparent floor. They saw a large man covered with curly, red hair stomp into the library. He wore a caftan of rich, blue silk emblazoned with a bright gold design. "FURST," he screamed.

He walked over to the circulation desk and relentlessly rang a bell until a small man, also covered with curly, red hair, came running from a back room. He, too, wore a caftan, but it only reached as far as his knobby knees and appeared to be made of plain sackcloth.

"At your service, I am." The smaller man pulled the bell out of the larger one's hand and placed it out of reach, behind the desk.

"The book ordered, I want."

"Here, it is not."

"On Tuesday, you promised."

"Here, it is not," the little man said a tiny bit louder.

"It, where is?"

"Of our region, outside."

"Beyond us, it is?"

"By force, taken."

"Get it back, you will?"

"An army, I would need."

"Stop, this must."

"An army, I would need," the little man said a tiny bit louder.

"To the council, I will speak."

"With my regard, go forth."

"Furst," the larger man said, nodding his head.

"Dungen," the smaller man replied, nodding to the big man's back as he exited the library. When the wall slid back into place, the little man retreated.

Johanna and Jackson watched as he walked back in the direction of the antechamber.

"How odd," Johanna whispered.

"Did you understand any of that?"

"No. And I don't want to. I want to get back home."

"How are we going to do that?"

She gave it some thought. "I think we ran up the wrong alcove and through a different window."

"I'd be more than happy to look in the other alcoves to see if there are more windows. Too bad the walls aren't made out of glass."

"Don't do anything foolish," she warned.

"I won't." On impulse, he kissed the tip of her

nose and then winked as he slipped away.

The cupola formed a triquetra, three intersecting ellipses intertwined with a circle. The winding aisles snaked like a puzzle, and the points of the ellipses formed the alcoves. Johanna saw Jackson only for a second, as he crossed the far side of the cupola. She sighed with relief when he finally returned to where she waited. "So?"

"There's an identical hazy window at the end of each alcove."

"You're kidding ..."

"Not only that. There are similar windows in some of the hallways. That opens up a lot of possibilities, and we can only guess at picking the right one."

"From what you could see, did it look like we're in the wrong alcove?"

He shook his head. "As far as I can tell, this is the alcove we started out from."

"Great." The word belied her feeling of frustration.

"Look, when we ran in what we thought was the right direction, we ended up here, not back at home. So I'm thinking, even if we go through this same window, we shouldn't end up back in scary town."

"I think I'd rather take my chances talking to the little red-haired man. Maybe he knows something about these windows."

"And if he starts chasing us?"

"We run."

"Okay, let's go."

"Quietly."

Jackson nodded.

They crept down the stairs, and Johanna pulled Jackson toward the circulation desk. "Let's ring, so it doesn't look like we're invading his space."

"Where's the bell?"

She made a face. "I'm pretty sure he put it on a shelf." She walked around the circulation desk and slipped inside the gate leading behind the counter. She saw the bell and grabbed it, but didn't get a chance to ring it.

"Behind my circulation desk, what business have you?" The curator practically roared at her, not at all like the meek little man who had just cowered before his much-larger kinsman.

Johanna placed the bell on the counter. "I'm Johanna Charette, curator of the Library of Illumination ... uh ... another Library of Illumination. We came in through a window in one of the alcoves, and we're wondering if some sort of map exists that can help us get back to our own library."

The man just stared at her.

She gave it another try. "We're not supposed to be here. Can you help us?"

"Operating, the portals are." He said it barely above a whisper, with a look of dread upon his face.

"We mean you no harm," Johanna continued. "We just want to go home."

"Use the portals, why did you?"

"Know what they are, we did not," Jackson broke in.

Johanna poked him. "Why are you talking like that?"

"Because that's how he speaks. It's almost like Yoda from *Star Wars*."

"Want to go, where do you?" the man asked.

"Where are we now?"

"The Realm of Dramatica, this Library of Illumination is in."

That piqued Jackson's interest. "You're a realm? That's so cool!"

"A realm, you must be from," the curator said decisively.

Jackson looked at Johanna. "What realm are we from?"

"I have no idea."

"Of your library, what are the properties?"

"Do you mean the different levels of the books? Mostly twos and threes, although we recently had a four, and Casanova caused all kinds of havoc."

"Come alive, do your books?"

"Yes."

"Here, wait."

He disappeared into the antechamber, and returned a moment later with a large, tattered book, which had a heavy, metal padlock. He held the palm of his right hand about an inch above the lock, and it popped open.

Furst slowly turned the pages. Jackson leaned over to see what he was reading, but could not see any words. He whispered in Johanna's ear, "The pages are blank."

She smiled. "That's because you're not the curator."

"Right."

"Found it, I have," Furst said, with a satisfied smile. "Of the Eleventh Realm, Johanna Charette, you are. Fantasia, it is called."

"Really?"

"Fantasia? Fantastic. At least, I think it's fantastic that you found us," Jackson said. "The Eleventh Realm, huh?"

"And you said we are now in ...?" Johanna asked.

"In the Sixth Realm, Dramatica is."

"Wow," Jackson said. "We traveled five realms."

Johanna shook her head. "Like that means

anything to you."

"Well, at least this isn't like the scary library with the guy with the tentacles."

Furst paled. "Another library, you have been to?"

"Yeah. A scary place with obelisks instead of books, that's run by someone or something with tentacles."

Furst consulted the gold book.

Johanna watched his hand start to tremble. He looked at her with horror in his eyes. "Terroria, that is, the Twelfth Realm. Talk to the Library Council, I must. The Two Millennia War, Terroria started."

"Why did they start a war?" Johanna inquired.

"To take over all the libraries, they wanted. Very serious, this is."

"Can you tell us how to get back to our own library?" Jackson asked.

"Go, you cannot. Talk to the Library Council, you must."

JACKSON GNAWED ON his thumbnail. He leaned close to Johanna. "How long do you think they're going to keep us?"

"You actually look worried."

"It's just that I promised Logan I'd be there tomorrow for our community-service project. He's depending on me."

"You didn't tell me you're working on a project."

"Yeah, we have to do it to graduate. Logan and I got some of the local home-improvement stores to donate materials, and we're going to fix up the outside of Old Lady Caruthers's place, which is falling apart."

"It sounded wonderful until you ruined it all by calling her 'Old Lady' Caruthers."

"Point taken. Anyway, like I told you before, I'm handy around the house. So we're going to paint the exterior and replace the shutters, and Cassie's father is a contractor, so he volunteered to help us rebuild the porch. Chris is getting a few of his friends to chop up the broken front walkway, and Cassie's dad is going to show us how to pour concrete. Plus, Cassie and Brittany got the Mothers' Club to donate flowers and stuff that they're going to plant in front of the new porch and along the sidewalk. It's a lot of work, but we're hoping to finish it all in one day. I've got to be there. We made a commitment."

Johanna was impressed by the scope of work Jackson and Logan had taken on. Plus they managed to get promises and donations from others, to make the revitalization project a success. "You should shoot video of it and put it to music, so you can upload it to the Internet."

"I won't be able to shoot anything, because I'll be too busy working. But *you* can volunteer to shoot it." He put his arm around her. "It'll be fun."

"First, we have to get out of here," she said pragmatically.

"The next time I come up with a bright idea, like opening a library window, you have my permission to fire me."

"Thanks. I'll remember that."

IT DID NOT take long for the Dramatican Library Council to convene. Their library had a giant bell in an open tower over the entryway, and the peals immediately drew council members from all over the city. They dropped whatever they were doing to respond to the perceived emergency.

"For five hundred years, the bell has not rung,"

Furst told them. "Great danger, we are in."

The council members stared at Johanna and Jackson as they gathered around a table in Dramatica's version of the executive boardroom. The stone walls and leaded glass windows reminded Johanna of her own library; however, this one had a glass ceiling and a glass table.

Jackson knocked twice on the tabletop. "I like this. It's really cool."

Furst leaned over and whispered, "Secret deals made under the table, it is to prevent."

"Ahhh," Jackson answered.

"Explain," one of the council members demanded.

"Speak, you must," Furst told Johanna.

She stood up and looked at the assembly of people before her. They were all covered with curly red hair and wore caftans of varying degrees of richness. "I'm Johanna Charette, curator of the Library of Illumination on Fantasia." She looked at Furst for reassurance, and he nodded at her. "We found a small window that could not be seen from the outside of our library, and we tried to open it to see what was behind it. When we managed to do that, we were transported to another library, much like our own, except instead of books we found obelisks." This statement incited an increase in murmurings among the Library Council members. "When Jackson"—she pointed to her assistant—"went to find out where we were, someone or something with tentacles imprisoned him and placed him behind a force field." The sound level increased even more. "I saw him get pulled into the residence, but by the time I got there, I couldn't get inside. No one would come to the door, so to get their attention—and this pains me deeply to say—I threw one of their obelisks, breaking it." The murmuring grew quite loud.

"Here now, you are. Get away, how did you?"

She took a deep breath. "I was pulled into the residence after I broke the obelisk, but whatever dragged me inside must have rushed to inspect the damage, without bothering to secure me behind a force field. Jackson was immobilized, but because of something that happened recently in our own library, I managed to say the right thing to get the force field to release him.

"We left the residence and ran up to the cupola, where the window is located. We went back through it, but instead of returning to our own library, we ended up here."

"Through the window, did anyone see you leave?"

"We heard someone coming up the steps, but I don't know if he, or she, or it, saw us disappear through the window."

Torran, the largest of the Library Council members, stood. Gold embroidery covered every inch of his caftan, and jewels encrusted the neckline and edges. He had a deep, resonant voice. "The portals, you have breached."

"So they're like the portals from *Stargate*?" Jackson asked.

"A system of portals that connect all the libraries, it is said there exists. But hidden by the College of Overseers many years ago they were, when the Two Millennia War Terroria started. Seek to take over all the libraries, they did."

"Can you tell us how to get back to our own library?" Johanna asked.

"Breach the portals, we cannot. Know their true directions, we do not. Summon the College of Overseers, we must. Now."

"How do you do that?" Jackson asked.

"The Curator Key, Furst must engage."

Furst turned his head upward and looked through the glass ceiling to the very top of the cupola.

"Easy, it will not be," he mumbled.

"Do it, you must," Torran demanded.

Furst left the room, and the other council members trailed behind him. They talked among themselves as they waited, while the curator descended to a sub-level.

"What's this Curator Key they're talking about?" Jackson asked Johanna.

"I don't know. I could probably ask Mal's diary, but I don't have it with me. I didn't realize we were going on an excursion or precipitating a war."

"Sorry."

They heard scraping and turned to see Furst dragging a large ladder behind him. "Here, let me help you with that," Jackson said, picking up the back of the ladder. "Where are you taking it?"

Furst pointed straight up.

Jackson grimaced. He ended up on the lower end of the ladder as they lugged it up the cupola stairs, toward the highest point in the building.

"Place it across the railings, we must," Furst said, pointing to where he wanted Jackson to carry his end of the ladder. They extended it as far as it would go and laid it horizontally across the rails.

"Now what?"

"A rope, I must get." Furst disappeared down the stairs, pushing through the stream of council members who climbed up to watch. He returned several minutes later with a coil of rope. He tied one end into a lasso and the other around his waist. Then he climbed on top of the ladder.

"Whoa, whoa, whoa, what are you doing?" Jackson called out, grabbing the end of the ladder.

"Reach the hook with the rope, I must."

Furst started to crawl across the makeshift wooden bridge that now spanned the open space in the middle of the cupola. He moved very slowly. Jackson couldn't tell if Furst wobbled because of nerves, or because the ladder wasn't strong enough to hold his weight. None of Furst's countrymen moved to help him accomplish his task.

"Johanna," Jackson called out. "Can you grab the other end of the ladder and hold it still?"

"Will do," she responded, grabbing the opposite side.

The two teens watched as Furst shakily stood up in the middle of the ladder. He took the section of rope that he had tied into a lasso and threw it toward the uppermost part of the ceiling. It missed whatever target the curator had hoped it would catch onto, and fell downward, pulling Furst off balance. Everyone gasped as the curator fell. Furst managed to grab the edge of the ladder and clung to it as he dangled several stories above the library's main reading room.

—LOI—

C:L⟡ I

CHAPTER EIGHTEEN

THE LIBRARY COUNCIL members discussed Furst's dilemma in detail, but not one of them moved to help him.

Jackson climbed onto the edge of the ladder.

"What are you doing?" Johanna screamed.

"Someone's got to save him," he told her. "Hey, I'd appreciate a little help here," he yelled at the council members at large.

One of them, a man in a brown silk caftan without much ornamentation, grabbed hold of Jackson's end of the ladder. The teen crawled out to where Furst clung, all the while praying that the ladder was strong enough to support them both. He straddled the ladder when he reached the curator and locked his ankles together. Grabbing Furst by his arms, Jackson pulled him up high enough so the Dramatican could get a better grip.

Jackson contemplated his next move. Normally,

he would reach over and grab Furst's waistband to haul him up, but the man wore a caftan. Instead, the teen grabbed the rope Furst had attached to his waist. It had been tied with a slipknot, and Jackson could only reach the part that pulled it loose. As a last resort, the young man grabbed a handful of fabric from Furst's caftan and hauled him up, hoping the man wore underwear, or else Johanna would get an eyeful.

Furst managed to scramble back on the ladder to the cheers of the council members. As he sat catching his breath, he trembled as sweat oozed from every pore.

"What, exactly, are you trying to do?" Jackson asked.

Furst looked up and pointed. "A hook up at the top, there is. Try to lasso it to pull myself up, I did."

"Okay, first things first. Untie that rope from your waist and tie it to the ladder instead." Jackson took the lasso end in his hand. Taking a deep breath, he narrowed his eyes in concentration, and tossed it. Everyone released a collective sigh when the rope missed its mark. Jackson retrieved the line, which now dangled from the ladder, grabbed the lasso again, and thought about how Johanna never missed the trash bin when she free-tossed a wadded-up piece of paper across the length of the circulation desk. *I can do this,* he thought. He stared at the hook. He envisioned the lasso snagging it. He thought about how contacting the College of Overseers could pave the way for them to get back home. He raised his elbow so the noose hung open from his wrist and, without taking his eye off the hook, flung the rope upward. He watched as it climbed, willing it to snag the hook.

"That's what I'm talking about," he screamed, when the rope caught hold.

Enthusiastic shouts and whistles erupted from

the group.

Jackson looked at Furst, who had broken into a wide smile. "What do I need to do when I get up there?"

Furst's face fell. "You cannot. The curator, I am. Contact the college, only the curator can."

"Are you going to be okay doing this?"

"Know, I do not."

"Have you ever climbed a rope before?"

"No."

"We should have knotted the rope before we tossed it," he said, thinking out loud. He looked at Furst, who still looked scared. "Wait here."

Jackson untied the rope from the ladder and climbed to the top of it. He took a moment to study the Curator's Key. It wasn't a key at all, but an intricate dialing mechanism. The odd configuration of brass gears and ivory numbered buttons reminded him of Jules Verne's *Time Machine. I wonder if we have one of these.* Jackson shifted his gaze to the hook. It had been solidly integrated in the framework of the cupola. From up close, it was fairly large. He slowly slid back down to the ladder. "Do you have another rope?"

Furst nodded.

"Do you want to get it?"

Furst turned and tentatively stared at the end of the ladder.

"Better yet," Jackson continued, "tell me where it is, and I'll go and get it, that way you can save your energy for climbing it."

"Sub-level six, it is in. Next to the cellar stairs, it is."

"I'll be right back."

Jackson crawled to the edge of the ladder and jumped down onto the floor of the cupola. He didn't waste any time answering questions. He just ignored them all and ran down the stairs. The buzz level increased, as council members stared at Furst and called out their questions to him.

"Another rope, we need," he answered, not exactly knowing why they needed it.

Jackson returned a couple of minutes later, with the second coil of rope hanging from his shoulder. He crawled back on the ladder and formed a noose on one end and proceeded to tie knots at one-foot intervals. Then he scrambled up the rope that he'd already attached to the ceiling and secured the knotted line to the same hook.

He returned to Furst. "Those knots will keep you from sliding back down as you climb up. Just grab the rope above the knot, pull up your knees, and then wrap the loose end of the rope around one foot and use your other foot to hold it in place. Every time you straighten your legs, you'll be able to reach higher, and you just need to keep doing that until you reach the top."

Furst nodded. He grabbed the rope and used it to pull himself up to a standing position. He reached as high as he could and pulled up his knees as Jackson had advised, but had difficulty wrapping the rope around his foot and using the other foot to hold it in place. After three tries, he returned to a sitting position on the ladder. "Do it, I cannot. Doomed, we are."

Jackson gave it some thought. "You can do it," he said, with a smile. "Try it again."

Furst slowly stood up and grabbed the rope. Jackson stood up as well. When Furst pulled his feet up, Jackson looped the rope around one foot and pushed Furst's other foot into place. "Straighten your legs and move your hands higher," Jackson told him. Furst did, and Jackson climbed the second rope to help the man wrap his foot again. Together, the two men climbed the pair of ropes—student and teacher—until they reached the top.

"Okay, do your thing," Jackson said.

"Afraid to let go, I am," Furst replied, his voice filled with panic.

"You won't fall. I'll hold you in place. Are your feet tight against the rope?"

"Yes."

"Okay." Jackson pulled himself up and wrapped his legs around Furst's waist, holding him in place. "Do what you gotta do."

Furst tentatively let go with one hand and manipulated the dial. Jackson watched as the gears slowly turned, screeching with years of non-use.

"Descend, we must," Furst said nervously.

"Just loosen your grip a little at a time and slide."

Jackson released Furst and slid down the rope. The Dramatican curator slowly made his way down to the ladder, at the bottom of which Jackson waited to guide him in. Above them, the gears continued to turn as the opening in the cupola slowly grew larger. They headed in opposite directions, and when they each reached firm ground, Furst motioned Jackson to help him remove the ladder from the railing and place it out of the way. Then they stood and watched with the others as the cupola yawned wider.

METAL ON METAL clanged thunderously as the gears in Dramatica's cupola locked into place. The crowd gasped when a magnificent white light shot upward from the center medallion embedded in the library floor, straight through the opening in the roof. After a minute, the light stopped as suddenly as it had appeared.

"Now what?" Jackson asked.

"Look," Johanna said, pointing toward the various alcoves. A dozen men—nearly identical in appearance—emerged from the twelve portals. Each, one had a long, white beard and even longer, white hair that touched the floor. They all wore purple robes and matching miter hats.

"A plethora of popes," Jackson whispered.

Johanna jammed her elbow in his side. "Stop," she said under her breath.

Torran addressed the overseers. "Torran, I am, Dean of the Library Council."

𝄢 *Who is the curator?* the twelve overseers asked in unison.

Furst pushed forward through the throng of men.

"Furst, I am. Curator." He bowed deeply.

𝄢 *There is another.*

Furst looked for Johanna in the crowd and signaled for her to join him.

She walked over to where he stood and addressed the twelve men. "I am Johanna Charette, curator of a library in a different realm."

Ω *Realm Eleven.* She heard the words, as did everyone else, but did not know who spoke them.

❖*She breached the portals on Realm Twelve. We must extract Nero 51."*

The light shot up through the portal, and two of the overseers disappeared. When the light suddenly turned off, they retuned, flanking the curator known as Nero 51.

The Dramaticans gasped. Nero 51 had the body of a man, but his feet were larger and flatter—like swollen platypus feet—and he had multiple tentacles for arms that could stretch out to untold lengths. His wide head dipped in the middle, rising on either side over large black eyes that commanded more than half his face. He had a flat nose and a very small mouth.

He made a series of unintelligible sounds. One of the overseers waved his hand, and Nero 51's words instantly became understandable. "Terroria has been invaded," he declared, "and our property maliciously destroyed."

The overseers addressed Johanna. 🜍 *Why did you breach the portal and destroy library property?*

"We did not know about the portals or how they work. When we were unexpectedly transported to another world, my assistant Jackson wanted to explore it. But he was taken and locked in a force field."

"TAKEN? I did no such thing. I found him trying to break into my residence."

"I wasn't really trying to break into the residence," Jackson volunteered. "I only wanted to get Johanna's attention."

🜍 *You are Jackson?* the overseers asked in unison. "Yes."

They all nodded.

"Who is Jackson?" Nero 51 demanded. "A curator?"

🜍 *A curator-in-training.*

"A curator-in-training who has broken the laws of the Library of Illumination, just like his master." Nero 51 glared at Johanna. "I demand justice, with a trial on Terroria before a jury of Terrorians."

🜍 *Library law is regulated only by a jury populated by overseers. There will be no jury of Terrorians. But we will acquiesce to your request to have the trial on your home world. It is decided."*

Johanna felt a moment of nausea and realized she had unexpectedly been whisked through the portal to another library. She recognized the structure of the executive boardroom, and knew she was on Terroria when she saw the oily mist swirling in the air. It resembled the atmosphere inside the residence in which she found Jackson. Even here, shelves filled with obelisks of all shapes and sizes lined the walls. She looked around the room to see who had accompanied them to witness the proceedings. The twelve overseers were there, as well as Jackson, Furst, and Nero 51, but she was the only other person in the room. The Dramatican Library Council had been left behind.

℧ *Johanna Charette, state you story from the beginning, before breaching the portals.*

Once again, she could not tell where the voice originated. She looked at Jackson, startled to see that he, Furst, and Nero 51 were suspended in what appeared to be tubes of glass.

℧ *Do not be alarmed,"* the voice said. *"It is to prevent interruption, or the accidental disclosure of sensitive information not meant for the many.*

Johanna recounted how Jackson had discovered a window in the cupola that would not open and how he was sure there must be something like a safe hidden behind it. She explained how she had been skeptical but allowed him to try to remove the window after he promised to fix anything he broke. She explained how saying the word *Illumination* caused the window to fly open, and how Jackson repeating it had resulted in their transport to Terroria. She stated she was "scared" and her primary goal was to return home, but Jackson had a curious mind and a zest for exploring new places. She recounted everything that happened—from breaking the obelisk to escaping the residence—and finished by telling the overseers how surprised she and Jackson were to find themselves on Dramatica, when all they wanted to do was return home.

She revealed how Furst had explained that there were a dozen realms, plus the home world, Lumina, and that she came from Fantasia, Realm Eleven, which she hadn't known.

An overseer nodded, and Johanna found herself inside a glass tube. She watched as Jackson answered the overseers' questions, but could not hear what was said.

Jackson had a similar version of what had happened, except he gave more detail about being captured by Nero 51.

"It felt like a steel cable had wrapped around my arms, and when I saw all the tentacles he had, I was surprised he didn't wrap them around my legs as well, because I kicked as hard as I could, trying to get away. But then he reached for this huge weapon that looked like a rocket launcher, threw me against the wall, and fired it at me. I found myself locked behind a force field and couldn't move. He started clicking and whirring at me, but I couldn't tell what he was saying. I just knew he meant business, considering the number of weapons he had stacked up across the room. If that guy's going to war, I don't want to be the enemy."

Jackson found himself back inside the glass tube and watched as Nero 51 approached the overseers.

"THIS IS AN outrage," the Terrorian said in a low-pitched, threatening tone. "Those two *curators*," he sneered, "invaded my library and wreaked havoc. It is against library law. I demand that they be executed for breaking the peace of a million millennia."

FURST WAS THE last person to be interrogated. He spoke about how he had first found Johanna behind the circulation desk holding the bell, and how she said she was back there because the bell was not on the desk. He stated that she spoke the truth, because he had hidden the bell after Dungen gave him a headache by ringing it nonstop.

He was mystified that Johanna did not know anything about the various realms, but said, other than that, she seemed very knowledgeable about the layout of the library and its inner workings.

He talked about his decision to ask the Library Council for permission to contact the Board of Overseers, and that once the decision was made, how Jackson helped him climb to the dial at the top of the portal. He also detailed how the teen had saved his life when he lost his balance and nearly fell to his death.

Like the others, Furst was returned to a sound-proof holding tube after his testimony.

AFTER MUCH DELIBERATION, the College of Overseers agreed their decision would depend on the testimony of Johanna's mentor, whom they instantly summoned to corroborate the information they had been given. Mal was escorted to Terroria through one of the portals.

𝔰 *Malcolm Trees?*

"Yes."

𝔰 *It is said your charge had no knowledge of the confluence of realms. Did you not teach her?*

"I did not. I thought her too young to fully comprehend the importance of the information when she first became curator of the library. She is, by far, the youngest person ever to assume that role, although it must be noted, she has admirably mastered the proficiencies necessary to run such a, shall we say, *dynamic* institution. I had arranged for the provenance of the library system to be apportioned to her within the text of my eternal diary, which I know she refers to frequently. I had scheduled it to start in her twenty-first year. She is not even nineteen years old, and I did not want her youth to influence the possibility that she might overlook the importance of our history."

§ *This would bear out the testimony of Furst, who claims she entered Dramatica without knowledge of the realms or her place within them.*

"I am sorry to admit that I have been remiss."

§ *The boy, Jackson, is a curator-in-training?*

"Yes. Johanna hired him to help out at the library. After I witnessed his devotion to her and to the library, I—quite unknown to them—took the necessary steps to have the young man designated a curator-in-training. Like Johanna, his background makes him highly suitable for the position. Together, I believe they will grow into all that the job demands."

§ *You see them as equals, then?*

"Not exactly. The girl is intelligent and pragmatic, with excellent business sense and a love of literature. She is a natural-born leader of the levelheaded variety. Jackson, on the other hand, takes risks Johanna would never take. While this may seem foolhardy at times, his bravery, geniality, and ability to take charge of difficult situations and foresee their outcomes complement her leadership by making Johanna push her boundaries past what is comfortable. I believe they can accomplish great things together. In light of the rumored build-up of arms and unrest in some of the realms, I see them as the light of the future."

𝔖 *You have ascertained, then, the increasing possibility of conflict within the realms?*

"Yes. It is said the Terrorians are bartering ancient obelisks for weapons."

𝔖 *It would be detected.*

"Not if the obelisks were replaced by counterfeits."

There was a moment of silence. 𝔖 *That is all.*

Mal was escorted back to his point of origin.

—LOI—

C:L I

CHAPTER NINETEEN

❖ RECOUNT THE CHARGES *against Johanna Charette.*

    Ψ *Charge: Portal Breach.*

    ❖ *Acquitted: She had no knowledge of their existence.*

        ◉ *Duly noted.*

    Ψ *Charge: Destruction of LOI Property.*

    ❖ *Guilty: Johanna admitted to destroying property.*

    ◉ *Duly noted.*

    ❖ *Recount the charges against Jackson Roth.*

    Ψ *Charge: Portal Breach.*

    ❖ *Acquitted: He had no knowledge of their existence.*

        ◉ *Duly noted.*

    Ψ *Charge: Trespass.*

    ❖ *Acquitted: As a LOI curator-in-training, it is impossible to trespass on any LOI property.*

⌻ *Duly noted.*

Ψ *Charge: Illegal Entry of a Residence.*

❖ *Acquitted: The boy was pulled inside and detained by the resident.*

⌻ *Duly noted.*

⌨ *Johanna must be punished for the destruction of property.*

★ *Extenuating circumstances existed. Nero 51 ignored her communication, thus inviting the use of unorthodox methods to get his attention.*

⎙ *She broke the obelisk to save the boy, not knowing what fate awaited him, due to her ignorance of the realms.*

❖ *She must pay for her transgression. She is from Fantasia, based on Earth. It is decreed she work the equivalent of three Earth days on Terroria to repay the loss.*

Σ *Nero 51 will condemn the judgment as too light.*

❖ *Nero 51 is not an overseer.*

π *Johanna Charette will not like the judgment.*

❖ *Johanna Charette must pay for willful destruction of library property. And we need her to serve time on Terroria.*

☂ *Your decision, perhaps, is based on the boy's testimony about weapons, as well as other rumors that have come to light ...*

§ *Ahhh ... the counterfeits.*

❖ *You are correct.*

∾ *And the electromagnetic waves?*

❖ *We continue to monitor them.*

⎙ *And the boy, Jackson?*

❖ *He must remain on Earth to curate the Fantasian library.*

Ω *Shall we seal the portals?*

❖ *No. Johanna Charette must be able to return to her realm.*

■ *What if Nero 51 uses them to wage war?*

❖ *That is to be expected, and countered.*

The tubes vanished, and the four curators stood before the College of Overseers.

❖ *All charges have been acquitted, save one.*

Nero 51 took a threatening step forward. "How could all charges have been acquitted? I demand retribution."

❖ *All charges, save one.*

"And what charge is that?" The Terrorian sneered.

❖ *Johanna Charette, you have been found guilty of the willful destruction of LOI property. You are sentenced to work in the service of the library on Terroria for three Earth days.*

"No!" Nero 51 roared. "I do not want her on my world. She is a spy and must be executed!"

❖ *Nero 51, Johanna Charette has been sentenced to a period of service on your world. As a ward of Terroria for that given period of time, you must guarantee her safety, or lose all rights as curator of your realm.*

Nero 51 huffed and puffed like he was about to explode.

"If she's going there, I'm going with her," Jackson interjected. "It's my fault she broke the obelisk."

❖ *No. Jackson Roth, you have been acquitted of all charges. In the absence of Johanna Charette, you must assume the duties as curator of the Library of Illumination in the realm of Fantasia.*

"You can't let her go to Terroria alone."

❖ *It is the finding of the College of Overseers and cannot be overturned. Johanna Charette, you have an equal amount of time to prepare for your sentence: three Earth days. We will send an escort to accompany you to Terroria when the moment has arrived.*

The College of Overseers stood in unison.

♫ *Johanna   Charette,   Jackson   Roth,   Furst, accompany us. We will return you to your home worlds before we temporarily seal the portals,* the overseers said in unison.

"This is an outrage!" Nero 51 screamed at their retreating number. "I will not stand for it!"

Johanna and Jackson found themselves back in the alcove of oddities. "Do you think we're really home?" Jackson asked.

Johanna stooped and retrieved a chunk of their wood window frame from the floor. "Yes."

"You can't go to Terroria alone."

"I have to. You heard what the College of Overseers said."

"That Nero guy has it in for you. He wants to execute you."

"He can't without losing his curatorship, and I have the feeling that it's something he doesn't want to lose. So I'll be fine. I'll polish a few obelisks. I'll wash a few windows. Whatever."

"Who's that guy they brought in at the end?"

"Mal."

"That's Mal? Really? He looked so different."

"That's because you met him when he was only one hundred forty years old."

Jackson took a moment to think about what she had just said. "Why do you think they called him there?"

"I don't know, but I have every intention of asking him ... or at least his diary."

"Are you going to do that now?"

"Right now, all I want is a slice of pizza."

"Since I got you into this, I'll treat."

She linked her arm in his. "Let's go." She refrained from telling him how safe she felt while they walked arm-in-arm. If she did, he would argue with her about going to Terroria. Instead, she secretly welcomed the warmth and security that holding on to him offered, if only for a little while.

PICCOLO ITALIA DID not seem very busy for a Friday night. "Where is everyone?" Jackson asked.

Dante wiped his hands on his apron. "Been and gone. We close in fifteen minutes."

Jackson looked at the clock on the wall. "Do you believe it's already eleven fifteen?"

"Time flies when you're on trial," Johanna murmured.

"We can still get slices, can't we?" he asked.

"I've got three plain slices left and one mushroom."

"Ugh, I hate mushrooms." Jackson made a face.

"I'll eat the mushroom slice," Johanna offered.

"Okay." He turned to Dante. "We'll take them all. And a couple of colas."

Dante slipped the slices in the oven, while Johanna and Jackson slid into a red leatherette booth across from the counter.

"Anyway, I was thinking," Jackson started, "that once I tell—"

"Stop."

"What?"

"You're dangerous when you think."

"I'm going with you."

"You have school."

"I'll just tell Old Man Benson that you need me to go with you."

"To another world, where the beings have tentacles for arms and alien eyes? I don't think so."

"You can't go alone."

"I *will* go alone. And you *do* need to ask Mr. Benson for three days off from school, because you have to run the library while I'm gone."

"They should have sentenced me to hard labor on Terroria, instead of you. You were there because of me. Besides, I don't know how to run the library."

"Yes, you do. Nobody is asking you to do any bookbinding or to research special exhibitions while I'm gone. All you have to do is open the mail, save the bills for me, and process the requests to borrow books. The list of approved borrowers is on the computer. I'm sure you know where to find it, because you're the person who entered all that information. That's all you have to do for three days, besides answer the phone. Tell anyone asking for me that I was suddenly called out of town and that I'm expected back on Thursday. What could be easier?"

"I still think—"

"Pizza's up," Dante shouted.

"Get our food. Then tell me all about the project you and Logan have planned for this weekend."

THAT NIGHT, JOHANNA's dreams were peppered with nightmares about all the horrible things that could happen on Terroria. She slept fitfully, and it was after nine by the time she woke up. She checked her messages, prepared two book deliveries, and grabbed her camera before heading out.

When she arrived at Mrs. Caruthers's house, Jackson and Logan, along with what looked like half the neighborhood, were already busy scraping old paint off the siding and chopping up the broken sidewalk. Cassie walked around the house with a clipboard in hand, jotting down ideas for plants. Brittany and Chris painted new shutters, so they would be dry enough to handle when it came time to attach them to the windows.

Johanna walked over to Jackson's mom, who stood with Ava in their adjoining yard. "So what does Mrs. Caruthers think of all this?"

"She doesn't know. Jackson made a deal with someone over at the senior center to get her out of the house. She's apparently a gifted quilter. They asked her to give a class in quilt making and offered to pay her fifty dollars, so she happily agreed."

"That's pretty amazing. Where did the money come from?"

"It's from a senior-center program. They have a grant that pays experts to teach classes. I hope it goes well."

"Me, too. I'd better start shooting video. I promised Jackson I'd edit it to music so he could post it online."

Mrs. Roth sniffed back a tear. "They're really something, these kids. They did the same thing for me last year, and I was overwhelmed. I'm so proud of them. But don't let me keep you. Go take pictures."

It turned out to be a long day, but Ava supplied everyone with lemonade and water, and the Students for a Better Society club at the high school brought sandwiches and brownies for the crew. It turned into more of a celebration than anything else, and the camaraderie made everyone work a little harder.

BY LATE AFTERNOON, Chris and Jackson had finished attaching the shutters to the house, and stood back to admire their work. The only thing they had overlooked was how long it would take the new concrete sidewalk in the front yard to dry.

"I hope Mrs. Caruthers has a key to the back door," Chris said. "I'd hate to have to break a windowpane to get her inside her fixed-up house."

The crowd cheered when the senior-transit van pulled up in front of the house. Everyone waited anxiously for Mrs. Caruthers to get out of the vehicle, but after a very long interval, only the driver emerged.

"Is everything all right?" Mrs. Roth asked.

"She's crying. She wanted to know why all these people are standing in front of her house, and when I told her, she became very emotional. She needs a moment to compose herself."

Slowly, Mrs. Caruthers climbed out of the vehicle, her eyes bright with tears. Mrs. Roth pulled a tissue out of her pocket and offered it to the elderly woman.

"Thank you, dear." Mrs. Caruthers sighed deeply and made her way toward the front door.

Jackson reached for her arm. "I'm sorry, Mrs. Caruthers, you can't go in that way, for now. The cement is still wet. Do you have a key to the back?"

She nodded, and then her head movement changed from up and down to side to side. "Why ...?" She could not finish her thought.

Jackson turned on the charm. "You know, you're a pillar of this community." He slipped his arm around her shoulders. "And you've always watched out for us. This is just a gesture from your friends and neighbors that we're watching out for you, too, and we're here to help you. If you need help ..."

A giant tear rolled down the old woman's cheek. "Thank you, Jackson. This is the nicest thing anyone has ever done for me."

"Let me introduce you to everyone who helped out." Jackson called out each volunteer by name. He told her about every person's contribution to the project, and Mrs. Caruthers shook hands with each and every one of them, to thank them personally.

Johanna captured it all on video, glad that her tears did not splash onto the camera lens and blur the images.

JOHANNA STAYED OUT late with Jackson and his friends, celebrating the success of their community project, but in the back of her mind, she couldn't shake the fact that her sentence would begin in forty-eight hours.

It was after two in the morning when she finally crawled into bed. She yawned with exhaustion, but her looming incarceration prevented her from getting much sleep. Finally, she gave into her insomnia, brewed a pot of coffee, and grabbed Mal's diary.

"Mal, why were you on Terroria?"

She waited. After several minutes passed with no word from her mentor, she felt abandoned. Then, the pages riffled to a section near the end. The diary outlined how Mal had been summoned to appear before the Library of Illumination's College of Overseers to testify on behalf of Johanna, who had admitted to destroying Terrorian property. According to his diary entry:

> *I had initially thought the punishment too harsh, but then I discerned an undercurrent of deep concern among the overseers. It began when I testified about reports that I had heard about obelisks being counterfeited so the originals could be sold to finance weaponry.*

The overseers dismissed me, but more importantly, they did not dispute my testimony. I am sure the College of Overseers needs Johanna to serve her sentence on Terroria, so that she can act as its eyes and ears on that world. I am quite certain she is being planted as a spy.

Johanna's nerves tingled when she read Mal's words. *Counterfeits. Weapons. Spy.* She would have to keep her eyes and ears open for any indication of warmongering and subterfuge. Well, maybe not her ears, not unless the overseers reinstated her ability to understand the Terrorian language. *They'll have to, or else how am I supposed to know what Nero 51 expects of me?*

Three days. She planned to travel light. Nothing fancy—just a change of clothes, a toothbrush, and protein bars in a backpack. And water. She would need to bring her own water. She didn't even know if they *had* water on Terroria. She spent the rest of the day trying to find out as much as she could about the realm. She didn't expect it to be easy, but when she plugged Terroria into the library database, listings for it came right up. Finding them would be another matter. They were located on sub-level fifty-six. *Could that be in the basement?*

She picked up Mal's diary and consulted it again. "Where's sub-level fifty-six?"

The diary opened to a section she had never seen before. It contained page after page of detailed floor plans, starting with the cupola and ending with sub-level 1,311. The plans for most of the sub-levels looked the same. They were made up of countless rows of stacks filled with every book, pamphlet, drawing, musical composition, letter, treaty, mathematical equation, and other tangible collection of words, numbers, symbols and ideas the realms had ever known.

"How do I get down to sub-level fifty-six?" The pages shuffled again, and a picture of an archaic hand-crank elevator appeared. *Hand crank—for fifty-six levels? Going down might not be so bad, but coming back up would be a bitch.*

"Mal, do you know if it's hard to crank?"

A new entry by Mal appeared.

The original apparatus has been upgraded many times. The container was last replaced in the mid–nineteenth century with an open cage elevator that may look old but is in good working order. It is easy to operate. The hand crank has also been replaced, and the device is nuclear powered, just like everything else in the library.

Johanna breathed a sigh of relief.

"Are you okay?"

She jumped. She hadn't heard Jackson come in the back door. "I'm fine. I located books on Terroria on sub-level fifty-six."

"Where?"

"My thought exactly. If you come with me, we can find it together."

She led him down into the basement to the area where Mal's diary had indicated the existence of an elevator. A large cabinet containing library castoffs stood where the elevator should be. An old adding machine, a broken postage meter, and other obsolete office equipment that had seen better days filled the shelves.

"Look for a lever," she said.

They inspected every shelf, removing the junk

and piling it on the floor so they could spot the lever more easily.

"I don't see any," Jackson observed, while pressing on the backs of the shelves, looking for a way to get them to swing open.

"It's too dark in here." The absence of windows made it hard to see in shadowy corners. "See if that light still works."

Jackson inspected a tarnished brass frame encasing an old-fashioned light bulb. "I don't see any switch. Maybe I just need to tighten the bulb ... if I can get my fingers through these stupid bars." The frame made reaching the bulb difficult. "I wonder if this thing comes off," he said, twisting it. As he did so, the shelf slid open, sending up a cloud of dust.

"You're like an accidental genius," Johanna said, with a smile.

"Thanks ... I think."

Hidden behind the shelf was an ancient cage made of brass bars. It had a bronze medallion affixed to the front of it: *LOI.* Johanna pulled the door open and pushed aside an inner scissor-gate. She tentatively entered the elevator, and Jackson followed. They looked at the massive panel of numbers. The number 6 was already lit. The button for the lowest level said *1311.* She found the button for sub-level fifty-six and pushed it. The elevator lurched as it started its descent.

—LOI—

C:L●I

CHAPTER TWENTY

JOHANNA DIDN'T KNOW what to expect on sub-level fifty-six, but envisioned something dark, dirty, and in disrepair. Instead she found a comfortable space filled with abundant soft lighting and climate-controlled air. She located the section where the computer catalog system said she would find books on Terroria, and she soon chose one that looked promising.

"That was easy," Jackson said, as they headed back to the elevator.

"All things considered," she agreed, "we got off lucky."

They hopped on the elevator, and Jackson studied the buttons. "What floor? I've never seen an elevator in the library. Do you think there's a door hidden behind one of the shelves?"

"I'm pretty sure the basement is level six. Press that button. We can look for an elevator on the main floor after this is all over."

The cage made a creaking sound as it started to ascend. Jackson gazed at the staircase that wound around the elevator as it climbed. "Could you imagine if we had to walk up all these stairs to get back? There must be thousands of them. Tens of thousands, if the library really does go down to"—he inspected the button panel—"sub-level thirteen-hundred and eleven."

The cage suddenly stopped between floors, and the lights went out.

"No, no, no, no, no." Johanna huffed.

The lights suddenly turned on, and the elevator began moving again.

"Frit. My heart dropped to my stomach when that happened. I wouldn't want to be stuck down here. No one would even know where we were. We would starve to death. Maybe even have to kill one another for food." He thought about that for a second. "Don't worry, I could never do that to you. You could eat me first."

"Uh-huh." She left it at that.

"You're supposed to say that you would do the same thing for me."

"It grieves me to say that you would have to die alone, because the College of Overseers is coming tomorrow evening to escort me to my sentence, and I get the feeling that they would find me no matter where I am."

"That's probably true. You don't think they would leave me down there, do you?"

The elevator stopped. Johanna opened the scissor-gate and stepped out. "I guess we'll never know."

They sat together on the sofa. "Be prepared in case the Terrorians appear."

She opened the back cover and immediately

inspected the bottom of the endpaper. "It's a zero. We're safe."

"How do you know?"

"Mal's diary. I saw a section about how the library's collection has a hint about the book levels camouflaged in the endpapers." She turned the book and showed him a minute *0*.

"That could come in handy. When were you going to tell me?"

"I just read it this morning," she replied.

She paged through the *History of Terroria*. It gave details on Realm Twelve from its earliest days through the present, and included the curators who had overseen it. There was a section on Terrorians' major contributions to music, art, and literature, and a detailed geographical outline of the world and its natural resources. The book also touched upon the portals, and how all the libraries had full use of them for communicating with the other realms, until the Two Millennia War.

> *Terroria's impatience with some of the other realms, as well as its unbridled thirst for power, resulted in a scheme to take over the entire library system. The Terrorian Realm formed alliances with Adventura and Mysteriose to overturn the Council of Twelve (now defunct), a governing board formed by the curators of each of the realms. In a well-planned coup d'état, the three rogue curators seized control of the Council of Twelve and commanded their troops to use the portals to invade each library and take over its operation. The population of each realm resisted the invaders, but could not break the defenses of the well-protected libraries. The nine realms that*

refused to join with the Terrorians, Adventurites, and Mysterians suffered severe deprivation at the hands of their captors. The population on some worlds decreased by more than two-thirds.

The College of Overseers moved to seal the portals, isolating the rebels in nine separate battles. The overseers immediately convened the First Inter-Realm Peace Council. Rebel leaders agreed to attend, but as soon as the portals reopened, Terrorian curator Claff 8 ordered new troops to transport into the war zones and push for victory. He took two of the overseers prisoner and had them executed in a demonstration of power.

The remaining overseers escaped and sealed the portals again—scrambling their configuration so anyone breaching a portal would never be sure where he or she might emerge.

The war raged on until the overseers secretly built a one-way portal to a containment cell in Lumina. In a stunning use of reverse propaganda, the overseers leaked information that the portal doors would be opened so a secret emissary could travel between worlds, but in fact, no such visit had been planned. Instead, all the portals were reconfigured to lead only to the Luminan cell. In a stunning victory, all newly recruited rebel fighters, along with Claff 8, were captured. The Terrorian curator turned his weapon on himself, rather than become a prisoner. Many of the other fighters broke down and told the Luminans everything they knew about the military operation. Claff 8's allies were taken into custody and, after cross-examination, found guilty of treason and put to death.

Special Luminan troops traveled to each realm to restore order. A substantial amount of blood continued to be shed during the following half century, while Lumina battled to regain control of all the Libraries of Illumination. Once peace was established, new curators who swore loyalty to the College of Overseers were put into place, and the portals sealed. The Two Millennia War had ended, but would never be forgotten, especially by those realms that suffered the deepest losses. (For more information, refer to "The New Epoch" by Summeria 15.)

"Do you think the Terrorians still hold a bit of a grudge against the overseers?" Jackson asked.

"It's possible, although that was a very long time ago."

"Nero 51's living room had piles of stuff that looked like rocket launchers. They were huge."

"Did he say anything when he put you behind the force field?"

"Ik, ik, glug."

"Helpful."

"You asked."

"Mal is pretty sure they're counterfeiting obelisks to buy weapons, which would give credence to your observation of a stockpile of heavy artillery. Did you get a peek into any of the other rooms of the residence?"

"No. He slammed me inside that force field pretty quickly. And a moment later, you began banging on the door. Except, now that I think of it, I did see something that looked like a TV screen on the wall that he momentarily 'ik, ik, glugged' into. It may be some sort of communications device."

"I wonder if there's a book downstairs on the Terrorian language."

"Why? Are you planning to say 'how do you do' in Terrorian?"

"I'd like to know how they say words like *weapons, war, counterfeit,* and *invasion,* so that I'll know if they're talking about something other than literature."

"Well, if you're going to use the elevator, I'm going to stay behind. And if you're not back within a half-hour, I'll lasso the hook in *our* cupola and dial up the College of Overseers."

"Maybe I'd better take a flashlight and Mal's diary with me."

"You think Mal has a better chance of helping you than I do?"

"No. But I think he's an excellent backup plan."

Johanna checked the computer for a book on Terrorian language and syntax, and found one listed on sublevel fifty-six. "Fifty-six must be the Terrorian level."

She grabbed what she needed, and Jackson followed her down to the basement and watched as she twisted the light fixture.

"The way I figure it," Jackson reasoned "it should only take you one minute to get down there, three minutes to find the book, and another minute to get back up. After that, I'm calling in the troops."

"You promised me a half-hour—a few minutes ago."

"Just hurry."

Johanna entered the elevator. Before she could slide the scissor-gate shut, the lights blinked.

"See what I mean?" Jackson added.

"I'll be back before you know it."

* * *

A REALM AWAY, a society of select Terrorians met in secret. One member of the group, Zor 114, discussed how they might be able to hack into the portals and take control of their operation. He attempted a demonstration, but after a promising flash, it failed.

During those attempts, the power on twelve different worlds ... blinked.

JOHANNA FOUND THE language primer quickly and hurried back up to sub-level six. Jackson awaited her there, as promised.

"Four minutes. Not bad. Let's go back upstairs. For some reason, this place is giving me the creeps."

Johanna cracked open the book, thankful for another Level Zero designation. Jackson sat down next to her and read aloud from the middle of the page. "Ik, ock, uk: *I am; you are; he, she, or it is*. What are all these funny symbols?"

"The conjugation of ik, ock, uk, written in Terrorian."

"While you were down there, you should have looked for a Terrorian-English dictionary."

"Yeah. Why don't you just go download one on the iPad while I study this."

"Good one." He sat back and closed his eyes.

Johanna turned to the back of the book to see if a word list or glossary existed. She found what she wanted and looked up *weapons*. "Ergat."

"You gargling?"

"I'm saying the word for *weapon*. Ergat."

"That's an easy one. Wyatt Earp carried a gun. Mobsters called a gun a gat. 'Er' for Earp, 'gat' for gun."

She marveled at Jackson's ability to make anything

sound simple. "Cru."

"What's that?"

"*War.*"

"Okay, war is cruel. Just cut off the end. What's it say for 'counterfeit'?"

"Nothing. There's no listing in here for fake, phony, or even bogus."

"There's got to be some equivalent."

"Noh."

"There has to be."

"I didn't say 'no'—n-o—I said 'noh'—n-o-h—which means 'copy' or 'reproduction.'"

"Oh. That's a 'noh'-brainer."

She sighed, although the corners of her mouth turned up a little. "Guz."

"Does that mean they're going to cut out your gizzard and guzzle your blood?"

"Close. It means 'invade.'"

"What's the future tense of 'ik, ock, uk'?"

Johanna turned back the pages. "Iki, ocko, uku, ikin, ockon, ukin."

"Rhymes with ..."

"Stop it."

"Okay. If you hear someone say, 'Ikin guz,' it means we will invade."

"Porg."

"We will invade pork?"

"Porg means 'portal.'"

"How do you say 'takeover'?"

She turned the pages. "There's nothing listed for 'takeover,' but there is 'seg.'"

"What does that mean?"

"'Seize.' So if I hear anyone say, 'Ikin seg porg,' I'll know they're planning to seize the portals."

As Johanna tried to commit words to memory, Jackson made up little mnemonic devices to help her absorb them. She laughed at his attempts because they sounded goofy, but had to admit they actually helped her learn Terrorian.

"Do you know this one?" he asked. "Bli z' Bril."

"Cold?"

He smiled. "If you're talking about your answer, it *is* cold. 'Bli z' Bril' means 'Library of Illumination' in Terrorian."

WHEN THE CLOCK struck nine, Johanna kicked Jackson out. "Go home. You've got school tomorrow, and I've got to rest up so I can spend the day learning about Terroria and tying up loose ends here at the library."

"I'm thinking of taking tomorrow off."

"Don't. I need the time to get stuff done."

"I can help you."

"You can help me after school. We didn't get back here until around eleven on Friday night, so they won't be coming for me until late tomorrow. If you come straight after school, we'll have plenty of time to go over everything you'll need to do here while I'm away."

He made a face at her.

She pulled him over and kissed him. "Really, it's going to be all right."

"I hope so."

NORMALLY, JOHANNA DIDN'T mind Monday mornings, but this one filled her with anxiety. She dressed quickly and made herself a huge breakfast. She would be taking protein bars to Terroria to help her keep up her energy, but she wanted to make sure that she ate several hearty meals before leaving Exeter. Earth. Fantasia. Realm

Eleven. *Whew.* Everything she had learned in the past seventy-two hours boggled her mind.

She crammed everything she thought she'd need in her backpack, and placed it by the circulation desk. She packed Mal's diary, but then unpacked it to ask a question.

"Mal, if I leave Jackson my diary, will he be able to read it the way I can read yours, and ask questions?"

His words crawled across the page: *A curator has the ability to read the diary of either a mentor or a protégé.*

She grabbed her diary and quickly scanned it. Mal had given it to her when she became his protégé. She placed it on the circulation desk.

"How will I know if Jackson asks a question? Will I be able to see it?"

You will sense it. And once you consciously think of the answer, it will appear in your diary. It will be a mostly one-way conversation, however, because Jackson will have no way of knowing if you are trying to reach him.

"Thanks, Mal." She closed his diary and slipped it in her backpack. She kept busy for the rest of the day by doing chores around the library and memorizing as much Terrorian language and lore as possible.

"How's it going?"

She jumped when she heard Jackson's voice. "Is it that late already?"

"I had to ask Old Man ... uh ... Mr. Benson for the next few days off to take care of the library, and I asked if I could leave an hour early so you could *mentor* me. He's so happy about all the positive feedback he's getting about our community-service project that he was happy to oblige. It's like being a superstar. I can get anything I want right now."

"Help me with my Terrorian. Even better, sit down, relax, and think back to when Nero 51 grabbed you. I need you to tell me everything. What you saw, what you felt, what you smelled, what you heard."

"I thought we already went over all that?"

"You said he spoke to someone. Can you recall what he said?"

"I'll need to close my eyes for this."

Jackson sat on the sofa and put his head back. He envisioned the tentacles pulling him into the residence. He recalled the acrid, metallic smell—like a chemical lab—and while most of the Terrorian library was merely hazy, he remembered the residence contained an oily mist rising from the floor.

"It smelled really bad, like a solvent mixed with rotten eggs. I could actually taste it when I inhaled, but then he picked up a weapon and shot me, and I didn't really think about it after that."

"You didn't tell me he shot you."

"He didn't shoot me with bullets or arrows or anything like that. He shot me with a force field that locked me in place."

"What did the weapon look like?"

"Like all the other weapons piled up against the wall."

"How many were there?"

"A hundred, maybe? Didn't you see them?"

"I was too focused on getting you out of there."

"Yeah, well, if we hadn't made a run for it before Nero 51 returned, he would have probably used the same weapon on you."

"So their weapons can immobilize any enemy without killing them?"

"Yeah."

"Which means they want them alive."

"Yeah."

"Why?"

"Dinner? Slavery? Maybe they want people to work the mines. Or maybe, they want to brainwash them and turn them into soldiers, so their own people don't get killed on the front lines."

"The front lines ..."

"Yeah. I think they're planning something big. I didn't know what 'cru' meant at the time, but I'm sure Nero 51 said it to the communication device."

"Did he use the word *tec*?"

"Maybe. I don't remember. What does it mean?"

"'Spy.'"

"Did you learn anything touristy, like 'I'm thirsty' or 'where is the bathroom'?"

"No." She looked them up. "There is no word for 'thirsty.' Apparently Terrorians absorb liquid from the air." She thumbed through the book for several minutes while Jackson quietly looked on. "Ewww. They don't have bathrooms, either. That thick, hazy vapor is their 'waste product,' which is discarded through their feet. We walked through that stuff."

"Everyone walked through that stuff, including the overseers."

"This is going to be the longest three days of my life."

"You'd better pack a roll of toilet paper."

Johanna slumped back against the cushions.

Jackson picked up her hand. "I'll be with you every step of the way. I won't stop thinking about you until you return."

"Oh." She jumped off the sofa to fetch her diary. She handed it to him. "This is my diary. It has a lot in it about how things work in the library. If you're stuck and need to ask me a question, write it in the diary on the last page. I'll sense it and can tell you the answer if I know it. Check it often, even just to ask how I'm doing, so I can answer you, or else there's no way I can stay in touch with you."

"What about Mal's diary?"

"I'm taking it with me."

"What if they take it from you?"

Her eyes widened with alarm. "Do you think they'll do that?"

"If they think it's important to you, they might. If they think they can get secret information about our library, they might."

"I never thought of that. Maybe I should leave it here."

"Why don't you ask Mal?"

WHEN JOHANNA POSED the question, Mal did not reply, but she felt the diary shrinking in her hand. It finally stopped when it was a half inch wide and three-quarters of an inch long. A small, metal loop grew out of one corner, and a little glass peephole appeared in the front. She raised it to her eye and saw her last entry. "Mal, do you hear me?"

She peeked inside and saw the word *Yes*.

"I'll be right back." She practically flew up the stairs and went straight to her jewelry box. She returned with a gold chain that she attached to the book and then placed around her neck, slipping the tiny tome under her tee shirt. She smiled at Jackson. "I feel better, now."

He picked up Johanna's diary and slipped it in his back pocket. "Don't worry about me. I don't need a shrinking diary. I'll just carry you around au naturel."

The clock struck eight. And Johanna's stomach rumbled. "Pizza?"

"Okay. Relax. I'll run out and get it. You're getting a little jumpy."

"I'll call it in" she said, picking up her cell phone. As soon as Jackson left, she stuck the phone in her pocket. She sat on the sofa and closed her eyes.

Ω *This is no time to sleep, Johanna Charette. Your sentence has begun.*

—LOI—

C:L◈ I

CHAPTER TWENTY-ONE

A MOMENT LATER, Johanna and Overseer Plato Indelicat stood in front of the circulation desk on Terroria. Nero 51 was nowhere in sight. The overseer rang a large brass bell attached to the front of the desk.

"Uk infi," Nero 51 stated as he entered the area. The overseer waved his hand to enact a translation enchantment. *You're late.*

Ω *I have delivered Johanna Charette to you at the appointed hour. She is here to work off her sentence under the rules of the Arkan Peace Treaty, ratified after the Two Millennia War. She is to be treated in a civilized manner in accordance with her species, which is human. I will inspect her quarters, now.*

Nero 51 led the overseer to a small storage room toward the back of the library. It was empty except for the oily mist rising from the floor. The overseer waved his hand, and the mist vanished. A cot appeared, as well as a small sink and a toilet.

"You give preferences," Nero 51 practically shouted at him.

Ω I am giving her the minimum accommodations necessary for her species.

He turned to Johanna.

Ω This room will serve you for one-third of every twenty-four hour period that you are here. You may spend seven consecutive hours here in repose, and one full hour dividing the workday for your meal break. You have merely to say the word 'sustenance,' and a meal made up of foods common to Fantasia will appear on this table.

He waved his hand again, and a small table and a single chair appeared.

"You coddle the spy. Call me when she is ready to begin serving her sentence." Nero 51 left them alone.

Ω As you can tell, I have enacted a translation enchantment, so that you can understand what Nero 51 and his minions expect of you. I will be back in seventy-two hours to escort you home. Be Illuminated, Johanna Charette.

She dropped her backpack on the cot. The overseer disappeared, and Johanna found herself transported back to the front of the circulation desk. After waiting a moment, she rang the bell.

"You dare summon me."

"My sentence has begun."

A tentacle extended the width of the library to a utility closet and withdrew a rag and a jar of oily paste. "Polish the obelisks. If you dare to break one, you will be punished."

"I will need a ladder to reach the higher shelves."

"Find one," he snarled.

"I didn't want you to think I was snooping

around."

"Look in the utility closet."

"Thank you."

JOHANNA STARTED WITH the stacks to the right of the front door. She planned to work from top to bottom, but she wanted to determine what she was in for first. She selected an obelisk from a lower shelf. It was heavy, which she expected. The one that she had smashed had been just as heavy. As she opened the jar of paste, the noxious fumes nearly caused her to swoon. The odor resembled a cross between putrefied flesh and rotten fish, with a biting quality that stung her eyes and made them tear. She pulled her tee shirt up over her nose to filter the air, and did her best. The paste made the obelisks slippery, and she was afraid of dropping one, so when she climbed to the upper shelves, she tucked the obelisk inside her belt. She also learned a drop of polish went a long way, so she used as little as possible.

Johanna worked mindlessly, but the constant climbing to retrieve crystals made her back and knees ache. It didn't help that the Terrorian day started just when her day should have been ending. She had been at it for hours, and relief washed over her when she heard a voice out of nowhere say, Ω *Johanna Charette, you may take a one-hour meal break.*

She returned to her room and lay down on the cot. It turned out to be more comfortable than it looked. She thought back to Nero 51 accusing the overseer of coddling her, and wondered if it was true. It took a while before she felt her back muscles relax. She remained on the cot for a half-hour, then sat at the table and said, "Sustenance." A plate filled with carrots and peanuts appeared before her, as well as an old-fashioned tankard. She picked up the cup and sniffed. *Apple juice.* She consumed everything the overseers provided, and slipped a protein bar in her pocket.

Hardly a moment had passed when a voice said, Ω *Return to work.*

By the end of the day, she had polished most of the obelisks along the outer walls of the first story. It had been a massive effort, but hardly enough to make a small dent in the number of crystals in the building. She silently kept track of how many times she saw Nero 51. He spent a great deal of time in the antechamber and the residence, and she only saw him every couple of hours, when he would cross from one space to the other.

At the rate she was polishing obelisks, she would never reach the second level, or the curator's residence. She hoped to get a peek inside, or at least to eavesdrop on some snippet of conversation, but she may as well have been on an iceberg off the coast of Siberia, for all the good her proximity to the Terrorian war effort was doing.

BACK ON FANTASIA—as Jackson now liked to call it— sudden demands on his workload kept him on his toes. It started when the president of the library's board of directors called and demanded to speak to Johanna.

"She's out of town," Jackson explained.

"What do you mean, 'out of town'? We have no record of a request for time off."

"Her grandmother ... is dying," the teen fudged.

"Oh. Well. Who's taking her place?"

"I am, sir."

"And who are you?"

"Jackson Roth, Johanna's assistant." He paused. "You must know about me. I'm her curator-in-training. Just ask any of the overseers of the Library of Illumination

... uh ... foundation."

"Aren't you just a kid?"

"I'm the curator-in-training."

"Well, *Mr. Curator-In-Training*, some of the libraries in our neighboring communities are impressed with our facility's new information retrieval system. I've invited about two dozen of them to view a live demonstration of it on Thursday evening."

"No," Jackson said.

"Yes," the president of the board of directors stated emphatically. "I'm sure you can find money in your budget for some coffee and cookies. If we play our cards right, we could be named 'Library of the Year.' It's an honor that I would hate to see snatched away from us by a less prestigious facility that's still operating in the dark ages. We would be forced to *cut jobs* if that were to happen, if you get my drift."

"Right. A demonstration for a couple dozen people, with snacks, on Thursday evening," Jackson confirmed.

"At seven."

"Gotcha."

Click.

How hard can it be? He had helped Johanna set up evenings like this before. Clear out the furniture, set up some chairs, call the gourmet food shop in the village for coffee and cookies. *Easy peasy.*

He thought about the demonstration. How would he show all those people how easily the system worked? A large-screen TV would allow him to illustrate his workflow.

He called the president of the board of directors back.

"What is it?" The man sounded a little snarky.

"This is Jackson Roth, the curator-in-training at the Library of Illumination. There's the matter of a large-screen TV. I need one to stream our new digitized system, so your guests can see how well it works. Unfortunately, the library board rejected our request last fall. I'm so sorry, but that oversight will prevent me from demonstrating the system."

"What?"

"No TV, no ability to live stream my digital demonstration."

"That is not an option. Order the damn TV."

"Plus installation, of course."

"Just do it."

Jackson smiled. *This management stuff is easy.* He called The Guys Next Door—an appliance store in the village—and explained what he needed.

"What's the P.O. number?"

"We don't have a P.O. box. I'll give you the street address."

"Not post office—*purchase order*. What's the purchase-order number?"

"I'll have to get back to you." Jackson put down the phone and began to pace. It helped him think. Unfortunately, he lacked the experience or knowledge necessary to continue. *Johanna's diary.* It was right there in his back pocket. He dredged up a memory of her using it to contact Mal. He wrote down the words as he said them. "Johanna, how to you get a P.O. number?" *It stands for purchase order,* he added, just in case she was confused.

JOHANNA HEARD JACKSON's voice in her head.

She said aloud, "Why do you need a purchase order?"

After a minute she heard Jackson reply, "The president of the library board told me to get a TV for a demonstration that he's scheduled here. The Guys Next Door asked for a P.O. number."

"There's a pad in the top right drawer of my desk that says 'purchase order' on it. They're pre-numbered. Fill out the next blank page. Take the top copy to the president of the library board for his signature, then give it to The Guys Next Door."

"Thanks," she heard him say. "How are you doing?"

"It's okay. The overseers are making sure I'm treated humanely."

"Anything you need?"

"Diet Coke with ice."

"Right."

Her evening meal seemed astonishingly similar to chicken soup—at least, she hoped it was made out of chicken. It contained meat and a variety of vegetables, accompanied by something that looked like bread that had been run over by a truck. Surprisingly, her tankard held beer. She had never been much of a beer drinker, but after the day she had endured, it quenched her thirst.

She lay down on the cot to contemplate her next move, and felt something poking her—her cell phone. She switched it off and stuck it in her backpack. She would have no use for it here. The next thing she knew, the voice in her head warned her that her workday would begin in twenty minutes.

DAY TWO SEEMED tediously comparable to day one. After her midday break, Johanna saw Nero 51 go up to the second floor, followed by several other Terrorians. *I believe I'll continue polishing obelisks on the outer walls before working my way in to the interior stacks. Since I'm done down here ...*

She climbed up to the next level and began working on the crystals that lined the shelves next to the residence. She couldn't hear a word they said, which was really disappointing. *Maybe when they're done.* With luck, they would continue their conversation as they exited the apartment, and she would learn something of value.

Johanna's stomach growled. She pulled a protein bar from her pocket, but before she could remove the packaging, the door to the residence slid open. She shoved the bar behind the obelisks and grabbed a rag, polishing the closest crystal.

NERO 51 FUMED when he saw Johanna near his residence. *This Fantasian is nothing but trouble.* He wished he could delay his meeting until after she left, but the very fact she was on Terroria was the only thing keeping the portals from being permanently sealed. *We must be ready by tomorrow.* He cursed the overseers for putting a translation enchantment on his library. He would have to contact his followers and demand a night meeting at an outside location. They must prepare. He would be forced to leave the girl alone on the premises; however, anything she learned would not matter once they claimed victory.

He waited until she retreated to her room for the evening. Once he heard her door latch in to place—a precaution taken by the overseers—he walked to the front entrance and hit a switch on a control panel. Giant fans that blew warm, humid air into the library stopped running. *No use wasting precious humidity on the Fantasian.*

JOHANNA'S *SUSTENANCE* CONSISTED of a fish cake and

a hill of beans. *Edamame*. She thought of the protein bar that she had left on one of the shelves outside the residence. She held her breath as she opened her door, praying Nero 51 was not out inspecting her work. She popped her head out just in time to see him disappear out the front door.

Something struck her as odd. The mechanical sound that droned day and night suddenly stopped. She wondered what it meant.

NERO 51 ENTERED Building 7, a neighboring structure at the end of the block. Almost everyone he contacted had already assembled there. "Where is Heil 66?"

"Printing maps of the realms. They must be ready by morning."

Nero 51 nodded. "Before dusk tomorrow, our teams should be ready to amass outside each portal. They must be indistinguishable from the library patrons I have invited to a special fundraising event in the cupola. There should be no reason to question anyone being there."

The gathering had originally been organized as a bona fide meeting, and it proved to be fortuitous planning after the teenagers from Realm Eleven breached the portals. Nero 51 decided at the outset that the Fantasians were too young and stupid to be spies. His accusations were deliberately intended to keep the portals open, until Terrorians could use them to invade the other libraries. He knew the overseers would impart *justice*.

"You could not have planned better," Opel 29 stated. "If we had dialed the overseers as originally planned, they may have suspected our motives. Instead, we are reacting to an external intrusion, and the element of surprise will be ours."

Operation Final Darkness would begin in less

than twenty-four hours.

THE LEVER TO the residence was missing, just like when she had tried to rescue Jackson. She crossed her fingers. "Illumination." Nothing happened.

She took a deep breath. "Delumination." The door remained sealed.

She had never been within hearing distance when Nero 51 entered his apartment, yet something poked the back of her brain. For some reason, she conjured up an image of Jackson grinning. *What did he say?* She closed her eyes for a moment and scanned her memory for something he had said, which she should have known, but didn't.

Ahhh ... "Bli z' Bril."

The door vibrated as it slid out of the way. She tentatively entered the residence. The thick, oily mist inside the private quarters made her gag. She remembered what she had read about it and hated having to wade through it. A light would have been helpful, but she dared not use one, for fear of being caught. The building across the courtyard was lit, and let in just enough of a glow to illuminate the cache of weapons stacked against the wall. She did a quick count and moved into the next room. It also appeared to be filled with weapons, although it was difficult to tell because they obscured the window, eliminating it as a potential light source. The only reason why she could see at all was because the entry door remained open and the library proper was still illuminated.

She returned to the living room and looked for a desk. She found a short column shrouded in the haze that held several obelisks. It did not appear to have any drawers, and while she had taken the time to learn some Terrorian words, she had not learned the symbols that went with them, so she could not read the obelisks.

The room dimmed. Johanna glanced through the window and noticed the light from the other building had gone out. There was nothing more she could learn here. She slipped out the door, but it did not automatically close. "Bli z' Bril," she said aloud. As the residence door whooshed shut, the main door to the Library of Illumination creaked open. Nero 51 had returned, and Johanna stood immobilized—trapped—on the residence floor.

The Terrorian passed beneath her on his way to the curator's staircase. Johanna slipped to the front shelf that separated the apartment from the balcony overlooking the main reading room. If this library was a duplicate of her own, she'd find a tiny space between the end shelf and a front window. She scurried to it, pressed herself into the space, and held her breath.

"Bli z' Bril." *Swoosh.*

She waited for a second swoosh that would tell her the door had closed. She heard the latch snap into place, and quietly released her breath. *I just need to get to the staircase.* She waited a minute before stealthily sneaking to the spiral stairs. She had not paid attention to whether they squeaked, and prayed with each step she took. Downstairs, she hurried back to her room and heard the door latch loudly click into place. She wondered if Nero 51 heard it as well.

Johanna picked up Mal's diary. "What should I do if I found several rooms filled with weapons?" she whispered. She held the tiny book up to her eye and waited. After several minutes, a single line of type appeared.

Nothing. You are only there to serve out your sentence.

Johanna's face wrinkled. She thought the overseers wanted her to learn as much as she could about the Terrorian plot, but now Mal stated that she must merely serve her sentence. She slumped. *Did Mata Hari have to go through this?*

JACKSON ROLLED HIS shoulders. Even with the help of the dumbwaiter, removing enchanted books from the most accessible stacks turned out to be a back breaker. He had worked well into the evening, and had conked out on the sofa in the main reading room.

He spent most of the following morning re-populating the shelves with the old unenchanted books they had stored in the basement. *Good thing we never sold these back to Bebe's Bibliothèque.* He was almost done when he heard someone banging on the front door.

"Are you from The Guys Next Door?" It was a dumb question. Their uniforms had the company name emblazoned across them, and they stood next to a huge box decorated with a full-size picture of a sixty-inch flat-screen TV.

"Yeah. Where do you want it?"

Jackson surveyed the library. In the back of his mind, he had always thought it would be cool to have a TV rise out of the back of the circulation desk, but that would require special cabinetry. And a budget (he had learned about the importance of budgeting when he opened the petty-cash box the day before and found only $11.45 for coffee and cookies. The bill was actually four times that amount, and he ended up paying the difference with his own money). Regardless, the circulation desk seemed like the most logical place for a TV. "Put it here, facing those chairs."

"You got an antenna or cable hookup back here?"

It was another one of those questions he didn't know the answer to. "You go ahead and unpack it while I find out." He consulted Johanna's diary in the antechamber. He didn't want the repairmen to think he was some kind of nut when he asked it a question.

OUTSIDE THE TERRORIAN library, Heil 66 lumbered along, hidden in the shadows of the building across the way. He had been delayed making maps for the war effort, and needed to leave them for the troops gathering in Building 7. He saw Nero 51 reenter the library and knew he had missed that night's meeting. Seconds later, he saw a fleeting shadow in a second-floor library window. Nero 51 was strong, but not necessarily quick. Heil 66 doubted his compatriot could have reached the upper level so swiftly. He watched, waiting. The shadow appeared a second time, several minutes after the first darkening. The mapmaker waited to see if anyone would emerge from the Library of Illumination. Anyone trying to escape the building would have to use the front door, because the rear entrance had been sealed shortly after the start of the Two Millennia War and had never been reopened. The night was raw, and Heil 66 wrapped his unoccupied tentacles around his body to keep his moist emissions from evaporating.

An hour elapsed. There had been no further shadows nor disturbances of any kind, so the Terrorian continued on his journey. *It's probably nothing.* Still, as he hurried along to Building 7, he made a mental note to mention the shadows to Nero 51.

—LOI—

C:L ✦ I

JOHANNA SAT AT the edge of her cot staring into space. Jackson's voice broke the silence. "Do we have a cable hookup or TV antenna near the circulation desk?"

She had no idea, but she knew where to find the information. She asked Mal's diary. She waited several minutes for an answer.

No need. Any device inside the library will wirelessly absorb any transmission signals. Just plug it in and let it warm it up. No further setup is required.

She relayed the message to Jackson, wondering what she would find when she returned to the library. *My library.*

That night, Johanna slept restlessly. Her only solace was that at the end of her sentence, she could burrow beneath the blankets of her own bed.

Finally she fell asleep, but could not escape her

dreams.

She worked feverishly in the cupola of the Terrorian library, trying to clean obelisks. Every time she reached for one, it floated away. Nero 51 had ordered her to clean them all, or she would not be allowed to leave the Twelfth Realm. With her future at stake, Johanna chased the crystals around the cupola, trying to grab them, but as soon as she wrapped her fingers around one, it fell to the floor and shattered.

She panicked, sweat oozing from her pores. She tried picking up the broken pieces, but could barely see them through the hazy mist. Perspiration made her hands slippery, and the shards she found slipped through her fingers, cutting her hands and making them bleed. She managed to push the pieces off into a misty corner where she hoped they would not be discovered. She reached for another obelisk, but again, it eluded her. Try as she might, she could not grab on to it.

"Did I hear an obelisk break?" roared Nero 51.

She was so startled by his sudden appearance, her arm hit the shelf, and several of the crystal manuscripts crashed to the floor.

"She is willfully destroying library property," he shouted. "Off with her head."

Two other Terrorians appeared behind him, their tentacles snaking toward Johanna, to take her into custody. She tried to grab an

obelisk to hurl at her captors, but the crystals
continued to evade her grasp. Finally, she
snatched one out of the air and hurled it
at one of the Terrorians, but it bounced off
his chest and dropped to the floor, where it
bounced again, but didn't break. Amazement
overcame her. Instead of continuing her
attack, she dove for the unbroken obelisk. It
was fashioned out of a plastic-like material
that looked like the crystal obelisks but was
indestructible. "Counterfeits," she screamed.
"Fakes. Noh-nohs."

"Kill her now!"

Johanna felt a tentacle wrap around
her throat. Another held her wrists while a
third bound her feet. She gagged.

Ω *The workday will begin in twenty minutes.*

Johanna's eyes flew open. She reached for her
throat. The chain attached to Mal's diary had tangled
around her neck. She pulled it loose, got out of bed, and
splashed water on her face. *It was a dream.* She dropped
down onto the chair. "Sustenance." A bowl of cold gruel
and an apple appeared. The gruel had no taste, but it
filled her stomach and stopped it from growling. The
apple, at least, had flavor. She also received a tankard of
weak tea, but no honey or sugar to sweeten it. She drank
it to quench her thirst, knowing she had only one bottle
of water left.

The dream haunted her. She thought of the obelisk
that would not break. If the Terrorians had counterfeits,
where would they be? Not on a shelf where anyone could
find them. More than likely, they would be on a shelf that
no one looked at. *The Cupola?* True, it was a seldom-used

area of the library, but it meant carrying heavy obelisks up five flights of stairs. The least likely place would be among the main-floor stacks, the ones closest to the back wall, by the antiquities.

She berated herself for being so predictable. The obelisks she had polished were the most visible ones. Maybe today she would pick up a clue by investigating the ones buried in the stacks.

She exited her room. Nero 51 stood at the circulation desk, placing glass microscope slides into a box. *That can't be right.* They looked like microscope slides, but Johanna had a hunch they were documents of some sort.

She went to the utility closet and grabbed a rag and the jar of oily paste. She could feel Nero 51's eyes boring into the back of her head as she walked to an interior shelf and started polishing.

THE CURATOR SLIPPED the last bit of glass into a padded box. Time was of the essence, and he could not stop to bother about the girl, even though she was a nuisance. *Let her clean obelisks. She's not going to find anything. Even if she does, it's too late.*

He picked up the box and walked out the front door, switching off the humidity fans as he passed by. Terrorian soldiers awaited the information he carried—detailing the different realms, their curators, and the conditions rebel troops might face on each world. They had less than twenty-four hours to review maps and other forms of intelligence and complete their war preparations.

Nero 51 had grown up learning about the Two Millennia War and dreaming about the part he could have played in it. He imagined winning the war and being proclaimed "Grand Guardian of all the Libraries," a master of twelve different worlds—thirteen if you counted Lumina, the home of the Board of Overseers. He desired ultimate rule, and he would not allow some insignificant human female from Fantasia to disrupt his plans. *Johanna Charette, curator of the Eleventh Realm, I will make sure you are taken alive. I want to watch you being tortured. Yours will be a slow, painful death that will give me great pleasure.*

JACKSON ENTERED JOHANNA'S apartment. He felt uncomfortable being in her residence without her. He had debated asking her diary where he could find a blanket and a pillow, but didn't want to write something that might distract her—in a bad way. He knew they had to be there. Casanova had used them.

He stopped in front of two closed doors. He'd seen them during his previous visits to her home. He selected the one on the left and entered her private sanctuary. A four-poster bed dominated the space, and the comforter that topped it looked so fluffy, Jackson knew if he lay down on it he would sink halfway to the floor in a cloud of goose down. He looked around the room. Additional closed doors beckoned him. He pulled one open and found an en suite bathroom with a huge built-in tub. Creamy-white pillar candles decorated the back ledge, and he imagined them flickering, their light reflecting on the polished marble walls and mirrored surfaces while Johanna soaked in a mountain of bubbles. *No blanket or pillow in here.*

He pulled open the second door. It contained an L-shaped walk-in closet filled with very few clothes. Johanna dressed nicely, but he knew she didn't splurge on clothing the way Cassie and Brittany did. He sniffed.

Her closet smelled just like her—baby powder and roses. He looked at an empty hanging rod. *If I ever move in with Johanna, there's plenty of space for my stuff,* he thought, then shook his head. *Talk about a pipe dream.*

He walked back into the hallway and opened the other door. It was a linen closet, and sitting on the upper shelf, right at eye-level, he found a blanket and pillow. In the back of his mind he knew they would be there, but if he had opened that door first, he would not have had an excuse to explore her bedroom. *Tour over.* He grabbed the linens and carried them downstairs.

Jackson stretched out on the sofa. All he had left to do was test the visual presentation he had created for the group of visiting librarians, but that could wait until morning. *I've got it all under control,* he thought, before rolling onto his side and falling asleep.

JOHANNA NOTICED THE sudden silence when Nero 51 exited the building.

She continued polishing obelisks, but soon realized if she wanted to find what she sought, it would make more sense to pick the crystals up and hope the fakes felt different. She calculated fifty or sixty obelisks on each shelf, and hundreds of shelves. Thousands, even. She also had to consider the private book rooms, antiquities, erotica, periodicals ... she rubbed her temples as she felt the beginnings of a headache. *What if they're on a sub-level?*

She heard the front door open. She dipped a rag in the wax and polished another obelisk.

"Nero 51, are you here?"

"I told you he wouldn't be here," a second voice said. "He's probably already at Building 7."

"Where's the Fantasian creature? Shouldn't she

be here? I want to get a look at her. I hear she's hideous."

Johanna could hear the Terrorians flat feet slapping against the floor. She continued polishing.

"Oh. Here she is."

"What a pathetic little beast."

"I know. But she's the key to our victory. The portals wouldn't be open if she weren't here."

"Shhh!"

"She can't understand us. I doubt she can speak Terrorian."

"Just hold your tongue. Anyway, there's nothing for us here. Let's go meet the others."

Johanna focused on their words. *The portals are open because I'm here. And I'm the key to their victory.* When she heard the door open, she peeked around the edge of the stacks and watched them leave. She began grabbing obelisks at random, hoping to find one that would prove to be false. She wanted to be able to give the Board of Overseers the proof they needed. Unfortunately, the obelisks all looked alike, so she had to pay very close attention to make sure she made progress.

Ω *Johanna Charette, you may take a one-hour meal break.*

She finished the shelf she'd been working on and left her cleaning supplies there, so she would know where she left off. She needed sustenance, and she wanted to tell Mal what the Terrorians had said. She choked down dense, grainy bread with some kind of vegetable mash, and followed it with orange juice. *This cuisine will never earn a Michelin star.*

She detailed what she had heard in Mal's diary. "What should I do?"

She waited quite a while before a reply appeared. *Nothing. You are only there to serve out your sentence.*

She gritted her teeth. Her jaw clenched so tightly it gave her a headache. *I should have brought aspirin.*

Johanna left her room and looked around the library. It didn't look like anyone was there. She grabbed the rag and paste and climbed up to the second level. She placed her ear against the door of the residence, listening for any sounds coming from within. She heard nothing, and quietly said, "Bli z' Bril." The door opened, and she ducked inside.

The light of day brightened the room, and she tried to estimate the number of weapons. They were piled everywhere. She grabbed one from an inconspicuous area and left, but froze outside the door to the residence, her mind racing. The quickest way to her room was down the curator's staircase, but if Nero 51 walked in, he would surely take those stairs. Her intuition told her to take the stone steps by the front door. They would provide more cover once she got there, and she could ditch the gun behind the steps if she heard anyone enter. Using them, however, would force her to run around the very visible second balcony to the opposite end of the library, and then past the circulation desk on the main floor. That would be too much time out in the open. The Terrorians would not think twice about killing her.

Stop wasting time. By now she could have run down the stairs and been safely back in her room.

She heard a noise in the outer vestibule. She sprinted down the spiral stairs with the weapon raised above her head so it would not bang against the handrail. As she reached the bottom step, the front door screeched open. *The "juvenile" stacks should shield me from view.* She prayed she wouldn't be seen darting past the gaps that allowed light to flow throughout the space.

When she got into her room, she threw the weapon under her cot, sat down, and said, "Sustenance." A bowl filled with yogurt appeared, a ripe peach and a cup of coffee beside it. She bit a huge chunk out of the peach and felt its juice run down her chin as her heart pounded. She could hear it quite clearly, even if it wasn't as loud as the pounding on her door.

—LOI—

C:L◈I

CHAPTER TWENTY-THREE

"Come in," she called out, as she stuffed a spoon of yogurt in her mouth.

"You're supposed to be working." Nero 51's eyes darted around the room.

"If the overseers told me my break was over, I would have heard them." Even as she said it, she racked her brain trying to remember if the message might have been drowned out by her escapade.

Ω *Johanna Charette, your break period has ended.*

The announcement came as if on cue. She bit into the peach again before standing up. "I guess I'll save this for later."

"You will not," Nero 51 said, grabbing the uneaten food in a tentacle and stretching it out the door and across the main reading room to dump it in a trash bin. "Get to work."

Johanna glared at him, but did not defy him. He

took one last look around the room, which made her heart pound. Plato Indelicat had removed the mist that might prevent Nero 51 from seeing the weapon, yet he did not comment on it. She worried that he *had* seen it but failed to mention it because he wanted her to lapse into a false sense of security. She had no recourse but to get back to polishing obelisks.

The hairs on the back of her neck suddenly stood on end. She had left the cleaning tools upstairs by the ladder. If Nero 51 saw them, he would know she had been snooping near the residence. She disappeared behind a stack and wondered what her next move should be.

JACKSON SHOT OFF the sofa when the television turned itself on at sunrise. He stumbled and then realized where he was. He looked to see if he had rolled over on the remote control, but found it on the circulation desk where he'd left it the previous night. He shut off the TV and walked around the library to make sure everything was secure. The main level seemed fine, and the public portions of the other levels appeared to be clear. Up in the cupola, he inspected the portal window he and Johanna had used. It looked sealed, but how could it be if Johanna had to use it to return home? The notion that Nero 51 and his pals could come flying through it at any given moment made him shiver. *Thank God Johanna's coming home tonight and the portals will be sealed.*

His imagination shifted into overdrive. What if a few Terrorians slipped through with her when she returned and held them hostage? Would the College of Overseers even know if that happened? *They would have to know. One of them will probably escort Johanna home.* The Terrorians would have to take the overseer hostage as well, and then everyone would know what had happened, because it would mean the beginning of a revolutionary multi-world war.

Stop it. You're making yourself crazy. Although, craziness might explain his sudden desire to buy a gun—just in case.

"HAVE YOU LOST your mind? Who do you think is going to sell a gun to a seventeen-year-old?" Logan bellowed over the telephone.

"Lots of people our age get guns. I hear about them all the time."

"It's illegal."

"All right. Forget I ever mentioned it."

"No. I want to know why you need a gun."

"What part of 'just forget it' don't you understand?"

"All of it."

"I've got to get back to work." Jackson disconnected the call. The phone rang almost immediately, but the teen ignored it when he saw Logan's name on caller ID.

Jackson spent the next hour perfecting the details for that night's presentation. Johanna would probably walk in, right in the middle of it. He froze. If the Terrorians were planning anything, all those poor little librarians would get caught in the crossfire. Talk about rotten timing. In his estimation, the library board had picked the worst possible night for a demonstration. *Maybe if I call the president of the board of directors, I can appeal to the man's better sense.* Jackson dialed the number and waited for the president's secretary to put him on the line.

"Is everything ready for tonight?"

No "Hello, Jackson, how are you?" No small talk of any kind—just a command disguised as a question.

"Sir, I'm thinking tonight is not the best night for

the presentation."

"Tonight is the perfect night for it. And it's the only night for it. Tell me, Jackson, do you *like* working at the library?" The teen shivered when he heard the thinly veiled threat with an icy-cold delivery.

"I only mentioned it because Johanna is returning tonight, and as curator, she'll be very disappointed she wasn't part of the event."

"That's what she gets for leaving town without notice." *Click.*

Jackson did not have time to react to the click, because someone started banging on the door. He checked the security camera and sighed. *Logan.* "Illumination." The door slid open.

"I had a devil of a time finding this place," Logan said. "I was sure I knew how to get here, but the streets all seemed to lead me in a different direction."

"Yeah, that happens," Jackson answered.

"So, why do you want a gun?"

"There may be some trouble here tonight. The library board wants me to give a demonstration, but some ... uh ... unsavory characters may show up."

"'Unsavory characters'? At this library? I think you're reading too many of these books and not spending enough time in the real world."

"You can't repeat that to anyone, you know. My job is on the line."

Logan knew how much Jackson's family depended on his paycheck—not that he made a lot of money, but every little bit helped. "Marcus Hurble."

"What about him?"

"I heard he has a couple of guns he wants to sell. That was last week. I didn't pay much attention, because I'm not interested in buying one. But he may still have one to sell. Do you want me to find out?"

"You can't tell anybody."

"Right. How much do you want to spend?"

Jackson counted the money in his wallet. It contained every cent he owned. He wanted to buy a car, and hoped by the time he turned eighteen he might be able to scrape together enough money to get a used one. He hated parting with his hard-earned cash, but if trouble broke out tonight and he wasn't prepared, he might not even be around for his eighteenth birthday. He counted out five hundred dollars. "Do you think this is enough?"

"How do I know?"

"Just make sure the gun works."

"I'm not shooting it."

"Well ... don't buy something you haven't heard of, you know?"

"So you want an UZI ..."

Jackson didn't answer.

"Fine. I'll be back as soon as I can."

"Ammo," the curator-in-training blurted out. "You know if you load it, you can hurt someone."

"That's the idea."

JOHANNA HEARD NERO 51's footsteps fade as he headed toward the antechamber. She waited a few minutes, to allow him to become totally engrossed in whatever he was doing, before dashing up the spiral stairs and grabbing the cleaning supplies. She then scurried up the ladder to retrieve the protein bar she had hidden the day before.

"Looking for something?"

The sound of Nero 51's voice gave her chills. "Yes. I forgot my protein bar up here yesterday, and since you wouldn't let me to finish my lunch today, I need it to relieve my hunger."

He stared at her hands. "I don't see any such thing."

She reached behind the obelisks and pulled out the bar. "This."

"You are here to work, not to eat." He grabbed the protein bar and put it in his pocket. "I believe you were working downstairs."

"Yes."

"Take the ladder with you."

He obviously did not want her working on the second floor. *Maybe this is where he's hiding the fakes.*

JACKSON PACED IN wide circles around the circulation desk. It seemed like hours since Logan had left. The curator-in-training's stomach growled, but he didn't want to leave the library to get lunch, in case his friend returned while he was out. *Instead of a car, I should get a cell phone. Then I could text him.*

"Argh." He hit himself in the head for being so stupid. He picked up the phone on the circulation desk and dialed Logan's cell number. "Where are you?"

"Piccolo Italia. A guy's gotta have lunch."

"Good. Bring me a meatball hero. I'm starving. Did you have any luck with ... you know?"

"Yeah. I'll be there soon."

"Okay. Hurry."

The ticking of the grandfather clock drove Jackson crazy. It was still early, but he felt like every minute stretched into an hour. He had practically worn a groove in the floor by the time he heard Logan banging on the door. His friend carried two bags, a white one from the pizzeria and a brown one, which must have held the gun.

Logan handed him the white bag. "Eat while I tell you about my little jaunt into the world of handguns."

Jackson ripped the wrapper off his sandwich. "Spill."

"Marcus Hurble has been arrested."

"While you were there?"

"No. Last night. The cops say he robbed a church poor box. Mrs. Krebs, that little old lady who lives across the street from the rectory, told police she heard a gunshot and thought someone killed Reverend Blake. She claims she saw Hurble leaving the church. Reverend Blake is fine, but Hurble had a gun on him when the cops picked him up, so they charged him."

"I thought you said you got me a gun?"

"I did, but not from Hurble. I got it from Larry at Once A-Pawn A Time."

"That guy's a nut job. You didn't tell him it was for me, did you?"

"I told him it I needed it for target practice. He took down all my info ... or I guess I should say, my older brother's. If you ever shoot someone with this gun, he'll be the one they send up the river, and my life won't be worth a damn."

"So show me."

"Oh. And by the way, you owe me twenty bucks."

"It cost that much?"

"No," Logan answered, sliding a black case out of the bag and unlatching it. Inside, a 9mm Glock and an empty magazine sat embedded in the box's foam lining. "The gun was four hundred ninety-nine dollars. The ammo is what put you over the top."

Jackson inspected the Glock. "Did he show you how to use it?"

"It's a pawn shop, not a firing range. So no, he didn't show me how to use it."

"Did he at least show you how to load it?"

"No, because he didn't have any nine-millimeter rounds in stock. I had to go to Buy-Mart for that."

Jackson tensed. "Anybody could have seen you getting bullets at Buy-Mart. That's where my mother shops."

"It's Wednesday afternoon. Your mom is working. Everybody's mom is working. So you can stop working ... up a sweat. Can I use the computer?"

"Why?"

"So we can find out how to load a gun you shouldn't own with bullets you shouldn't have."

"Go ahead."

Twenty minutes later, the gun was loaded and the safety was securely in place.

THE COLLEGE OF Overseers sat in an ancient chamber, considering their options.

       ☙ *The girl has confirmed the existence of weapons.*

       ❖ *Yes.*

       ■ *Do we have evidence of the sale of antiquities?*

       Ψ *No counterfeits have been reported.*

       Σ *Our hands are tied.*

       ♠ *The Terrorians will strike.*

       π *We cannot prevent them from taking action.*

       ❋ *We do have options.*

       § *Yes.*

       ☙ *We must turn on the resonator.*

       ★ *A visit to each of the realms is essential.*

       ◍ *We will begin immediately, with the exception of Terroria. Plato Indelicat will travel there at the appointed time and escort the girl back to her own world.*

       Ω *I do not see Pru Tellerence. Who will visit Dramatica?*

❖ *I will go to Dramatica. Stay illuminated, my brethren.*

IT WAS TIME for Johanna's seven-hour rest period. Upon its completion, she would be escorted home. *Why can't they just let me go home now?* She thought it, but she didn't really mean it. She needed the time to look for counterfeits.

She listened carefully for the telltale signs of Nero 51's departure. She could barely hear the squeak of the front door from her room, but when the giant humidifier stopped churning, she knew for sure he had gone. She asked for sustenance, and quickly ate the potato-and-bean soup provided. The tankard contained lemon-flavored water, which she was glad of, because beer would have slowed her down. She noticed a light go on in the building across the courtyard. *That must be Building 7.* She would have to keep checking to make sure the light did not go out while she investigated the residence floor.

TWO HOURS LATER, Johanna yawned. She had examined thousands of obelisks, and still hadn't found anything. Suddenly, she heard the humidifier fans sputter to life. She glanced across the vast opening in the center of the library and out the window. The light in Building 7 still burned. She dropped to the floor just as the front door opened, and dozens of Terrorians entered the library and headed toward her quarters.

Johanna did not hesitate. She stuffed the rag and paste in the back of the shelf and wriggled across the floor on her stomach. She heard feet slapping against steps as the Terrorians climbed the curator's staircase. Johanna rolled across the floor as fast as she could, straight into the old, stone stairwell adjacent to the front entrance.

She heard someone say, "Bli z' Bril." They were apparently more interested in Nero 51's residence than her quarters.

She crept down the stairs, but remained hidden in the stairwell. If she crouched in the dimly lit corner, she could watch the main part of the library, unobserved. Before long, she saw a parade of Terrorians carry weapons out the main entrance. They walked in unified precision, as if one brain commanded everyone's movement. Only one Terrorian at the end of the line marched a hair out of step. *He won't last long,* she thought. *They'll probably execute him for missing a beat.* By the time the last of them exited, those who had been at the front of the procession returned to transport even more weapons. She knew the retrieval of arms had ended when the humidifier again went silent.

Johanna wanted to contact Mal, but first, she needed to clean up loose ends. She climbed the stairs, and tried to remember which shelf she had hidden the rag and paste on. She grabbed them in haste, clumsily knocking over an obelisk. If anyone had been in the library, they would have heard her gasp. She could not afford to break another crystal and incite the wrath of Nero 51. She looked at it lying on its side, unbroken. *Curious.*

She picked it up. It felt as heavy as the others, but not in the same way. She picked up a second obelisk and immediately knew it was real. The crystal was uniformly heavy. But all the weight of the unbroken figurine was in the base. *I'm such a fool.* She had probably picked up dozens of fakes, but disregarded them because they had felt as heavy as crystal. She took the counterfeit back to her room and got out Mal's diary.

"Mal, I found a fake obelisk. It looks like crystal,

but I knocked it over by accident and it didn't break. What should I do?"

His answer did not arrive for more than an hour.

Nothing. You are only there to serve your sentence.

Mal could be so exasperating. Surely she could do something. She grabbed her backpack and looked for her cell phone. Her battery had lost a lot of its juice, but she only needed enough power to take a few pictures. She photographed the obelisk from several different angles, so she could describe it in her diary, which she knew Mal read regularly. She also took several pictures of the weapon she had ... uh ... confiscated. *Stolen is such an ugly word.*

She didn't know what else she could do. She looked at her phone—6:00 a.m. In two more hours, it would be time to return home.

JACKSON SLIPPED THE loaded gun in his waistband, just like he had seen on TV. *I hope I don't shoot off any body parts. That would be embarrassing. And painful.* Everything was ready to go.

R-R-R-I-I-I-N-N-N-G-G-G! He answered the phone. "Library of Illumination."

"Yeah. I'm from Delectable Comestibles. You placed an order?"

"Yes."

"Could you open the front door? I've been standing here for fifteen minutes and still haven't figured out how to get in."

"Illumination." The wall slid open. "Right in here," Jackson said, leading the man to a table he had dragged up from the basement. He had considered using the circulation desk for serving coffee, but the television took up a lot of space.

While the man set out the refreshments, Jackson switched on the TV to warm it up.

"That's it. Sign here." The caterer handed Jackson the invoice.

"Thanks." Jackson took a ten-dollar bill out of his pocket and tipped the guy. He was going broke as curator-in-training, and wished he had never pried open that stupid window.

THE SCREECHING SOUND of metal upon metal disrupted the silence in Libraries of Illumination on each of eleven worlds. Curators looked up to find their cupolas opening, and stared at the blinding light shooting up from their LOI medallions—straight through the sudden openings in their roofs. A moment later, the light went out as a member of the College of Overseers greeted each world's steward. Most of the curators expressed outrage when they learned Terrorians had stockpiled weapons and the threat of war was imminent.

HUNDREDS OF TERRORIAN soldiers amassed outside Building 7. They had been training all year for this moment, and were fired up. Nero 51 had promised them they would be handsomely rewarded for helping Terroria establish itself as the prime sovereign of the twelve literary worlds.

Inside Building 7, a quartermaster outfitted each Terrorian with a weapon and two crystals, one with their orders on it and another with a map of the library they were assigned to seize. The return of the Fantasian to her own world meant all the portals would be in a specific alignment, allowing the Terrorians to know which realm each portal would lead to.

In the courtyard, soldiers assembled into twelve

flanks, with three leaders at the head of each. Nero 51 emerged from Building 7 and stood in the middle of a wide loggia facing them.

"Terrorians. For many millennia, our realm has waited patiently to reclaim its position as prime sovereign of the Libraries of Illumination. It is an honor we held for two millennia, only to have it snatched away by a united force of rabble-rousers who refused to recognize our indomitable spirit and natural ability to lead. Nine worlds against our one forced us to sacrifice our position of power, if not our dignity.

"It has long been my dream to restore our great world to its true destiny as leader of all Libraries of Illumination." Nero 51 smiled in the strangled way in which Terrorians contorted their faces to impart any semblance of benign cordiality. "To succeed in our endeavor, we must do something that at first may seem reprehensible, but is ultimately necessary. Your primary objective is the destruction of every piece of documented literature in each of the libraries, as soon as you have secured the site. Once the other library systems have been wiped clean of all knowledge, their outlying books and papers will cease to exist. Their records will be eradicated. They will be devoid of all facts, fiction, figures, histories, music, art, plans, manuals, maps—any and all information that has ever been recorded will cease to exist for them. The compendium of universal literature on Terroria will be the only surviving resource for all our worlds, and will provide us with the ultimate power to rule the others—consummate knowledge.

"Maul 232, take our 'fundraisers' to the cupola, immediately. May I remind you that this is supposed to be a social event, so mingle amiably. When the time comes, you will find weapons inside my residence.

"Advance teams, prepare to take your places. We are moments away from glory. Use your weapons' force-field initiators to prevent our adversaries from detaining you. Humane conquest is the key to obtaining support. Those who yield to *our* ways will be *conditioned* to serve Terroria. However, there may be some who prefer to spill blood rather than accept the magnanimity of our governance.

"If you must, do not hesitate to use the Omicron Key." He turned a key on the side of his weapon and took aim at Heil 66. A black-and-white beam shot out of the armament, disintegrating the Terrorian. "Heil 66 claimed dedication to our cause, yet delayed giving me crucial information about a spy planted by the overseers in our library until just moments ago. He disregarded the prime directive, and has paid the ultimate price.

"If you must, eradicate all who resist."

—LOI—

C:L⟠I

CHAPTER TWENTY-FOUR

Overseers, except Pru Tellerence and Plato Indelicat, arrived at their designated realms carrying large, flat boxes containing translucent screens. The overseers did their best to calm the librarians by discussing their precautions against the possibilities of what might occur, but without overwhelming success.

"How could you allow this to happen?" most curators asked.

𝔖 *We did not allow this to transpire. We simply did not prevent it.*

Their answer confused the curators. The overseers sought to distract them by asking their help to position the screens across from the portals. The shiny, paper-thin attachments easily adhered to the walls, and once in place, could not be detected.

"What will that do?" one curator asked.

𝔖 *It will make the Terrorians reflect on their*

actions.

"From what I've read about Terrorians, they're not a species that embraces reflection. They have more of a 'kill first, ask questions later' attitude."

𝄢 *That, unfortunately, is accurate.*

JACKSON MOVED OUT of sight when he heard the cupola screech. Having witnessed it on Dramatica, he knew it meant the portals were opening. He should have been excited at the prospect of Johanna returning, but it was much too early. *If Terrorians are invading the library, I'm not going to be an easy target.* He slipped inside the coat closet and held his breath. Relief washed over him when he saw an overseer approach the circulation desk. Jackson walked out to greet him. "Where's Johanna?"

◉ *I am Selium Sorium. I'm here to assist in Johanna Charette's return.*

Someone pounding on the front door interrupted them. The overseer waved his hand, and the door slid open. The president of the library board of directors was on the other side, with his wife and a pair of librarians from a nearby village. The president stared at the overseer, then grabbed Jackson by the arm and pulled him out of earshot. "What the hell is this, a masquerade ball?"

Jackson pulled his arm away. "That man," he said, nodding at Selium Sorium, "is a very important member of this library's College of Overseers, and I suggest you don't insult him."

"If he's so important, why haven't *I* ever met him?"

Jackson felt momentarily bewildered until the answer formed in his consciousness. "You're in charge of development for the management and growth of the library. However, Mr. Sorium oversees its *literary* endowments. After all, there would be no library if there was no collection of literature."

As far as the board president was concerned, the word *endowment* was spelled M-O-N-E-Y. He glared at Jackson before he walked over to the elderly man in the odd costume and introduced himself.

Jackson smiled. *That should keep him out of my hair.* He turned to see a librarian lean over the top of the circulation desk and pick up a slender volume of *The Strange Case of Dr. Jekyll and Mr. Hyde.* It was a Level Two book that had just been returned that afternoon. "Excuse me," he said, as he rushed to her side and pulled the small book out of her hand before she could open it. "If you start reading that," he joked, "you'll never pay any attention to me. Why don't you find a seat up front? We'll be starting in just a minute."

"I was just looking for a little something to occupy my time."

Oh, it will keep you occupied, he thought. He stuffed the book in his jacket pocket and continued greeting guests, while keeping an eye on the crowd to make sure "curiosity did not kill the cat."

NERO 51 CHECKED his timepiece. It was time for Operation Final Darkness to commence. He raised his weapon into the air while pulling a sliding lever on its side, a feature not included on most of the other arms. Suddenly, everyone's weapon glowed with an eerie purple light.

"To the portals!" he cried.

THE LIBRARIANS IN the Fantasian reading room settled in for the presentation.

Selium Sorium nodded at Jackson.

The teen took his cue. "Good evening, everyone.

Are you ready to see how to convert your system into one that's designed for the twenty-first century?"

Some of the librarians applauded. One man shook his head and said out loud, "I hope this isn't a waste of time, because our system is already computerized." Other librarians whose organizations had also converted to computer nodded in agreement.

"I know most of you have already switched to online public-access catalogs. That's not what we're discussing. We're here to talk about wirelessly retrieving information from anywhere—a car, your back yard, or even a cruise ship at sea. Tonight, we're talking about serving our communities with cutting-edge technology. In today's society, the keyword is 'instant gratification.'"

Jackson used a remote control to bring the giant TV screen to life. It showed banks of library tables filled with sleek computers—with nary a book in sight. "These computers will access our library's full array of knowledge, as well as connect to online creative editing programs for video, photos, music, and text. We like to call it our 'digital hub.'" He took a deep breath. "And if we're very lucky, maybe we can talk the president of our board of directors into approving this." An image of a three-dimensional printer filled the screen.

Jackson saw the board president scowl, but forged ahead. "With our wireless and online capabilities *and* a 3-D printer, we can become *research central*—a think tank that fosters creativity, invention, and innovative solutions to take us into the future."

"What happens when your hard drive fails?" someone asked.

"Lock the doors," another person called out, inciting giggles and snickers.

"Here at the Library of Illumination, we save all

our information to multiple cloud servers, and retrieve it wirelessly using these." He waved an iPad in the air.

"Does that work when you've got no electricity or modem?" someone asked.

"It does if you have a mobile hot spot—which is easy enough to get."

The audience buzzed. Jackson grinned as he changed the slide and pointed to the screen. An image with a graphic about cloud computing appeared, and then pixilated before changing to video of a scary-looking alien with a huge weapon. Everyone laughed except Jackson and Selium Sorium, who immediately recognized a Terrorian soldier.

JOHANNA SAT ON the edge of her cot, wearing her backpack. Inside, she had packed the fake obelisk. She rebalanced the stolen Terrorian weapon, now braced against her shoulder. She almost abandoned her choice to use it when it started emitting a purple glow, but changed her mind when she heard the humidifiers roar to life.

The Terrorians embraced precision. Johanna had witnessed it when they marched in unison to recover the weapons stored in Nero 51's residence. It would not surprise her if the curator activated all the guns at the same time, resulting in the subtle purple light.

She took a deep breath. If anyone entered the room, other than an overseer, she planned to immobilize that person and everyone who followed. She didn't really know how the weapon worked, but it looked fairly straightforward; it had a wider end, a narrower end, and a double ring that reminded her of a partial eclipse, which she surmised was the trigger. She shivered—not because she felt cold but because she was anxious. *What if this thing doesn't shoot? What if they execute me? Who will take care of the library? What about Jackson? Is that why they made him a curator-in-training, because they already knew I wouldn't be returning?*

Her door suddenly opened, and without thought she pulled the trigger, and the weapon fired.

ON EVERY REALM, Terrorian advance teams dove through the portals with their weapons at the ready. A scout on each team stepped forward to survey the open space that exposed each library's aboveground levels, looking for signs of resistance. A second member of the team covered the scout, while the third warrior stood guard over the portal. On the other side of the openings, troops began amassing, ready to launch into battle. They stood poised, awaiting the go-ahead from the advance teams.

In most cases, the libraries were quiet. However, some exceptions existed.

OPEL 29 WAS motivated by the possibility of confrontation. Like many members of his species, his eagerness manifested itself as secretions from overactive glands—much like sweat. He signaled his Terrorian partners that they should hold their positions until he got an idea of what they might be up against. He leaned over the cupola walkway and was instantly stunned by what he saw. *How can this be?* Below sat an army of Fantasians, waiting to take them on. He wiped excess secretions from his brow with a tentacle, which sent a hail of minuscule droplets onto the people below. One of them turned to look up, and Opel 29 immediately jerked back.

"DO YOU HAVE a sprinkler system in here? I think it's leaking," a librarian said.

Jackson took a deep breath. "I'll go see what it is."

"Wait," the overseer said in a normal voice, rather than transferring his thoughts inside everyone's head. "These people are interested in what you have to say. I will check on the upper level."

"No," the president of the board of directors declared. "If anyone's going to check on the condition of this library, I'll do it." He pushed past the overseer and headed toward the cupola stairs.

◍ *Oh, dear.*

Jackson could hear the overseer's thoughts in his head.

◍ *This has "catastrophe" written all over it.*

THE FORCE OF the blast from the Terrorian weapon threw Johanna forward. She collided with Plato Indelicat, who grabbed the young woman to steady her. The wall behind the cot glowed. The overseer moved to touch it.

Ω *You have enveloped the wall in a force field.*

"Delumination," Johanna stated. The force field continued to glow.

Ω *The Terrorians have obviously reconfigured the key to their force fields.*

"Bril," Johanna tried.

Ω *Bril means "illuminate," not "deluminate." Dril.*

The overseer's attempt failed.

Ω *As I have said, they have altered the code for deactivating the shield. Little matter. The Terrorians will deal with it when they come back. It is time to go to the portal.*

Johanna picked up the weapon and turned it around. "At least now I know which end to aim."

Plato Indelicat warily eyed the young woman.

Ω *Be illuminated, Johanna Charette. There will be Terrorians on your world.*

* * *

THE LEADER OF the Terrorian advance team assigned to Dramatica descended to the main floor of the library. He could hear Furst humming in the antechamber. He twirled a tentacle in an upward spiral, motioning the others to begin moving through the portals to the cupola. A dozen soldiers had crossed when the Terrorian scout heard Furst push back his chair. His tentacle suddenly dropped, and the troops stilled, awaiting further instruction.

The team leader stepped back behind a shelf.

Furst's humming got louder as he approached the main reading room, but then ended in a series of sniffs.

The team leader readied his weapon.

Furst rounded the corner, and then he spotted the Terrorian. His red, curly hair pulled into tight, wiry corkscrews, and he flexed his knees.

The Terrorian aimed his weapon.

❖ *That is ill-advised.*

The words he heard did not deter the soldier from pulling the trigger.

ON EACH OF the worlds, curators experienced similar events. They had been instructed to go about their normal routines, while the overseers used an enchantment on themselves to shrink to the size of one of Johanna's protein bars. At that height, they looked more like figurines than people, and could often observe what was going on undisturbed. Even the curators disregarded the overseers' presence.

JACKSON FOUND IT difficult to concentrate as he continued his presentation to the librarians. He could hear the president stomping up the cupola staircase as it rose like a patinated metal helix through the five uppermost levels of the library. Every so often, the footsteps stopped as the president paused to catch his breath.

High above him, the Terrorians watched and waited, ready to suspend their first victim behind an impenetrable force field.

JOHANNA BEGAN TO exit her quarters but stopped when she heard countless troops of Terrorian soldiers stomping up the cupola stairs. She slammed the door to her chamber, with Plato Indelicat and herself still inside. "The Terrorians are all heading to the cupola. How will we get past them to the portals?"

Ω *We will wait. Terrorians are an impatient breed. They will waste no time traversing the portals to force their will on beings from other realms. Once they have done that, we will return to Fantasia.*

"But they'll already be there, doing lord knows what to my library."

Ω *I suggest you leave the weapon behind. There is the possibility that other Terrorians will follow. Being caught with one of their weapons could mean certain death. You would be perceived as a spy and never be allowed to leave this place. Without the weapon, you are merely a Fantasian who has served a sentence and is being escorted home. They will allow the charade to continue until you reach your home planet, just so they can relish your sudden realization of domination rather than escape.*

"How nice of them."

Ω *Come. The footsteps have ceased.*

They climbed to the cupola and made their way to the portal to Fantasia. They saw no sign of the Terrorians. The troops had all transported to the other libraries. Johanna took a deep breath and said, "Illuminate." When nothing happened, Plato Indelicat repeated the command, and the pair immediately transported to the other side.

ON TERRORIA, NERO 51 lifted a tankard of fermented merk. "T' cra!"

Members of his inner circle echoed his toast. "T' cra." *To victory.*

It would not be long before reports filtered in from the troops, declaring their positions and successes. Nero 51 used a tentacle to wipe the foamy head of the sudsy spirits from his mouth. His plan had been perfectly executed. Every man had been thoroughly trained and appropriately dispatched. One member of each advance team was fluent in the language of the realm being invaded. The timing had been perfect. The only imperfection scratching the smooth surface of his plan was Heil 66. He had been a member of the inner circle, and yet had withheld information about a spy. Nero 51 wanted to believe the shadow Heil 66 had seen belonged to Johanna Charette, but the information had come too late to interrogate the girl. *What if someone else spied on me?* It made Nero 51 uneasy.

"I am going to withdraw in preparation for victory," he told the others. He handed them a small black box with three buttons. "Please buzz me when you have heard from our soldiers on every world. Press the white button for total victory, the purple button for partial victory, and the red button for retreat."

"So fancy, Nero 51. Why not just have us meet you at the library when we hear from the troops?"

"I will be contemplating victory and fine-tuning our plans for the future—in a place of meditation. It will be easier to contact me in this manner." He raised one of his right tentacles. "T' cra!" He worked his way toward the exit, entwining tentacles with each member of his inner circle in a show of solidarity.

Back inside his library, Nero 51 descended to the basement and moved the bookcase leading to the sub-levels. Like all the Libraries of Illumination, his had been designed with 1,311 floors, most of them underground. However, he had taken the initiative to create a secret passage on level 333 that led to a living compartment only he knew about. He had used it as his personal residence for years, and had stocked it well, with everything he could possibly need. He preferred to use his official quarters on the residence level as a command post. It was the perfect place to store munitions and pertinent information about the invasion, to keep them close at hand.

He settled into a comfortable position and looked at the bank of lights near the ceiling, white, purple, and red. He could relax here, undisturbed, while remaining informed about Terrorian exploits on distant realms. He closed his eyes and sank into deep meditation.

—LOI—

C:L I

CHAPTER TWENTY-FIVE

"What the ...?"

Even before the president of the board of directors had finished his sentence, a Terrorian trooper took aim and fired his weapon. The blast caused a high-pitched squeal that reverberated throughout the library and caused the president, as well as Jackson and their guests on the main floor, to slump over or drop to the ground, cover their ears, and suffer the pain. The pitch of the audio signal had a much different effect on the Terrorian who fired his weapon. It caused the weapon to reverse action, locking the shooter in a force field.

The other soldiers did not immediately comprehend what had happened to their team leader. Instead, they saw the president of the library board still moving, so several of them took aim and fired.

Terrorians began freezing in place, unable to move after firing their weapons. One of the remaining soldiers threw his weapon down and raced down the stairs, intent on strangling any Fantasians he met with his bare tentacles.

JACKSON STRUGGLED UP from the floor, even though his ears continued to ring. If Johanna returned now, he feared she would get caught in the crossfire. He raced up the stairs to the cupola, only to find his way blocked by a Terrorian. The soldier extended his tentacles, as Jackson stepped back and reached into his waistband. The teen removed the gun and fired a shot before the Terrorian knocked the Glock out of his hand and it clattered down the long staircase. The bullet hit the Terrorian, and a spray of blood covered Jackson in a purple haze. The soldier squealed in pain, but did not give up.

Another tentacle snaked toward Jackson. He stuffed his hand in his jacket pocket, looking for a screw-driver or pen—anything he could use as a weapon. His fingers closed over the slender volume of *The Strange Case of Dr. Jekyll and Mr. Hyde*, and he pulled out the book.

The Terrorian knocked it out of his hand, but Mr. Hyde suddenly sprang from the pages of the open book, carrying a heavy cane with a blood-covered handle. He used it to beat the startled Terrorian until the soldier went limp. Jackson ducked, grabbed the book, and quickly closed it. He slipped it back in his pocket before he climbed over the inert soldier and continued up the stairs.

THE LAST FEW troopers on Fantasia realized their weapons had been turned against them and tried to retreat, but the portal suddenly flashed, and Plato Indelicat and Johanna appeared.

Without thinking, one of the soldiers fired his weapon, causing Johanna to drop to the ground, writhing from the pitch of audio feedback. The warrior immediately found himself locked behind a force field. His fellow soldiers dropped their weapons, grabbed the overseer, and jumped back through the portal to Terroria. They dragged Plato Indelicat through their library, out onto the toxic streets of the Twelfth Realm, and into Building 7—a location that they felt would give them greater control over their hostage.

Members of the Inner Circle grew disturbed when they heard about the defeat of their plan, but remained hopeful that a hostage would aid their negotiations with the College of Overseers.

Troops on other realms reported similar outcomes. Soldiers found themselves suddenly immobilized by force fields. A warrior in the Numericon library switched on his weapon's Omicron Key and was vaporized when he fired at Pi, curator of the Tenth Realm. The few Terrorian troopers who managed to retreat all had similar tales to tell.

Jackson quickly recuperated from the second earsplitting blast, and reached the cupola in time to see Johanna recover from the effects of the Terrorian weapons. He helped her off the ground and slipped his arms around her, glad to see she was okay.

She pushed him away. "I've got to save Plato Indelicat," she screamed, and disappeared back through the portal.

His mouth hung open—just for a moment. He leaned over the cupola railing and yelled to the crowd below: "Tonight's demonstration has been canceled due to unforeseen technical difficulties. Please exit in an orderly fashion." Then he jumped through the portal.

ON TERRORIA, JOHANNA's footsteps pounded down the cupola stairs. Jackson followed as fast as he could, often taking two steps at a time to catch up to her. He saw her run into a utility closet and reemerge with a weapon.

"You can't shoot that," he said. "You'll end up caught in a force field."

Johanna studied the gun. "Did the overseers do anything strange before the Terrorians arrived?"

"Yeah. They stuck a bunch of shiny white papers on the walls by the portals, but they had nothing on them. You couldn't even see them."

"That high-pitched tone ... did you hear that when Nero 51 grabbed you outside his residence and put you in a force field?"

Jackson shook his head. "No."

"Okay. I'm thinking those shiny white papers had something to do with the way the guns backfired. But I'm also thinking the overseers wouldn't have bothered sticking them here on Terroria, where they might have been discovered. So this weapon is probably going to work just the way we expect it to."

"If you say so. Do you think the overseer is here? I don't hear anyone."

Johanna ran to a window and looked over at Building 7. "No, but I bet I know where they took him. Follow me."

The two of them ran into the street, but immediately retreated, coughing and gagging. "What is that smell?" Jackson moaned.

"I don't know. I never strayed outside of the library. I only know that every time the Terrorians entered, they'd turn on a blower that makes a real racket. That's how I knew when Nero 51 was in residence."

"Is there some kind of secret passageway to the building you want to go to?"

"Nope. We've got to go out there, but it's just across the courtyard. We can hold our breath that long."

"Right. We deplete our oxygen supply while we run into a building that's full of armed Terrorians, with a weapon that may backfire."

She nodded. "Pretty much."

"Okay. Let's do it."

They both took a deep breath and headed out.

SELIUM SORIUM MADE sure everyone who had attended Jackson's presentation left the building safely. The president of the board of directors babbled about being attacked by some "armed monstrosity," but the overseer convinced everyone that the man had hit his head when he fell. He encouraged the president's wife to have her husband checked for a concussion.

Finally alone, the overseer closed his eyes to commune with his brethren. Ten of his colleagues gave positive reports on the worlds they observed; however, they now knew Plato Indelicat had been taken hostage.

❖ *That is a setback.*

The overseers possessed supernatural powers that enabled them to communicate, transport themselves, and alter the perception of their appearance. They had also undergone a special longevicus ritual to extend their lives tenfold. As the guardians of all knowledge, they relied on those gifts to maintain their existence. However, the overseers were not immortal. The Original Thirteen, save one, had passed on. Overseers could be fatally injured, and Plato Indelicat would have to use his wits wisely to continue his state of being.

JOHANNA AND JACKSON heard the pandemonium erupting inside Building 7 before they even reached the door. They hid in the shadows as someone exited, and spotted a cloakroom just inside the vestibule. A diminutive Terrorian, possibly a woman or a child, appeared to be in charge of it. The discussion in the main hall became more and more heated, and the tiny Terrorian got up and joined the crowd to get a better look.

"Come on." Johanna pulled Jackson inside the grimy cloakroom.

"It smells almost as bad in here as it does outside," he whispered.

"Yeah. This is what Terrorians smell like. And if we smell like them, they may not notice us." She grabbed a cloak from the corner and threw it over her shoulders, covering the weapon. She pulled the hood over her hair and tugged it down to conceal her face.

Jackson did the same. "There are no arm holes."

"Look again. There are four on each side—they're just smaller—for tentacles."

The teens moved out of the coatroom but stayed in the shadows near the door. Most of the Terrorians, by contrast, pushed forward to get right into the middle of the discussion.

"Did you learn any more Terrorian here?" Jackson whispered.

"No. Plato Indelicat performed a translation enchantment so I would be able to understand the Terrorians when they ordered me around."

"So everything was in English?"

"Everything except the passphrase to get into the residence."

"Did you figure it out?"

"Lucky for me, someone taught it to me before I started my sentence."

"Who did that?" he asked, amazed.

"You."

The roar of the crowd increased, and a pair of Terrorian soldiers marched Plato Indelicat to the front of the room.

Jackson leaned toward Johanna. "It sounds like a freakin' cricket convention."

"I wish we knew what they were saying." She stared at Plato Indelicat, trying to read his face. A moment later, an English translation enchantment took effect.

"What did you do?" Jackson whispered.

"He knows we're here. He must have read our thoughts."

MANY OF THE younger Terrorians called for Plato Indelicat's execution. Older residents claimed they needed him as a hostage to use as a bargaining chip. With Plato Indelicat incarcerated on Terroria, the possibility that they could exchange the overseer for the troops who remained immobilized in force fields on distant worlds still existed. But more importantly, the portals might remain open, keeping the hope of a future victory alive.

A Terrorian soldier interrogated the overseer about why their weapons had backfired. Plato Indelicat did not answer his questions. A nearby soldier picked up a weapon and swung it at the overseer. He swung high, and the weapon knocked Plato Indelicat's hat off his head.

The overseer suddenly grew agitated, and struggled to pull away from the soldiers who held him in place, but they kept a firm grip on him. Another soldier stuck his weapon inside the hat and raised it above his head—a symbol of their small victory in capturing the overseer. The crowd cheered, barely noticing that Plato Indelicat had started to wither.

Johanna turned to Jackson. "We've got to do something before the Terrorians tear him to pieces."

"What do you suggest?"

"I don't know, but we'd better act soon."

Someone shouted a command from the center of the crowd. "We must take him to Nero 51. He'll know what do."

"Where is Nero 51?" a soldier asked.

"Planning our future path to victory in the Library of Illumination. We must take the prisoner to the library."

"Let's get out of here," Johanna said. "We've got a better chance of saving Plato Indelicat in the library than we do here."

"How do you figure that?"

"We know the lay of the land. They'll be afraid to shoot their guns in there. And the portals are nearby."

"So all we've got to do is run up five noisy flights of ancient stairs with an old man in tow? Piece of cake."

They slipped out of Building 7 with the crowd and made their way to the library. Inside, Johanna grabbed Jackson and dragged him into the corner of the stone stairwell.

"We'll be safer in here," she whispered.

On the other side of the wall, the mob got restless when Nero 51 did not answer the bell they used to summon him.

"The box," a member of the Inner Circle said. "Where is the box he gave us?"

Another member held it up. "I have it right here."

"Good. Press the button."

"Which one?"

"Well, we weren't completely victorious, so don't press the white one."

"Do you think I should press the purple one for partial victory?"

"Uhhh ... We haven't really taken control of any of the libraries. The few troops who have returned—retreated."

"So you think I should press the red button?"

"That would be the most accurate assessment of what has happened. He deserves to know that."

The Inner Circle member pressed the red button, and almost immediately Building 7 exploded, blowing out the windows on one side of the library and shaking the structure to its core. Stunned Terrorians squealed as they dove for cover.

"Now!" Johanna said, and ran into the fray, grabbing Plato Indelicat and dragging him to the cupola steps.

Jackson followed close behind her. They began running up the stairs, but the overseer's robe, his advanced years, and his delicate condition slowed them down.

"Can you carry him?" she asked. Jackson threw the overseer over his shoulder like a bag of laundry, and Johanna pushed him ahead of her. "Run," she cried.

A RED LIGHT blinked on sub-level 333. Nero 51 rose in a rage. What could his troops have done to lead to total defeat? He felt the subterranean cavity he had built shudder. *Building 7 has been destroyed. It serves them right for ruining my plan.*

THE EXPLOSION STUNNED the Terrorians. Some were knocked unconscious by the percussion, but a few raised their heads in time to see *aliens* grab the overseer and drag him away. Many Terrorians felt defeated and did not rush to pursue the interlopers, but a few seized the moment, believing the aliens had bombed Building 7 and were now escaping with Terroria's hostage. They clambered up the stairs, their fat, flat feet slapping the metal treads.

JACKSON WAS STRONG, but rushing up five flights of narrow, spiral stairs carrying a man over his shoulder took its toll. He could feel the Terrorian pursuers. Their added weight on the staircase made it shudder. He hoped that whatever held the stairway in place had been designed to withstand the weight load.

"They're gaining on us," Johanna shouted. "Can you go any faster?"

"No." He knew it wasn't the answer she wanted to hear, but he had to tell her the truth.

"Here goes nothing," she said, as she turned and raised the Terrorian weapon to her shoulder. She barely had time to aim before she pulled the trigger. A force field encased the closest Terrorian, blocking the ones who followed. She turned and ran, catching up to Jackson and Plato Indelicat at the portals.

"Illuminate," Jackson yelled.

Nothing happened.

Johanna echoed his command. "Illuminate!"

The portals remained closed.

"Plato," she cried. The overseer was unconscious. She gently tapped his cheek. "Please, Plato, you've got to help us. How do we open the portals?"

The overseer's eyes fluttered. He mumbled something difficult to understand.

"What is he saying?"

Johanna looked confused. "I think he said, 'The

key is in the might.'"

"What does that mean?" Jackson asked.

"I don't know, but I hear them coming up the stairs, so they must have gotten around the soldier I shot.

"Please, Plato," she begged. "There must be a word that will open the portals."

He looked at her through clouded, gray eyes.

Ω *Totalis illuminatio.*

Instantly, they transported to their own world, where Selium Sorium met them.

⍟ *Totalis tenebris.*

The portals slammed shut.

"We saved him," she cried triumphantly.

⍟ *He will be laid to rest with those who have come before.*

"What are you talking about?" Jackson gently placed Plato Indelicat on the floor.

⍟ *He is no more.*

"You mean, he's dead? He can't be dead. We saved him," Jackson stated.

Johanna's face clouded over. "How could he die?"

⍟ *We are grateful that his body has been returned to us. You have provided a great service, Johanna Charette. And you, Jackson Roth.*

"How can you say that? Why don't you help him?" She suddenly felt empty inside.

⍟ *You have provided us with information about Terrorian arms and confirmed violations against the Library of Illumination through the illegal trade of precious artifacts.*

Jackson looked around at the Terrorians still suspended behind force fields. "What about them?"

⍟ *They will be taken to Lumina for trial.*

"So the portals are still open?"

◍ *We have effectively sealed them for now.*

Johanna's brow furrowed. "How will you get to Lumina?"

◍ *Like this.*

Selium Sorium, the body of Plato Indelicat, and more than a half dozen Terrorian soldiers disappeared.

Johanna and Jackson looked around in astonishment, and then at each other.

"It's over," Jackson said, as he wrapped her in his arms and gave her a bear hug. "It's over," he repeated, "and you're home."

Tears streamed from her eyes, and she began to sob.

"Don't cry." Jackson rubbed her back. "You helped avert a war. You did everything in your power to rescue an overseer. You survived! You should be overjoyed by your accomplishments. And then there's your crowning achievement."

"What's that?" She looked up at him.

"I will never, ever again say, 'I bet there's something hidden behind this wall.'"

She smiled, but she could not shake the sensation of doom she felt. The Terrorians had been planning an all-out war, and she didn't think they would easily abandon their plan.

To the contrary, whatever Johanna and Jackson had unwittingly become embroiled in had just begun.

—THE END, IT IS NOT—

Turn the page for a preview of the next
Library of Illumination adventure ...

THE OVERSEERS

Coming soon from Artiqua Press

C:L❂I

The Overseer

"THAT'S THE LAST of them," Jackson said with finality, as he pushed a stack of books toward Johanna. "Once you've read these, you'll know everything there is to know about the realm of Terroria. Although why you want to become an expert on *planet evil* is beyond me."

Johanna shook her head. "That's why I'm the curator and you're just my assistant."

"Hey, hey, hey, didn't you hear what they said when we stood trial for breaching the portals? I'm a *curator-in-training*. I'm the one waiting in the wings to pick up the pieces."

"Well then, you'd better read some of these, too," she said as she pushed the pile of Terrorian history books she'd already read, towards him. "Then we'll both be prepared."

"Prepared for what?"

"I'm not sure." She felt her nerve endings jitter. "But it never hurts to be prepared. You never know what can happen."

As if on cue, the middle of the venerable library began to wobble and shimmer, like the air that hovers above a hot roadway on a steamy summer day. Suddenly, a 22nd century time machine appeared. It was the same one that Johanna's predecessor Mal had used to transport Casanova back to 18th century Venice, after the legendary lover suddenly popped out of a book in the library, and stayed. Mal smiled as he stepped out. His appearance had changed in the short weeks since Johanna and Jackson had last seen him.

"Are you growing a beard?" Johanna walked over to her mentor and gave him a hug. Mal had been in charge of the library for nearly four hundred years, and had only relinquished his stewardship after he had personally trained Johanna to deal with the intrusions, oddities and aftermath of *living* literature.

Mal stroked his face and smiled. "It was a little itchy at first, but I'm getting used to it now."

"It makes you look older," she observed.

"Yeah," Jackson said. "You used to look four-hundred and thirty years old and now you look four-hundred and thirty-one."

"Don't listen to him." Johanna placed her arm protectively around Mal's shoulder. "You don't look a day over eighty."

Mal smiled. "I come with sad news, and with happy news."

"I think the actual saying is, 'I have some good news and some bad news,'" Jackson quipped.

Mal slowly inhaled. "Sadly, we will say our final goodbyes to Plato Indelicat tomorrow, when he will be enshrined following a celebration of his life and a memorial to his death. On a more positive note, his replacement will be inducted into the College of Overseers on the following afternoon."

"Will anyone ever be able to take his place?" Johanna wondered out loud.

"Where do overseers come from anyway?" Jackson asked. "Is there a special place filled with them, like *Overseers-R-Us*? Do they have to supply their own hats? I know Plato Indelicat was pretty sad after the Terrorians knocked his pope hat off his head."

Mal's eyes grew more focused. "Can you tell me what became of Plato Indelicat's headpiece?"

Jackson shook his head. "Not really."

"We were too busy trying to stay ahead of the crowd," Johanna added. "They had turned into a lynch mob and we didn't want to become hostages, too."

"So it remains on Terroria."

"Unless it was destroyed in the explosion."

"Yeah," Jackson agreed. "The last place we saw it was in the building around the corner from the library, and that place was blown to smithereens, which was really good for us, because that's how we escaped."

Johanna took Mal's hand. "So, what's the happy news, Mal?"

"I've been selected as one of the candidates for the vacant overseer position."

"*One* of the candidates," Johanna noted. "Who are the others?"

"Well, of course, you wouldn't know them

because they're from other worlds, but there's Prophet IAN c. from Adventura, who is the current library curator, there. You may have met Torran, the head of the Library Council on Dramatica, who has declared himself a contender although I don't know how good *his* chances are. And then there's Dame Erato, the former curator of Romantica, who relocated to Lumina and has reinvented herself as something of an inspirational insider. She and Prophet IAN c. are both strong competitors."

"Do you think you have a chance?" Jackson asked.

"I have my strengths. But ultimately, it will be whomever the overseers believe brings the most needed assets to the college at this point in time. Whether that resource is political, administrative, militaristic or inspirational remains to be seen.

"There will be a challenge among the four of us, and any others who choose to declare themselves by noon tomorrow. I was hoping the two of you would remain after the memorial service to cheer me on."

"We're invited to Plato Indelicat's memorial service?" Johanna's eyes widened.

"Of course," Mal answered. "That's why I'm here."

Jackson nodded solemnly. "Cool."

"I've got to stay behind and take care of the library, Mal," Johanna sighed. "We can't both be gone at the same time."

"The library will be closed. All the Libraries of Illumination will cease operations for two days as a sign of respect for Plato Indelicat, and will not reopen until a new overseer has been sworn in."

"That seals the deal for me," Jackson said with a smile.

"Where is this all happening?" Johanna asked.

"Everything takes place on Lumina."

Of course it would; where else could it be held? Still, she was surprised that she and Jackson were invited. "The overseers sealed the portals after the Terrorians tried to take over the libraries. How will we get there if the portals are sealed?"

"I will escort you both."

"In that?" Jackson asked, not trying to hide his excitement.

"Absolutely. There's nothing like traveling in a time machine." Mal wiggled his eyebrows and grinned.

Jackson entered the time machine and looked around. "It's like standing inside a bubble." There was no floor, no doors and no visible controls. He touched the surface. It was firm, and warm, and as smooth as glass.

Johanna idly began straightening out the circulation desk. "Why would we need a time machine at all, if we're traveling in the present?"

"Because, it will take us back to a time when the portals were *open* so we can travel to Lumina, and then zigzag us back to the present." He tapped on the outside of the bubble twice, and exchanged places with Jackson. "I'll be back tomorrow morning at ten sharp." He pointed a finger at the *curator-in-training*, then laughed and shook his head, lowering his finger. "You won't be late."

"You've got that right," Jackson answered. "I'll get here by nine, so I don't miss anything."

Mal waved. The air around the time machine seemed to melt for a second before it disappeared.

"Lumina," Jackson said in awe. We've been to three realms, including our own, and now we're going to

Lumina. I'd never even been out of the country before we discovered the portals, but now I'll be traveling off world for the third time. How cool is that?"

"We're going to a funeral, and then Mal's challenge. It's not like we're attending a big rock concert on New Year's Eve."

"I know, but it's still the most amazing thing that has ever happened to me." He shrugged one shoulder and leaned over to kiss her. "Actually, you're the 'most amazing' thing that ever happened to me. If you had never come to the school and asked me if I wanted to work in the library, I'd probably be tossing pizzas at Piccolo Italia. Free pizza is nice, but not as nice as traveling to other realms with you.

He pushed the books on Terroria aside. "Do you think we have any books downstairs on Lumina? I think I'd like to study up on that world, before we leave tomorrow."

"Sometimes, you surprise me," Johanna laughed.

He winked at her. "Refreshing, isn't it?"

THERE WERE PLENTY of books about Lumina—many with pictures—and Jackson was enthralled by everything he read. "I can't believe most of their world is covered in water."

"I don't know if it's most of the world. The cities are built on numerous outcroppings that jut way above the surface."

"Yeah, but look at this picture of the capital. The bottom of that giant *outcropping* looks like it rests on legs. The middle is open and I bet you can sail a tanker right through it."

"Kind of like a subway traveling under a city."

"No, this is way cooler than a subway. Besides, anyone riding in a subway would drown unless by subway you mean submarine."

"The golden city on top of the rocks makes it look so ethereal." Johanna ran her finger across a picture in *Lumina: Past and Present.* Instantly, a miniature three-dimensional version of the capitol city of Lumi appeared, complete with clouds above and water below.

Jackson moved closer and stared at a rock leg supporting the city. "Look. This one has a door."

Johanna walked over to see what he was talking about. "I would have loved this as a kid. What a perfect dollhouse. I never owned one, but I saw one once in a museum and I thought it was the most wonderful thing in the world."

As they watched, a round wooden tub with a dozen oarsmen sitting around its radius rowed up to the tiny entrance. One of the oarsmen unlocked the door and a group of tiny Luminans climbed out of the tub and disappeared inside, allowing the door to slam shut with a resounding thud.

"Can you believe this?" Jackson laughed.

Johanna started to laugh but instead, gasped. As they watched, a group of men appeared from under the surface of the water, swam up to the tub, and began pulling at the oars and tossing them away, so the oarsmen wouldn't be able to row. The tiny sailors grappled with their attackers, but one by one, many of them were pulled under the water. A few managed to hang onto their oars and moved into the middle of the tub where they used them to fight off their assailants. One attacker hoisted himself onto the vessel and soon learned he had made a big mistake.

"Holy... frit. Look at him," Jackson cried. "He's a fish!"

Johanna squinted. "I think the correct term is a *merman*."

"Like Ethel Merman, the singer those guys at *The Comedy Club* are always impersonating?"

"No. Like the male equivalent to a mermaid."

"I knew that."

"Um hmm."

While they were talking, the oarsmen beat the brazen merman to a pulp, and pushed his body overboard—a sign of what other underwater creatures could expect, if they were thinking of hijacking a boat. The attack was over and in a single blink, the bodies of the fallen oarsmen and the beaten merman all disappeared under the surface of the murky water.

Johanna slammed the book shut. "I could have done without that."

"Yeah. But this isn't a storybook. It's a textbook that describes how things are on Lumina. And apparently, everything isn't fun and games in the golden city."

"Let's just hope we don't have to travel anywhere on the water while we're there."

B-R-R-R-I-I-I-N-N-N-G-G-G!

A phone call from *Book Services* informed them they had just received a scholarly request for research information and ancient texts. The order kept Johanna and Jackson busy for the rest of the afternoon. When they were done, Johanna sent Jackson home. She needed a little time to pack. Besides, she didn't want to start talking about Lumina again. She was still feeling uneasy about the attack they had witnessed when the book came to life, and it reminded her about the potential for an attack by Terrorians, if any of them were actually invited to the memorial service. She hoped not, but that wasn't her decision to make. The thought of running into Nero 51 again turned a trip that should be meaningful and interesting into a duty that filled her with dread.

THAT NIGHT, AS Johanna snuggled under the duvet in her bedroom, she opened Mal's diary and asked him if Nero 51 would also be on Lumina. Except for the time when she was serving her sentence on Terroria, Mal's answers to her requests had always been immediate, but tonight she dozed off waiting for his reply. When she awakened in the middle of the night, he still had not answered her. She glanced over at her clock. It was two in the morning. She had asked Mal her question more than three hours ago. He had never taken so long to respond. Johanna dozed off again, but continued to wake up every hour or so to check for Mal's answer. At 7:00 a.m. she threw off the covers and arose for the day. A quick check told her that Mal still hadn't answered her question.

She selected a long tan and black chevron print sweater and paired it with a short black skirt and black boots. She studied herself in the mirror. *Funeral attire.* She added a belt and a scarf. *Stylish funeral attire.* She packed something more lighthearted for the induction ceremony for the new overseer, as well as extra clothing to relax in. And then she waited. It was still too early for Mal to show up, although Jackson was probably on his way.

She grabbed Mal's diary to see if he had finally answered her question, but the last page of the diary remained blank. She threw the book in her bag and sighed. The library was closed and she was all packed and ready to go, and now she was forced to wait. She did the only thing left that felt natural. She paced.

A HALF-HOUR LATER, the back door flew open and Jackson breezed in. "I know I'm late, but I really needed to eat something, so I stopped to pick up some coffee and donuts. Unfortunately, everyone in town had the same idea. I thought of saying 'screw it,' but who knows when we'll get to eat again?"

Johanna was staring at him. "Is that a tie?"

"Yeah. You like it?" He stroked the narrow strip of black leather with pride. Jackson wore it over a light blue shirt and khakis. Everything else he needed was in the backpack slung over his shoulder.

"I don't think I've ever seen you wear a tie before."

"I don't think I've ever owned a tie before. I bought this one on my way home last night. It's *real* leather."

She gently touched the black leather and then straightened out the knot. "You look very nice. I like it."

He grinned. "Now all I have to do is make sure I don't spill any coffee on myself. Just to be safe, I didn't buy any jelly or cream-filled donuts. Why take chances?"

"Why, indeed?" She removed a plain cruller from the bag of treats. They chatted amiably until the grandfather clock struck ten. Johanna gulped down her coffee and used her hand to sweep the donut crumbs into the paper bag. "Mal will be here any second."

Jackson wasn't eager to rush through his morning

meal and took his time as Johanna fussed. The minutes ticked by. When he was done, he threw his coffee cup and crumbs in the trash bag, and then brought it out back to the dumpster. The clock was chiming the quarter hour when he returned.

Johanna frowned. "He's late."

"So the guy got hung up. Maybe he's making an 'under the counter' deal for the transport of human cargo.'"

Johanna didn't answer.

"That's what Mal said when he picked up Casanova. Don't you remember? He said he had to bargain with the people at Lloyds of London?"

"Don't you understand? Mal is always punctual. He's very dependable. His schedule runs like clockwork. But then, last night, he didn't answer a question I asked his diary. And now he's late. Something's wrong."

Jackson studied her face. She looked like she was on the verge of tears. He pulled her into a hug. "Don't worry. It won't matter if he's late. It's a *time machine,* and no matter what time he gets here, we can travel back to the perfect moment in time to go through the portals."

He rubbed her back to calm her and slowly felt her start to relax, but she grew tense again, when the clock chimed the half-hour.

—LOI—

ABOUT THE AUTHOR

C. A. Pack is the author of *Code Name: Evangeline* and the *Evangeline's Ghost* series, as well as the series of novelettes that make up *The Library of Illumination*. She is currently working on *The Second Chronicles of Illumination,* recounting the War of the Realms.

The author is an award-winning journalist, and former assignment manager/anchor at *LI News Tonight* in New York, and has worked as a news writer at WNBC-TV, and Cablevision's News 12 Long Island.

A member of International ThrillerWriters, and Sisters in Crime, she is also a former president of the Press Club of Long Island. She lives in Westbury, NY, with her husband, a couple of picky parrots, and dozens of imaginary characters who are constantly demanding page space.